Around the World
Fairy Tales

Around the World Fairy Tales

Retold by
Vratislav Šťovíček

Translated by
Vera Gissing

Illustrations by
Zdeňka Krejčová

Cathay Books

First published 1981 by
Cathay Books
59 Grosvenor Street
London W1
Reprinted 1985

Retold by Vratislav Šťovíček
Translated by Vera Gissing
Graphic design by Aleš Krejča
This edition © Artia 1981

ISBN 0 86178 062 0

Printed in Czechoslovakia by Svoboda, Prague
1/20/01/51-02

Contents

East of the Sun, West of the Moon

(The Tales of the East Wind)

Far, far away, where the rainbow rises, beyond nine mountains and nine rivers there lived in ancient times a poor father and a sad mother. All they owned was a cottage built of turf and twigs where they lived with their brood of hungry children. How these poor people wished there was enough food for them all, but good fortune never smiled on them—until one day when a snow storm howled in the sky a great polar bear hammered at their door.

'Good people, I bring you riches,' he growled, pouring a pile of gold before them. 'Good fortune will never leave you if you give me your youngest and most beautiful daughter for my bride.'

The poor parents burst into tears. They so wanted to see their children enjoy at least a spoonful of warm soup each day, but how could they give up their dearest youngest daughter to a great white bear with sharp teeth and threatening claws? But their brave daughter did not hesitate.

'Do not weep,' she said to her father and mother. 'I shall become the wife of this white bear and thus bring good fortune to you and my brothers and sisters.' And so saying, she gathered her few poor rags into a bundle and walked into the snow with the polar bear.

They walked on and on, wherever the snow flakes led them till they came to the black mountains. There the white bear tore open a rock with his huge paws, and a glittering palace appeared before the maiden's astonished eyes. It was built of gold and precious jewels and in its rainbow-coloured chambers fragile flowers danced on tiptoe, admiring themselves in crystal mirrors and whispering, 'Oh, how beautiful we are!'

The bear led the maiden into a magnificent hall, clapped his hands and cried, 'This now is your home, my bride!' And as he spoke, all the dancing flowers gathered round, bowing deeply and whispering sweetly, 'Oh, how beautiful she is!'

That night, when the maiden sank to her golden bed, the polar bear's breath blew out every candle and all the stars beyond the windows. 'You must not dare to kindle a single spark of light,' he warned, 'or ill fortune will befall us.'

Suddenly the astonished maiden felt the touch of gentle hands on her hair and

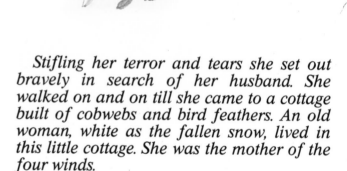

heard the strains of a lullaby sung by a human voice of great beauty. 'What is this strange magic?' she wondered. 'This is no bear which lulls me to sleep.' And that night she dreamt beautiful dreams, sweet as a mother's caress.

And so day followed day and night followed night. The maiden grew fond of the kind bear and looked forward to his nightly lullaby, but one night curiosity got the better of her. She placed a small icicle in each eye, so that her eyelids would not close and when her husband fell asleep before finishing his song, she leant over him with a lighted candle. Wonder of wonders! Instead of a great polar bear she saw a handsome golden-haired prince, smiling at her in his sleep. Just then three drops of wax fell from the slanting candle onto his chest.

'Oh, wretched woman,' he cried, 'I am a bewitched prince from a distant land. An evil stepmother has turned me into a bear and only in darkness can I become a man. But no one must see my face until the hour when the curse will end. You did not heed my warning. As punishment we now must part.' And the prince's face dissolved like a snowflake. Only his voice could be heard from afar.

'Where can I find you, my prince?' the maid cried despairingly.

'Far, far away, to the east of the sun and west of the moon a crystal palace stands on a glass island drifting in a transparent sea. There I shall be imprisoned by the witch, my wicked stepmother.' As his words died away, the golden palace dissolved in a misty cloud and the maiden found herself standing alone on a black rock in the depths of a dark forest.

Stifling her terror and tears she set out bravely in search of her husband. She walked on and on till she came to a cottage built of cobwebs and bird feathers. An old woman, white as the fallen snow, lived in this little cottage. She was the mother of the four winds.

'I know what grieves you,' she said, 'yet I cannot help you. But I can ask if my sons, the four winds, know the way.' Then the old woman took a handful of golden grain from her apron and tossed it into the sky. Thereupon a little fellow with a bird's beak and butterfly wings flew down from the east, pecked at the golden grain and curled up in the old woman's lap. This curious fellow was her youngest son.

'East Wind, my son, tell us the way to the castle in the transparent sea, which lies to the east of the sun and west of the moon,' begged the old woman. 'There the wicked stepmother keeps the handsome prince her prisoner.'

'I roam the world close to the sun and the stars, but I know of no such place,' replied the East Wind. 'Perhaps the journeys of South Wind, my brother, have led him to the enchanted castle.'

'Will the South Wind come soon?' asked the unhappy maiden.

'When the sun at noon chases away the shadows, you will see that son sitting on my knee,' replied the old woman, combing her youngest son's locks which were as red as

the sunrise. 'Do not fear, my dear,' she comforted. 'And while we wait, the East Wind
will tell us stories. Do not lose heart, but listen! And you, my son, begin.' And the East
Wind told his first story —

The Twelve Princesses

Long, long ago a powerful king ruled over his kingdom. This king had twelve daughters, each one prettier than the last, and the youngest, Princess Lina, was the prettiest of all. Her cheeks were like the morning sky, her hair shone like gold and her smile was as dazzling as the sun. She was so beautiful it was no wonder that Michael, the royal gardener, fell in love with her at first sight.

Having so many daughters gave the old king much anxiety and he could scarcely keep them in rich robes, fine slippers and precious jewels. But his greatest worry was that each morning it was almost impossible to wake them. They stretched and yawned, their cheeks as white as death, and even Princess Lina could hardly open her eyes. As if that was not enough, each morning their satin slippers were so tattered and torn that all their little toes stuck out.

'I wonder where they go night after night,' their angry father muttered to himself, and so that he could rest in peace, he locked them up from then on in their bedroom at night with three golden keys and three silver bolts. But believe it or not, the next morning his daughters were again limp with weariness, falling asleep wherever they went, their toes and heels again peeping out of their new shoes.

In vain the king asked which paths those shoes had trodden. The princesses could not tell. They did not remember, they said. They were worn out and ready for bed, was all they would tell him. This made their father so furious that he proclaimed throughout his own and all neighbouring kingdoms that he would give one daughter and half his realm to any prince who would stop the princesses leaving their bedroom.

But it was useless. Each day a prince arrived at the palace and each one in turn was locked in with the princesses. By morning the prince had vanished.

Eleven days passed and eleven princes disappeared. The king's daughters swore they knew nothing, that they had slept throughout the night. But every morning their slippers were in ribbons, and heavy-eyed, they yawned wearily wherever they went. Everyone was baffled and their father could find no more princes willing to guard his daughters and disappear in the night. The king became more and more worried. What was he to do?

One day Michael the royal gardener who was secretly in love with the youngest and most beautiful Princess Lina, was watering the rose beds. Suddenly a tiny fairy emerged from a blossom and began to bathe in a droplet of water. 'Where did you come from?' asked Michael in wonder.

'This is where I and my sisters live,' said the fairy. 'And as you look after our homes, I will give you a present of two magic bushes. One is a rose bush, the other a jasmine. Under your window, prepare a little bed with a golden rake, plant them and water them with a silver watering can. When the bushes grow to this height,' and the fairy showed how high by standing on tiptoe, 'they will fulfil your every wish.'

Michael the gardener thanked her and did exactly as he was told. For seven days he watered the bed with the silver watering can and raked it with the golden rake.

Meantime, the princesses still fell asleep in the daytime, and every morning their slippers were still full of holes. And so this went on till the king was almost at his wits' end and from morning till night he thundered and raved with worry and rage.

When the magic bushes had grown to the height of the fairy on tiptoe, Michael the gardener spoke to the rose bush. 'Pretty little bush,' he said, 'make me invisible!'

There was a soft rustling in the bush, and a rose blossom fell to the ground. Michael the gardener put it in his buttonhole, and leaning over the well in the garden as if it was a mirror he looked down into the water.

He was amazed that he could see nothing.

His wish had come true and he was invisible. As it was already turning dark, Michael ran at once to the princesses' bedroom and waited for the king to lock them in with the three golden keys and the three silver bolts.

The moment this was done, the princesses jumped from their beds, put on new satin slippers and new costly dresses and stood in a line from the youngest to the eldest. The eldest princess then touched a corner of their bedroom with a little diamond twig and at once a little

11

door appeared. It led to a glass staircase. One by one, the princesses slipped quickly down the stairs. Michael of course was hot on their heels. As he hurried after them, afraid the door might close in his face, he trod on the hem of Princess Lina's dress.

'Someone is following us,' Lina cried fearfully. 'He trod on my dress.'

But the eldest princess quietened her. 'Your dress probably caught on a nail,' she said, without even glancing round.

The glass staircase led the princesses and the invisible Michael into a magic wood. It was filled with diamond bushes, trees studded with rubies and ferns sparkling with sapphires. When they had passed through the wood, they found themselves on the bank of a lake where twelve little boats were anchored, each one with a silk canopy embroidered in moonbeams. Next to each boat a handsome prince sat waiting. Each prince rose and helped a princess into her boat. But poor Princess Lina had no one to help her, for there were only eleven princes. How hard she tried, how hard she had to work on her oars. For at the back of her boat sat the invisible Michael. No wonder she lagged behind the others, and no wonder she nearly wept with weariness. But at last they stopped at a large water-lily leaf on which stood a palace built of fish scales. The rooms in the palace were lit by fireflies, and pages dressed in crab shells and dragon-fly wings were handing out water-lily goblets. Whoever took a sip from one of these forgot the rest of the world and danced and danced till morning light, for the goblets held a magic spell. All the princesses danced with their partners: only Princess Lina had to dance alone. Michael the gardener wasted no time. Taking her round the waist, he spun her round and round, till her skirts whirled and swirled.

'Sisters, sisters, someone is dancing with me,' cried the astonished princess. But the others calmed her. 'It is only the midnight breeze,' they said. So Michael and Lina danced all through the night. In the morning the princesses bade their suitors farewell and returned to their bedroom. On the way, Michael broke off a ruby, a diamond and a sapphire twig.

The following day the princesses could not be wakened and once again their slippers were torn to ribbons, so that their toes peeped out. But Michael the gardener smiled happily. He wove a beautiful garland of flowers and placed the three twigs in it. Then he took the garland to the youngest Princess Lina.

'Sisters, the gardener knows our secret,' cried the frightened Lina, when she saw the three precious twigs. The bewitched princesses turned as pale as death, so afraid were they that the gardener would tell all to their father, the king. What were they to do?

'We shall take him to the magic palace and make him drink from a water-lily goblet,' the eldest princess said at last. 'He will then forget the rest of the world, and you, sister Lina, will at last have a dancing partner.'

Princess Lina burst into tears because she would have only a poor gardener as a suitor. But the invisible Michael, who without their knowing it, had listened to every word, hurried to the jasmine bush and begged to be turned into a handsome prince. When Michael leant over the well, he could hardly believe his own eyes, for now indeed he was a handsome prince. He wasted no time in being presented to the king. When he asked to be allowed to guard the disobedient princesses, the king was so overjoyed he could find no words to thank him. As for Princess Lina, she could not take her eyes off the handsome prince.

That evening, the moment the bedroom door was locked with the three golden keys and the three silver bolts, she embraced her guard and led him down the secret stairs to the magic palace. There the princess offered him the water-lily goblet.

'Drink, my suitor, drink the magic potion of love and forgetfulness,' Lina tempted him.

But Michael tossed it aside and cried, 'I know a goblet which is more beautiful than this one,

and a potion more magical.' With that he kissed Princess Lina on the lips. Immediately the earth shook and rumbled and the wondrous palace with its lake and the diamond wood disappeared as if someone had waved a magic wand. To Michael the gardener's astonishment, eleven princes and twelve princesses were kneeling before him, thanking him for breaking the spell of the water-lily.

And so Michael the gardener became a king. He would have liked to thank the little fairy of the rose blossom and the magic bushes for granting his wishes, but alas, both the fairy and the bushes had vanished forever.

The Gipsy Baron

Once upon a time there were three gipsies and greater rascals it would have been hard to find anywhere. Work they shirked always and would not do, yet neither would they eat dry bread. And so it was their time was spent in thinking up ways and means of tricking the unwary that they might live and eat well.

One day at dusk, as they squatted round their fire planning mischief, a traveller came by leading a bear.

'What is a gipsy for, if not for seeing into the future!' cried the traveller. 'Read my palm, you vagabonds! Tell me my fate and what I can't escape. If I like what you foretell, I'll pay you well!'

The traveller did not have to ask twice. As soon as he stretched out his palm to have his future read, the eldest and smartest of the gipsies started tearing out his hair and wailing, 'Alas, alas! You poor, unfortunate fellow! A terrible fate awaits you. You will not see the morning light, for it is written in your palm that tonight your bear will have you for supper. There is no way for you to escape.'

The man was terrified, so terrified in fact that he turned on the bear. 'You ungrateful, wicked beast,' he cried. 'You glutton! You envied me when I dined on roast beef or mutton or baked ham and stuffed pancakes. You wanted too to drink wine like me. You are a villain. Just because I eat rich food, you want to eat me!' And turning to the gipsies, he implored them to keep the bear.

The gipsies pretended to hesitate, but when the man at last offered to give them money besides for saving his life, they relented. As soon as their visitor had left them, the three roared with laughter at their cleverness in fooling the stupid man. But they were already working out new plans to trick unwary people. The eldest gipsy thought it would be an excellent idea to teach the bear to speak Hungarian. They tried hard to make the bear talk, helping it along with a smack and a whack here or a tickle and a titbit there, but the bear was not clever enough for them. All it learned was 'igen, igen', which, in our language, means 'yes, yes'.

When the gipsies saw that they were not going to get any further with the lessons in Hungarian, they turned to something else. One night they waylaid and robbed a rich man from the city, taking his best clothes, his gold pince-nez and his snuff box. Then they dressed up the bear in all his finery. On his paws they put white gloves, and even taught him to wipe his nose with a handkerchief. With the pince-nez balanced on the tip of his nose, he could easily have passed for a nobleman. His furry cheeks were shaved and a frilly handkerchief was tucked into his top pocket. Hiding the bear under canvas on a horse-drawn cart, they set off to visit the richest merchant in the nearby town.

'Open up, shopkeeper!' one gipsy cried. 'The gipsy baron himself is here to buy. He is on his way to a wedding and wants to prepare a great feast in his castle on the Danube!'

The shopkeeper was amazed to see such a nobleman accompanied by three barefoot ragamuffins. They bowed to the floor before him, then they swept it clean and set him down upon a brocade cushion by a barrel filled with jam on the one side and a large cheese on the other.

Next the ruffians started to shout orders at the merchant, telling him what to load onto their cart, so that they would not go to the wedding empty-handed. 'But,' muttered the bewildered merchant, scratching his ear, for he had had dealings with many gipsies in the past, 'who is going to pay for my excellent wares?'

'Can't you see? Our baron, of course! He is going to marry the gipsy princess, so he will buy all your stock,' the gipsies cried indignantly, at the same time nudging the bear in the ribs. 'Will you pay, sir?' they shouted in his ear.

'Igen,' growled the bear, who now had one paw in the barrel of jam and the other in the cheese.

'Strange manners for such a nobleman,'

thought the merchant, but by then the gipsies were bombarding the bear with questions. 'Another sack of flour? Some dripping? A jug of honey perhaps? Gherkins? Bacon and corn?'

'Igen, igen, igen,' growled the noble bear, licking his lips. The merchant, quite convinced, was now busily helping to load everything onto the cart. He was at the same time counting how much extra money he would make that night.

When everything had been loaded and the shop was quite bare, the gipsies said, 'Keep an eye on the noble baron for us. Let him sleep a while. He has eaten well, so his tongue is somewhat heavy, and his head is heavy too. When he awakes, he will pay you well!'

By then the bear was indeed snoring loudly and happily. The shopkeeper rubbed his hands in glee at the splendid sale he had made, and he bade farewell to the gipsies.

The merchant waited and waited for the baron to awake. Hour after hour passed until in the end he lost patience. Grabbing the wealthy nobleman by his collar, he shouted in his ear, 'Pay up at once, Baron, or I shall have you arrested.' With a great rumble, the bear awoke, picked up the astonished merchant and rammed him up to the neck in the barrel of jam.

'Glory be! This is no baron, but a bear! Those rascally gipsies have fooled me again.'

'Igen,' agreed the bear in Hungarian as he too shuffled off into the night.

Prince Miaow

In a high greenwood there once stood a palace on stilts, and everyone who wanted to enter the palace — and there were thousands — had to climb a very tall ladder. It was such a huge palace that the entire kingdom could squeeze into it. Every nook and cranny was filled with an uncle or an aunt, a grandfather or grandmother, a father, a mother, and scores of children. Over this kingdom there ruled a brother and his five sisters.

One day the youngest sister told her older sister to whisper to her older sister to ask her older sister to mention to the eldest sister that it was time their brother, the king, should get married. And so all five sisters sent him to the neighbouring kingdom to seek a bride. He set off with a buffalo, three hens and three coconuts and brought back a fair princess as his bride. They climbed up the ladder and moved into the kingdom where every nook and cranny was filled with uncles and aunts, grandfathers and grandmothers, fathers and mothers, with scores of children and the five sisters too.

A son was born to the king and his princess. But to the astonishment of all, the minute the baby opened his eyes, he pursed his lips and cried, 'Miaow'.

The youngest sister told her older sister to tell her older sister to whisper to her older sister to say to the eldest sister that, belive it or not, the baby had the face of a kitten. So they called him Prince Miaow. His father, the king, was so ashamed he set off at once to find another bride, muttering that he refused to have kittens for children.

He said this to his youngest sister, so that she could tell her older sister to pass it on to all the other sisters.

The princess, his wife, wept till her heart nearly broke. Nobody knew why her son looked like a kitten, and though the magician who lived in the palace tried, he could not turn him into a real boy. Prince Miaow was not unhappy, for people liked him as he was. But dogs hated him and every day he had to climb to the top of the highest tree to keep out of their way.

As the days passed, his mother, the princess, wept more and more and the cat boy was sorry for her. He cuddled up to her one day, purring and miaowing.

'Don't cry, Mother,' he whispered. 'I'll be a mighty king one day.' But his mother would not be comforted. 'Only mice are afraid of you, my furry prince,' she sobbed, while tears as big as peas rolled down her cheeks.

When Prince Miaow grew into a cat man, he

went to his youngest aunt and asked her to tell all his other aunts that his father was returning at last and bringing with him a new bride. The aunts were surprised that he could know this, but Prince Miaow only smiled and miaowed.

'How I know I shall not say, but my nose tells me that they are on their way, miaow, miaow, miaow.'

He told everyone to go and meet his father who was returning to rule them and they all went out to greet him and his new bride. Prince Miaow bowed deeply before her and miaowed, 'Miaow, miaow, miaow, don't be ashamed of your tomcat stepson, for soon you will have a furry daughter and I shall have a furry sister.'

When his father heard these words he grew so angry he wanted to kill his cat son there and then. But the people stopped him. They were afraid such an act would bring ill fortune upon them.

Soon great celebrations took place in the village. The king and his bride invited everyone in the kingdom to the wedding, everyone except Prince Miaow and his mother — so ashamed were they of him.

'Don't cry, Mother,' Prince Miaow whispered consolingly. 'One day I shall be a mighty king.'

'But only mice are afraid of you,' sighed his mother and went off to tend the buffalo. When this was done, she sat down under a palm tree and with tears in her eyes recited sad poems to her son. One went like this: My furry son might think himself a knight. As he licks milk and rice — but all he can fight are mice!

Prince Miaow listened, said not a word, just smiled.

'I am off to find a bride, Mother,' he announced one day.

'But who would have you, my tomcat boy?' his mother asked wistfully. Her only answer was a happy miaow from her son.

Prince Miaow followed the mice who ran in front of him until at last he came to another kingdom. The king was squatting on his heels by a ladder, sighing with despair. 'Where do all those mice come from?' he groaned. 'They've eaten all our rice, they've got into all our cornlofts. How can I keep order in my kingdom?'

The tomcat prince at once offered to drive the mice out of the kingdom, if the king agreed to give him one of his daughters for a wife.

'Which of my daughters will take a cat prince for a husband?' the king cried. 'One of you must agree or my kingdom will be overrun by mice.'

The princesses looked out and squealed in horror at the sight of so many mice. Then the

king's youngest daughter stepped forward, although she was the one who most feared mice.

The king smiled with pleasure and relief. Thereupon the cat prince stamped his feet, snarled and spat and the mice scattered in all directions. In a few seconds there was not a single mouse to be seen.

'What can I do now for you?' asked the prince. The king sent him to work in the fields,

and later when his task was finished, Prince
Miaow went to bathe in the lake. His bride, the
youngest princess, was secretly watching from
a distance. To her amazement she saw him pull
the cat skin from his face and turn into the most
handsome youth. Furthermore, he began to sing
without a single miaow.

The princess ran home as fast as her legs
would carry her and promised her father, the
king, that most certainly she would marry the
furry-faced prince. The king ordered the big
drum to be beaten to announce the glad news to
his entire kingdom.

Great celebrations were held and everyone

danced and rejoiced. But behind her back the
other sisters laughed at the youngest princess.

And so Prince Miaow was married to the
daughter of a rich king. Full of happiness he
took her home to his mother who still lived in
that cottage on stilts far up in the greenwood.
They climbed in up the ladder and Prince
Miaow presented his bride proudly to his
mother who was so amazed that she stopped
weeping.

'Why do you hide your true face from me?'
the princess asked her tomcat husband one day.

The prince was surprised. 'How do you know
what I really look like?' he asked.

'A prickly shell sometimes hides delicious fruit,' the princess replied. 'My good husband, do not let your mother suffer further. She has wept so many tears for you. Now it is time for you to work whatever magic is necessary in order to turn your face into that of a man.'

'Very well,' Prince Miaow agreed. 'Drain the milk from seven coconuts, weave seven mats and light seven fires in seven hearths. The milk you must pour into seven wells, the mats you must make into seven beds for seven lizards, and the fires you must take to seven old women. They must then throw the red hot cinders into my face!'

The princess went off in search of the seven coconuts. She drained the milk into seven hearths. Then she wove seven mats, and gave them to seven lizards to use as beds. Finally, she lit seven fires and sought out seven old women to throw the red hot cinders into Prince Miaow's face.

When the old women carried out his strange request, the furry skin caught fire and the prince plunged his face into the seven wells full of co-conut milk. At the same moment the mats turned into stables, the lizards into buffalo and the tomcat prince into the most handsome young man. The princess was amazed at all the wonderful transformations that were taking place before her eyes.

'The spirits gave me a cat's face so that I could test which people were cruel and which kind and wise. Those of you who were good to me will fare well. But those who wished me harm will suffer misfortune in return.' So spoke the prince.

In a trice his father's home burned to the ground, the buffalo fell dead in their pen and fleas bit the king's second wife with all their might till she ran screaming into the forest never to return. The king came like a beggar to his tomcat son and his mother, asking for food and drink. The prince would not listen, but his mother said, 'Forgive him, my son, for you are now a mighty king.'

And the prince to please her, forgave his old father.

And they all lived happily together as before in the palace on stilts far up in the greenwood. It was such a huge palace that a whole kingdom could squeeze into it.

Prince Miaow and his princess had five pretty little girls — not with fur, but with curls, and they also had a little son. Their happiness was complete and their children were all good and kind to everyone they met.

Urashima

Somewhere in the middle of the vast ocean lies an island where people say the sun sets. In ancient times a young fisherman lived on this island. His name was Urashima. Each morning he set sail with a happy song on his lips and wait for fish of all colours to swim into his net. There were days when the catch was good, and he and his parents smiled and were happy. Then came a time when it seemed that the sea had turned against Urashima. Day after day, from dawn till dusk he sat in his boat in the clear blue waters, but not a single fish swam into his net. Urashima's songs grew sadder and sadder.

'Do not fret, my son, all will be well again,' his mother would say, trying to cheer him, but Urashima refused to smile.

Then one morning he hoisted his white sail once again, saying to himself, 'If today I am unlucky and catch no fish to feed my father and my mother, I shall let the sea take me where it will.'

All day he waited with his net outspread and not a single fish did he catch. He was beginning to despair, when suddenly something flashed in the water beneath him and the net tightened with such force that his little boat almost keeled over. When Urashima saw what he had caught, he could hardly believe his eyes. Twisting and tossing in the net was a fish no fisherman had ever seen before. It shone as if made of solid silver, its fins were studded with pearls and on its head a gold crown glittered.

'At long last we shall be rich,' Urashima thought joyfully, already working out the value of his magnificent catch. But the fish gazed at him so wistfully, with eyes which seemed almost human, that in the end the young man could not bear to kill it. Next moment he had thrown it back into the ocean.

'What have I done!' he cried. 'I cannot return home once again empty-handed. I wish the cruel sea would swallow me!'

Suddenly he heard a mysterious voice calling him. 'Urashima, kind Urashima!' The fisherman stared about him, but there was nothing to be seen, except a gigantic sea turtle swimming slowly round his boat.

'The king of all oceans has sent me,' said the turtle in a human voice, 'to thank you for letting his only daughter, the silver fish, go free. As a reward he invites you to visit him in his underwater kingdom.'

'How can I, a simple fisherman, swim down to the sea-bed?' Urashima replied. 'I would surely drown.'

But the turtle said, 'Salt water and sea creatures will not harm you, for you are under the protection of their king. Come, sit astride my back and I will take you to my master.' Urashima obeyed. They dived deeper and deeper and the water parted before them like a glass arch, and shoals of sharks guarded their way. They swam into a strange world of coloured lights, through wondrous gardens of sea anemones and coral caves. Octopus, with their long arms, smoothed their path through thickets of seaweed and rainbow-coloured fish fanned them with their frilly fins.

The old turtle told Urashima how the king's daughter had wandered too far from the underwater palace, till she was trapped in his net.

'I am the princess's old nurse,' she said. 'Had you not given her her freedom, I would have been punished, so I too thank you with all my heart.'

Urashima had no idea how long they swam. But all at once a dazzling blue glare flared from the sea-bed and before them stood the gateway

with the frilly fins into lively maidens with flowing veils and fish-scale hair. Their shark guards became knights, who, when they smiled, showed not teeth, but sharp daggers in their menacing mouths.

'Whoever enters the gate of the underwater palace loses his fish form and turns into a being similar to a man,' explained the turtle. 'Do not be afraid, Urashima, for here no one is allowed to do anyone harm. Sharks live in peace with cod and herrings, eels and sea snakes play happily in gardens with the youngest fish. Such is the law here.'

Suddenly shell-trumpets played a triumphant fanfare and a beautiful princess, the daughter of the king of the seas, appeared, accompanied by her maidens. Smiling, she took Urashima by the hand and led him through exquisite chambers to

to the underwater palace which was built of scarlet coral and shining pearls.

At their approach, the palace guards in sword-fish armour raised golden lanterns lit by the glow of tiny blue fish. Bowing, they opened the heavy gates made of diamond turtle shells and whale fins. Then the sea with a mighty roar closed behind them.

The wonders of this underwater kingdom amazed Urashima. The old turtle turned before his very eyes into a grand old lady and the little fish shells round Urashima's neck and set him on a chair of sea foam. Music like the murmur of the outgoing tide played and pearl tables laden with delicious food and wine appeared before him.

As Urashima ate, the princess told him strange tales of the underwater kingdom. But the young man grew restless. He thought of his parents and longed to return to them. In vain the princess begged him to stay but realizing at last that he would not change his mind, she led him to a room filled with wondrous treasures. She picked from a pile of gold and jewels an ordinary shell.

'This is a precious gift to remember me by,' she said. 'A magic stone lies in this shell — my father's most valuable jewel. You need only whisper your wish to the shell and the magic jewel will fulfil it. But you must not try to prise open the shell, for like the face of my noble father, the king of all seas, no one must look upon it.'

Urashima thanked the princess, bade her farewell and as the palace gates closed behind him, he climbed once more onto the back of the old turtle and soon found himself back on his native shore.

'Heed the princess's advice! Do not try to open the shell which contains the magic stone,' the old turtle called, as she disappeared into the deep.

The happy Urashima ran towards his parents' cottage, but it seemed as if the earth had swallowed it up. In vain he stared about him. The region seemed familiar, yet vastly different. Where a small copse grew by the banks of the creek there now stood a huge forest, and the slender young trees on the hillside now had thick and gnarled trunks.

'Can you tell me where I can find the parents of fisherman Urashima?' he called to a passer-by, but the man replied with a shrug of the shoulders, 'I have never heard that name.'

Urashima ran to the village. It had changed beyond recognition and he met only strangers. No one remembered his parents. Eventually he met a hundred-year-old monk. 'Urashima?' he muttered with surprise. 'I recall hearing of a young fisherman of that name, who one day many years ago disappeared into the sea. My parents told me of it.' It was then that Urashima realized that while he was in the underwater palace, above on earth many, many years had flown by. He sank into the grass and cried bitterly. Then he remembered the magic shell.

'If only our cottage stood here once more, if

a screen which glittered with scarlet corals, pearls and sea flowers.

'My noble father must remain unseen,' she whispered to Urashima. 'Anyone who looks upon his face will perish.'

From behind the screen came the roar of a voice which was like the crash of the incoming tide on a rocky shore.

'With all my heart I thank you, Urashima, for returning my daughter to me. Stay here as my guest for as long as you wish.' While the king spoke, invisible hands placed a necklace of gold only I could see my parents again,' he whispered. At that moment a gigantic wave crashed onto the shore and when the water had subsided, there stood the old cottage with his happy parents on the doorstep. Urashima told them his strange story and all that happened to him in the underwater kingdom.

The whole village gathered to listen and the kind fisherman with the help of the magic shell offered them food and drink and made all their dearest wishes come true.

The governor of that region heard of Urashima and one day he sent his officials to see him. 'Tell us, Urashima, can your magic shell bring money?' they asked, after hearing the young fisherman's tale. A few whispered words to the shell and two heaps of gold coins fell from it in front of the astonished officials.

'Aha,' they cried. 'We have caught you breaking the law, Urashima. Only the emperor has the right to issue money. We must therefore confiscate your magic shell.'

Overcome by curiosity, they began to prise it open with their knives. Urashima tried to warn them but it was too late. The shell cracked in their impatient hands and the magic blue jewel was dazzling the eyes of the governor's men. Then it turned into a cloud of smoke which hid the faces of Urashima and his parents. Their hair turned as white as snow and their skin became dry and wrinkled as if they had lived for hundreds of years. The sea grew angry and a mighty tidal wave swept over the land carrying every living thing with it into the depths of the sea.

And so Urashima, his parents and his home disappeared for ever. But the sea birds say that he grew young again in the palace of the sea princess and that he lives there happily to this day never growing any older.

The Brave Clever Tailor

There once lived a little tailor called Thread who had a thin, frail body and a very small head. Though he was quick and nimble, he was so tiny he would have drowned in a thimble, so light that he could swing on a spider's web and so thin that he could squeeze through a wedding ring. A gentle breeze or a sudden sneeze would send him flying, but even when things were at their most trying, he would boast and brag about his own cleverness. This little tailor was sitting by the stove one day, surrounded by his many children, mending a pair of the mayor's best trousers and muttering under his breath, 'There's no justice in this world! Some people have plates laden with cakes, while the few crumbs others are blessed with get nibbled by flies! Just wait, you sly fly beauties. I'll show you I am someone to be reckoned with!' As if out of spite, more and more flies were settling on his table, hoping for a bite. Tailor Thread, furious at the sight, swung the mayor's trousers above his head and at one blow twenty flies lay dead.

'Now who would think me capable of such a feat?' the tailor swaggered, his chest swelling with pride. Feeling daring, he hopped into the mayor's best trousers, muttering that he was not going to spend his whole life pricking his fingers with needles, and being so poor he could scarcely make ends meet. On and on he chattered and complained, complained and chattered until at last he talked himself to a standstill. Then turning to his eldest son he told him to write in his best handwriting on a little wooden pendant these words,

'Twenty at one blow!'

Then he called his wife and children, gave each one a peck on the cheek and a pat on the head and with the pendant round his neck, he set off to seek his fortune.

It was just as well there was no wind blowing from the fields that day, otherwise he would most likely have been swept to the very edge of the world. At a brisk pace he marched along with his head held high as proudly as a peacock, and wherever he went, people put their heads together and whispered, 'Look at him! Look at him! Who would have thought he could do it? Such a little, thin fellow, yet he killed twenty at one blow!' And with great respect they stepped aside to let him pass. Naturally the tailor grew more and more vain.

It so happened that the little tailor came face to face with a devil. The devil looked just as one would expect — bedraggled, sooty and smelly, with pointed horns, a moth-eaten tail sticking out of his breeches and a hoof on one foot.

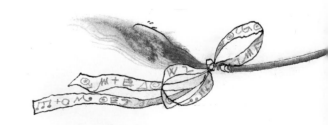

Tailor Thread gasped and stopped dead. But his courage quickly returned and he raged and stormed in a voice like the faint tweet of a tiny sparrow.

'Out of my way, you horny, mangy creature,' he cried at last and proudly he stuck the pendant with the inscription in front of the devil's nose. The devil balanced his glasses on the tip of his nose, and licking the corner of his grubby mouth with his sharp little tongue, he slowly began to read, 'Twenty at one blow!'

'Where did a scoundrel like you learn to read?' thundered the tailor, his voice like the twitter of a finch. 'I'll lead you by the ear back to school!'

That scared the devil. 'What harm have I done you?' he stuttered, trying to calm the fuming tailor. 'Besides, I could use a strong fellow like you. In hell I have scores of children so lazy they have no idea how to fend for themselves. Come into my service! All you'll have to do will be to fetch water and wood, so that I can take things easier in my old age. If you take on this work for three years, I shall give you a sack full of devil-gold!'

The brave, little tailor readily agreed, shrugged his shoulders and went to serve the devil.

'Who is this?' cried the devil's old wife, when she saw Tailor Thread. 'This is to be our new labourer? Why, he looks like a bent blade of grass! He seems to end where he begins. Look at his skinny legs — even mosquitoes would be ashamed of them!' While the woman went on, the devil tried to catch her eye, worried that her silly prattle would anger the tailor who with one blow had wiped out a round twenty.

The old woman stopped at last and handed Tailor Thread a leather flask. 'Off with you to the river and fill this with water!'

Poor little tailor! It was hard enough for him to lift the empty flask, far less a full one. Sadly he staggered out of hell towards the river, complaining, 'The minute one problem is behind me, another jumps on my back!' He had travelled far and he was tired and out of breath, so he sat down on the river bank and absentmindedly raked the soil with a stick.

'Why are you wasting time?' cried the devil, who had come looking for him. 'The old woman is waiting for the water!'

'I thought how ridiculous it was to wear myself out going back and forth with that flask all day,' Tailor Thread explained. 'I am working out a plan to alter the flow of the river so that it goes straight into hell. Then you will have more than enough water to last you for years and years!'

The devil was horrified. 'I would rather do the

25

job myself than let that happen. All the dirt in hell would be washed away, and our children would catch cold from so much cleanliness. You had better leave this to me and go to the forest and cut down some trees.' Tailor Thread went. Time passed and he did not return. The old woman sent the devil to look for him. He found the little man tying all the trees together with rope.

'What are you doing, you idiot? Our fires are nearly out and you are playing about with bits of string. Why are you not cutting down these trees?'

'I do not want to spend all my days dragging piles of timber,' said the tailor curtly. 'It is much better to tie all the trees together and take the whole forest into hell at the same time.'

'What madness!' cried the devil shrilly. 'With all those trees about, there would be room for nothing else down there. I tell you I shall just do this job myself too.'

With that the devil gripped the very tip of the highest tree and bent it right over to the ground. 'Hold it a minute, something is biting my back,' he said to the tailor. The latter was pleased to oblige, but of course the moment the devil let

go his hold on the tree to scratch his back, it sprang back and the frail little tailor shot into the air like a stone from a catapult. Over the forest, over the pond and over the next field he flew, until at last he landed with a thud in the high grass, scaring a young rabbit out of its warren.

'Stop, stop!' Tailor Thread cried, but the terrified rabbit shot off like a bullet.

'That was bad luck,' sighed the tailor to the devil, when he appeared. 'I leapt right to the edge of the world for that rabbit, and the scoundrel dared to escape.'

The terrified devil ran for all he was worth back to hell. 'Let another devil take that tailor; we do not want him. He slays twenty at one blow, alters the course of a river single-handed, carries a whole forest on his back and to top it all thinks nothing of leaping to the edge of the world for a mere rabbit. Let us pay him off and release him from our service before he can do any more damage.'

'I protest,' said the strongest and the most miserly devil. 'Let him first match his strength against mine! Then we shall see who is the stronger; this tailor or me.'

The next morning the strongest devil said to Tailor Thread, 'Come and match your strength against mine! The one who cracks this whip with the most force wins. If you are the winner, I shall carry you home together with your sack full of devil-gold.'

'Why not?' the tailor agreed. 'You go first.'

The devil cracked the whip with such force that rocks cracked and Tailor Thread fell into the river with fright.

'My turn now,' he said, when he had scrambled out of the water. 'But, first close your eyes, so that they do not fall out at the crack of my whip.'

The stupid devil closed his eyes and the tailor hit him on the head with a stone, so hard that the devil fell unconscious to the ground. 'I am the winner,' cried Tailor Thread, when at last the devil came round.

And so the devil had to carry the tailor and his sack of gold all the way home.

When they arrived the tailor's wife was stuffing a sack with dry leaves to make a bed for their goat.

'Believe it or not,' the tailor remarked, 'my wife and children are stronger than I!' Unnoticed, he had exchanged the sack of gold for the sack of leaves. He asked his wife and children to throw the sack of gold he had brought into the attic. As it was full of leaves, they tossed it into the loft as if it was filled with feathers. Thereupon the devil took to his heels and soon he was only a cloud of dust disappearing into the distance. On the way to hell he met a wolf.

'Ha, ha, ha,' laughed the wolf, 'how easily you have been tricked. Come with me and I shall help you to steal back that sack of gold.'

The miserly devil agreed, but as he was suspicious by nature, he insisted they should both be harnessed to a donkey yoke for fear the wily wolf might outwit him and run off with the gold.

As they approached the tailor's cottage, his children were playing outside.

'Look at those funny beasts,' cried the youngest child.

'Let's tie them to our little wagon,' shouted the cleverest.

'We can pull their tails,' yelled the naughtiest. The devil and the wolf did not wait to hear more, but ran for their lives.

And so Tailor Thread — and his family — outwitted two devils and a wolf. And that brave little tailor who one day had dared to hop into the mayor's best trousers was elected mayor himself and wore mayor's trousers to the end of his days and nobody ever managed to trick him.

The Magic Rattle

In a far away land among dense green forests the Indian people lived, hunting for food with blowpipe and arrows.

Once upon time a young hunter named Vovo lived in this land. He was good and he was kind but as a hunter he had little skill. His three sisters were married to the three best hunters in the whole village, and as Vovo rarely trapped or killed anything in the forest, they laughed and sneered at him nastily and called him a clumsy oaf. The young man became more and more unhappy.

One day Vovo found a nest full of baby birds in the forest. 'I'll show my brothers-in-law, that I am a fine hunter,' he muttered, his arrow pointing straight at the bird's nest.

But the baby birds cried out to him, 'Do not kill us, Vovo and we will reward you handsomely. Take the hollow gourd from under our nest. When you want to catch fish, plunge it in the river and half fill it with water. Remember the gourd must be only half full.'

Vovo thanked the birds and ran off at once to the river, where he did what he had been told to do. The moment the gourd was in the water, the river started to pour into it, and soon the water round him only came up to Vovo's ankles. And everywhere he looked fish were leaping and tossing in the shallows. By then the gourd was half filled, and Vovo began to gather in his catch. When he had as many fish as he could carry, he set off for home in high spirits. Instead of praising him, his brothers-in-law only scowled at him in envy. When Vovo let them into the secret of the magic gourd they pestered him until at last he gave it to them.

The first day they followed his advice and half filled the gourd. Their catch was so great they could hardly drag the fish to the village. But the next day their greed took over. Hoping for an even bigger catch, they plunged the gourd into the river and filled it to the brim. No sooner had they done this than the water poured back into the river with such force that the greedy men were almost drowned. The magic gourd was carried away by the current and the brothers-in-law turned in fury on Vovo, blaming him for nearly killing them with his magic.

Vovo sadly walked along the river following the current and searching for his lost gift. Suddenly there was a hum of wings above and a bird's cry floated down to him.

'In vain you search, Vovo,' it said. 'The fish have carried off your gourd. But as you spared the lives of the baby birds, we will give you a magic arrow. When you use it, your aim will be true. But remember to insert the arrow only half-way into your blowpipe!' As the bird finished speaking, a bright little arrow fell at Vovo's feet. The young man did not hesitate, but placed the arrow half-way down his blowpipe, as the bird had told him, and shot at random. Straight away ducks and geese and a host of other wild birds fell at his feet.

Once again the good-natured Vovo allowed his brothers-in-law to persuade him to tell his secret and to lend them the magic arrow. Just as before, for a time the brothers-in-law did what Vovo told them, inserting the arrow only half-way into the blowpipe. Then again they were overcome with greed and they pushed the

this magic rattle, but beware: each day you may rattle it only once.' With that the magic rattle on which secret signs were painted landed at Vovo's feet. The minute he shook the rattle, deer, tapirs and wild pigs ran out of the thicket, falling before him as if struck by lightning.

But Vovo was doomed not to keep the rattle for long. His wicked brothers-in-law robbed him of it, and as they wanted to be known as the greatest hunters of the forest, they did not heed Vovo's warning, but shook the magic rattle a second time. Immediately wild beasts sprang upon them from the bushes — caimans, pumas, jaguars — and this time the greedy hunters did not escape the fury of the forest.

When his brothers-in-law failed to return, Vovo set out to search for them. In the dense undergrowth all he found was his magic rattle and a heap of bones. Straightaway he knew that his brothers-in-law once again and for the last time had not listened to him. He brought the sad tidings to the village and ever afterwards he told no one the secret of the magic rattle. For him it never lost its amazing powers and Vovo became renowned throughout the land as the greatest hunter of the forest.

arrow down fully into their blowpipe. The moment they fired, wild vultures and eagles swooped upon them out of the sky, attacking them so fiercely with claws and beaks that it was a miracle the hunters escaped with their lives.

Yet again they turned on Vovo in fury and blamed him for nearly killing them with his magic. The unhappy young man turned away and wandered into the forest in search of the magic arrow, lost by his greedy brothers-in-law in their flight.

'Your bird brothers have taken your arrow,' chirped a bird voice from above. 'But as you had pity on us, we will give you one more gift. Take

The Enchantress Medusa

Once upon a time there was a powerful king, envied by all other rulers for his fame and riches. But he was not a happy king, for there was no one to whom he could leave his kingdom. He took no pleasure in life and entertainment, but spent all his days on his knees in the royal chapel praying for an heir. Year followed year but the cradle in the royal chamber remained empty.

Then one day, when the king was sighing as usual over his fate, he heard a gentle voice whisper, 'I shall fulfil your wish, oh King, but first you must decide whether you want a son who will die, or a daughter who will run away?'

The king asked the mysterious voice to give him a day to make his choice and hastened to consult his ministers. They put their heads together and stayed with their heads together till the eldest councillor, who had the greatest brain in the kingdom, pronounced, 'What can one do with milk that is spilled? What can one do with a son who does not live? It is far better to have a dove loose in the world, and an empty cage in the royal palace. Tell the mysterious voice to grant you a daughter, oh King!'

Thus it came to pass that less than a year later a beautiful baby girl lay in the royal cradle. The king built a castle in a deserted garden for the princess, and round it a wall which reached to the sky, and beyond it he had a moat dug which was as deep as an abyss. The waters of all the rivers of his kingdom flowed into it. There was only one golden bridge where the moat could be crossed and only one golden gate leading into the castle. There was only one gold key to open the lock of the gate, and the king carried it with him constantly. All this he did so that his daughter could not escape. But it was useless.

One day, when the princess was grown up, the king lost the key from his pocket. A young prince from the neighbouring kingdom found it and tried it in the lock of the golden gate in the high wall. And so it was that the princess met her bridegroom.

The prince took the king's daughter to his kingdom and when the king heard that his daughter had escaped, he vowed vengeance on the princess and her bridegroom. But he dared not enter the neighbouring kingdom.

The days passed and the princess gave birth to a little son. He grew day by day, and before long he had become a handsome youth. The young prince asked questions about his grandfather.

'Your grandfather was very angry when I left him to marry your father,' said his mother. 'Beware that his anger does not fall upon your head!'

But the young prince did not heed his mother's warning, and one day he set out to see the old king.

'Get out of my sight,' fumed the king, when his grandson bowed before his throne. 'I have neither a daughter nor a grandson. I have been forsaken. But if you insist in proving your love and loyalty to me, bring me the head of the enchantress Medusa. Then you shall indeed rule over my kingdom.'

And the king laughed harshly.

People spoke only in whispers of the cruel sorceress Medusa; nobody dared to say her name aloud. They said she was evil, yet so beautiful, that whoever looked upon her turned to stone. The young prince was not afraid. He mounted his horse and went to seek the palace of the beautiful enchantress and carry out the mission set by his grandfather.

In vain he asked everyone he met vhere she was to be found. As soon as he mentioned her name, people fled in fear. One day he came upon a frail old man at the foot of a steep mountain. He was huddled by the path, trying to protect his eyes with his hands from wild birds who were attacking them with their beaks. He would surely have died if the prince had not come to his rescue and drawn his sword and killed his attackers.

'Thank you with all my heart for saving me,' said the old man. 'I can read people's thoughts and therefore I know where you are going. Without my help you would never reach Medusa's palace.' The old man whistled and a winged horse flew down from the sky.

'The enchantress Medusa lives in a palace built of the teeth of poisonous snakes. It lies beyond impassable mountains, beyond uncrossable rivers. But my winged horse will take you there safely,' said the old man. 'Just remember never to look at the sorceress, not even out of the corner of your eye, or you will turn to stone.'

'How can I cut off her head if I cannot look at her?' the prince asked. 'It may be best to give up and return home.'

The old man reassured him with a smile. 'Do not fear! Behind a glass mountain two old women live in a glass house. They own a magic mirror. They can observe the whole world in this mirror, even the sun and the stars. Yet neither the heat of the sun nor the frost of the stars can harm them, for the mirror turns everything that is extraordinary into ordinary, everything that is monstrous into insignificant. Steal it from these women and when you reach Medusa's palace, do not look at her directly, but watch her only in the magic mirror. Then her evil beauty will not harm you in any way.'

The prince thanked the old man, bade him goodbye, and flew off on the winged horse into the sky.

As they soared over the glass mountain, he saw two strange-looking old women strolling in the garden of the glass house. In their hands they held the magic mirror. The winged horse descended and the prince saw that they had only one eye between them, which they lent to each other. The prince dismounted, wondering how he could capture the mirror.

Just then one of the women said, 'Lend me our eye, dear sister, for I want to see what is new in the world.' The other woman plucked the eye from her brow and was about to hand it over. At that moment when neither could see, the prince stretched out his hand and took the eye.

'When will you give me that eye?' snapped the first old woman crossly.

'But I put it in the palm of your hand,' protested the second. As they started to quarrel and grope for the eye, the mirror was put down on the ground and this was what the prince had been waiting for. Swooping on the magic mirror, he again jumped into the saddle and rose into the clouds.

The winged horse flew on and on, till at last the prince saw far below the palace built of the teeth of poisonous snakes and surrounded by a forest of stone. As far as the eye could see, everything was of stone. Trees and flowers, beasts and birds, all had been turned to stone by the enchantress Medusa.

The prince flew down into the courtyard and cried, 'Enchantress Medusa, I have come for your head!' Spine-chilling laughter resembling the hissing of snakes came from within the palace. After a moment Medusa walked into the courtyard.

'Look into my eyes, handsome youth,' she tempted him. But the prince refused and watched her only in the magic mirror. As the sorceress came near, he tossed his scarf over her and with one swift blow cut off her head.

Springs of poisonous blood gushed from her body and instantly changed into a score of snakes which turned hissing on the prince. He

would have paid dearly for his bravery if it had not been for the winged horse. As if by a magic command the mount, the prince and the severed head rose into the sky, and soon the palace was out of sight.

Suddenly far below there appeared by the seashore a city shrouded in black. 'What a strange sight that is,' said the prince, and flew down to look more closely.

Kneeling by the sea and weeping bitterly, he saw a beautiful maiden dressed in black. 'Fly for your life,' she cried to the prince. 'I am the daughter of the king of this land and today the seven-headed dragon of the sea is to come for me!'

But the prince was not afraid. 'Out with you, monster! Come and fight!' he cried. Great waves crashed against the shore and the dragon with seven heads rose out of the sea.

'Who dares to challenge me?' he thundered, tongues of fire leaping from his seven mouths. The prince did not hesitate, but pulled the scarf from Medusa's head. As soon as the dragon's eyes fell upon it, he turned to stone.

The whole kingdom rejoiced and the happy king gave his rescued daughter as a bride to the brave prince, together with gold, silver and precious jewels.

Time passed and then one day the prince again visited his grandfather. The old king was amazed, for he thought his grandson must have surely perished in all his adventures.

'Show me Medusa's head!' he cried. 'If you have come empty-handed I shall throw you into a dungeon!' The prince warned the king what would happen to him but the old man insisted on seeing the head. Reluctantly the prince pulled off the scarf and held high the severed head. In that instant the king was turned to stone. It is still said that it was a just punishment for not learning how to forgive.

The brave prince and his bride reigned wisely and well and were loved by their people. As for the winged horse, the magic mirror and Medusa's head — they vanished forever.

The Master Pupil

Once upon a time in a distant land in the depths of a forest there stood a little hut. This was the home of a hermit who was very wise. He was so wise he could read ancient books and the night sky. He knew the language of woodland flowers, of birds and fishes and trees. He knew how to sleep on his back and on his knees, in shorts, he was so wise and knew so much, that he could not remember all the things he had learned in his lifetime. So he always had to start learning everything again from the very beginning, till he found out what he had forgotten and before he forgot again what he had found out. This is how it went on forever and ever. He was renowned in the district for his wisdom and knowledge, and scores of pupils would come to his little hut to learn the secrets of the world.

The hermit's fame reached the ears of the parents of a young lad whose nickname was Gorger.

'My dear boy,' his father said, 'if only human wisdom could be measured by tomfoolery, tricks and pranks, then you would indeed be voted the greatest brain on earth. But a disobedient rascal like yourself does not turn into a noble, learned man when he refuses to listen to his parents or to read holy books. As your head is as empty as your everlastingly hungry stomach, we shall send you to this wise hermit. Perhaps he will teach you the meaning of moderation, obedience and learning.'

Gorger did not argue, but ate as much food as he could before starting out on his journey and off he went to stay with the hermit.

The good hermit did his best to fill the boy's head with wisdom and knowledge, but alas, most of it went in one ear and out the other. It was no wonder Gorger did not listen, for his stomach was so empty, he could think of nothing else but his mother's cooking. Food was not important to the old hermit. He made do with anything the forest provided. A handful of berries now and then, a mouthful of water from the spring, a few nuts were enough to satisfy him. But poor Gorger was so hungry he could scarcely listen to the wise words of his master for the rumblings and whistling of his stomach.

One day the hermit turned to him with a frown. 'Listen to me, you disobedient pupil,' he said. 'Everything I tell you goes right through your head, yet your greedy eyes devour everything in sight. Take this basket and go and beg for food in the village. No one will refuse to give to a pupil of mine.'

Gorger gladly did as he was told. One villager gave him a bun, another gave him two, and

yet another even gave him four. Before very long the basket was filled to the brim with buns and cakes. The sight gladdened his heart and Gorger licked his lips as he sniffed the wonderful smell of fresh baking. Who could resist it?

The ravenous Gorger sat down in the shade of a fig tree and thought to himself. 'My master is a good and godly man. He is sure to give me half of these buns and cakes. So why shouldn't I take my share now?' And before anyone could have counted to five, Gorger had gobbled half the basketful. He did not take one too many, just his fair share. Oh, how delicious they were!

The lad rose and continued on his way. He went on and on, the delicious taste of the buns and cakes still fresh on his tongue. Suddenly his mouth started to water again.

'When I give my teacher the rest of the cakes, he is sure to give me a half,' he thought to himself. 'So why shouldn't I help myself now?' With that, half the basketful disappeared down his throat. Now it was only a quarter full. You would think that Gorger had had enough now. But no!

'My teacher is sure to give me half of these buns and cakes when I get back to his little hut,' he said to cheer himself. And again he divided

the contents of the basket in two, and like lightning gobbled up his half.

And so he went on, dividing what was left again and again, till there was only one little bun in the basket.

'Well,' Gorger muttered, 'when I give my teacher this bun, he is sure to divide it in two.' And in one bite half of the last bun vanished. So Gorger went back to the hermit with only half a bun.

'Is this all you have been given?' the holy man asked in amazement.

'Oh no, I had a full basket,' Gorger truthfully replied. 'The rest I ate on the way, but always taking only the half you would have given me, for you are so good and kind.'

'Upon my word,' said the hermit in wonder. 'How could you eat them all?'

'How? Like this!' Gorger replied, and the last half bun disappeared before the hermit's eyes.

'Return home, dear Gorger,' said the old man, shaking his head sadly. 'Tell your parents I taught you nothing, but that you taught me much wisdom. An empty stomach contains more craftiness than a crammed head.' And the hungry hermit went off into the forest to collect a handful of berries for supper.

Jack and the Beanstalk

Beyond mountains and valleys and endless rivers and a thousand brooks, there once stood a little cottage where young Jack lived. He had no father, just a tired, hardworking mother whose hair was as grey as cobwebs and whose face was lined by the many tears she had shed. She was the kindest mother in the world and every morning Jack swore that he would do as he was told. This was not easy, for he was very lazy.

One sunny day his mother sat Jack on her lap, stroked his head and sighed, 'Jack, my son, life is hard. The flour bin is empty, our last apple has rotted in the cellar and all we have left in the pantry is an empty jar. There is only one thing to do. Tomorrow you must take our cow to market and sell her. But as we have nothing else left, you must make sure that no one cheats you, or we shall starve to death.'

Little Jack put on the one wooden clog left by his grandfather, pulled the remains of a tattered hat left by his father onto his head, and giving his mother a kiss, he set off with the cow for the town. He was very near to tears, for he loved the little cow very much.

On the road he met a strange old man. He was tattered, untidy and grubby. On his head there were horns, just like goat's, and his feet were the wrong way round, the left on the right side, and the right on the left. If he had not smiled kindly at Jack, the lad would surely have taken to his heels.

'Where are you going, little one?' asked the old man, a glint in his eyes. Bravely, Jack told him he was going to the town to sell his cow.

'There is no need to walk all that way. I will buy her from you,' said the old man. 'You will be paid handsomely.'

'Why not?' Jack agreed. 'One buyer is as good as another. But you are not to cheat me, or my mother will be angry.'

The strange man then opened his purse and took out a dry bean pod. 'Inside you will find magic beans,' he explained. 'When you plant them, they will grow right up to the sky!'

Jack could hardly wait to break the pod open, and when he saw the lovely coloured beans he could hardly tear his eyes away. He gave the cow to the old man and ran home to his mother as fast as his legs would carry him.

'Mother will be pleased that I did not let anyone cheat me,' he thought happily as he ran. But his mother wrung her hands in despair, when Jack showed her the beans, and cried.

'Oh, you stupid boy! Oh, you little fool! Now we shall surely starve!'

In her anger she threw all the beans out of the window into the garden.

Poor Jack! He had been so happy and now everything had gone wrong. Miserable and tired, he wandered into the garden, where at last he fell asleep. Then he had the strangest dream. He felt as if something was lifting him upwards, higher and higher, till his head began to spin. He awoke in fright and found to his astonishment that he was lying upon an enormous leaf which was supported by a gigantic beanstalk. And the stalk kept on growing, till Jack was going through black clouds and his cottage was a tiny speck below. Jack started to climb down by jumping from leaf to leaf. But the more he hurried, the faster the beanstalk grew, so Jack simply could not get any nearer to the ground.

So he shrugged his shoulders and said to himself, 'I may as well find out what is up there above the clouds.' And he climbed up the beanstalk as if it was a ladder. And as he climbed, the stalk stopped growing.

When Jack reached the very top, he gasped in astonishment. Far and wide, as far as the eye could see stretched a shining blue countryside with blue mountains, blue rivers and brooks. Even the grass, trees and flowers were blue like the sky. There was a blue path that led from the tip of the beanstalk to an enormous blue house. Jack had never seen such a huge house. Full of curiosity, he was walking towards it, when suddenly a hideous giantess appeared in the doorway. Her mouth went all the way round her face, her teeth were like yellow shovels and the one eye in the centre of her brow looked like a pancake. Jack barely reached up to her ankles.

'Look at that, a little man,' she cried joyfully, trapping Jack with her cap as if he were a butterfly. 'I need a scrap of a fellow like you to thread my needle.' Poor Jack did not dare to refuse, so he lifted the thread which was as thick as a log and jumped through the eye of the needle.

'Thank you, boy,' said the giantess, stroking

Jack's head so hard he went head over heels. 'I shall fry you an egg for your dinner, but then you must leave before my husband, the terrible man-eating giant returns.'

The giantess had just broken the shells of eggs as big as barrels when the ground shook and the giant stalked into the room. Jack scarcely had time to hide under an egg shell.

'I smell the strangest smell,' roared the giant. 'There's a human person here I can tell! He smells like an Englishman. Put him in the frying pan!'

Jack's heart was in his mouth, but the giantess calmed her husband and set the eggs before him. The giant swallowed them, frying pan and all, then stretched out on his bed. He ordered his wife to bring him a purse of gold, so that he could play with the coins. In his hands they tinkled merrily, and soon the giant fell into a deep sleep. Little Jack crept out from under the egg shell, seized the purse and ran for all he was worth. But the gold coins started to shout, 'Wake up, giant, can't you see that young thief is about to flee?'

The giant leapt from his bed, but by then Jack was climbing down the beanstalk, leaping from leaf to leaf like a squirrel.

'Just wait till I catch you,' stormed the giant from above, but by then Jack was safe in his mother's arms and she was not at all angry, so glad was she to see him and the purse of gold. Now they could be happy.

Before long Jack's inquisitiveness got the better of him and he climbed the beanstalk for the second time.

'A grateful guest you were,' grumbled the giantess when she saw him. 'Are you not the scoundrel who stole our purse of gold?'

'How can you think such a thing of me! It must have been someone else,' Jack answered indignantly.

The giantess believed him and told him to shell some peas for her. As soon as Jack began to work, the giant appeared. He sniffed and smelled and raved and ranted, but he did not find Jack, for the giantess had hidden him under a saucepan. When the giant had eaten, he fell on his bed and asked for his gold harp which played silver songs. Soon his snores were like the blowing of a gale. Jack crept out and tiptoed to his bedside, snatched the gold harp and raced to the beanstalk. 'Wake up giant, can't you see that young thief is about to flee?' cried the harp. But before the sleepy giant was quite awake, Jack was back with his mother.

'Just wait till I catch you,' the man-eating

giant thundered out of the clouds, but Jack only smiled and played silver songs on the golden harp.

For a time Jack was content to stay at home, but then one day he again climbed the beanstalk to the giant's house.

'You are the rascal who stole our golden harp,' cried the angry giantess.

'How can you think such a thing,' replied Jack, 'it must have been a boy from the village.' The giantess believed him and asked Jack to find her thimble which had fallen into a crack in the floor. Just then the giant came in sniffing and snarling. But he did not find Jack who had curled himself into a ball and was hiding in the thimble. Soon the giant was lying on his bed, this time playing with a golden hen, which laid golden eggs. The moment his eyes were shut, Jack seized the hen and raced for the beanstalk.

'Wake up, giant, can't you see that young thief is about to flee?' cried the hen. The giant jumped into his seven-league boots and rushed out in pursuit. This time he did not stop at the end of the blue path, but rolled down the beanstalk hot on Jack's heels.

Jack had just reached the safety of his mother's arms when he heard a crunching sound behind him. Lo and behold! The beanstalk had snapped under the giant's weight and he had fallen with a tremendous thud into the garden and been turned into a heap of stones.

After that Jack and his mother lived happily thanks to the hen that laid the golden eggs.

One day the strange old man suddenly appeared at their cottage. 'I am bringing back your little cow,' he said with a smile. 'She has been missing you.'

'Moo,' agreed the cow, giving a little curtsey.

The Magic Almond

There are little islands which lie in the middle of the ocean and when you fall asleep, it is to one of these that you drift. The tide which breaks upon their shores can tell many a tale like the one I shall tell you now.

Once long ago there lived on a little island a young man. He was called Sirini. He also had a beautiful sister who alas had married a very lazy fellow. So lazy was he that he refused to close his eyes at night because it was too much trouble to open them again next morning. And if, perhaps he chanced to fall asleep and dream of work, he was so exhausted, he had to rest in bed three days at least.

One day Sirini asked this idle fellow to come and work in the field. It needed a lot of persuasion from his wife to get him to stand up on his two feet, to push him onto the path and force him to move at all. Sirini had long since been in the field, digging and sowing, sweat pouring from his brow. But of the idler there was still no trace. Not till the sun was almost overhead did the fellow stagger into the shade of an almond tree which grew in one corner of the field. He looked at the field and said happily, 'Well, well, well, already a lot of work has been done, no wonder all the bones in my body are aching.' As all that gazing around made him terribly hungry, he returned home to eat his wife's good food.

'Where is Sirini?' his wife asked.

'Oh, that lazy fellow,' the idler muttered. 'He is sweating from so much idling, he cannot be bothered even to come home to eat. I suppose I must rest for him too.' With that her husband stretched out on his back and slept like the dead.

The next day the two men returned to the field and everything that had happened the day before happened again. Sirini toiled and the loafer lay under the almond tree, unwilling even to raise his eyes. But when he did look up he saw lovely ripe almonds in the branches above. His greedy eyes ate them up, but his mouth remained empty. He would need to stand and stretch up his arm. But he had done enough work with his eyes so he just rose and went slowly home to the food his wife had prepared.

'Sirini?' he yawned at his wife's question. 'That loafer! Sweat is pouring from him with laziness. He didn't even look up at the almonds in the tree.' And the idler fell flat on his back and slept.

The third day Sirini returned to the field and worked so hard he could hardly stand on his feet. At noon when he had almost worked over the whole field, his sister's husband appeared. Squatting under the almond tree, he was just able to look up.

'Almonds, I see!' he muttered very slowly, so as not to tire himself. His hungry eyes ate and ate, till that idler's body ached with the hard work. Now that he was doing such tiring work, he forced himself to rise to his feet and stretch up his hand to pick the ripe almonds. He ate with his eyes, he ate with his mouth, but soon the effort made him so weary that he fell flat on his back and slept like a log.

The patient Sirini had had enough. He picked a lovely almond, the biggest one on the tree and put a spell in it. He put it on the ground beside his sleeping brother-in-law and covered it with a pile of ordinary almonds.

When at last the lazy fellow awoke and saw the scrumptious feast, he sighed. 'How hard I must have worked in my sleep!' he muttered to himself. 'No wonder my whole body is aching.' With that he began to eat. What an effort that was! He ate with his eyes, he ate with his mouth, and among the other almonds he swallowed the magic one. Then very strange things began to happen to the idle fellow.

When he sighed with contentment at having eaten so well, a loud voice inside him suddenly yelled. 'Oh, how excellently well I have eaten today!'

The idler was scared, fearing that a thief was hidden among the branches of the almond tree, so he cried with all his might, 'Help! A thief!' He tried whistling to attract Sirini's attention, and the magic almond inside him whistled louder still.

Now he realized that the strange noises were coming from his own stomach.

He tried pinching his stomach hoping to quieten that terrible voice, but the almond only pinched him harder from inside, making him hop with the pain. The almond in his stomach began to hop too, till the idler, screaming with terror took to his heels and raced for home. Inside the almond too started to run. Round and round his stomach it went, faster and faster. When the lazybones in his hurry fell head over heels, the almond also fell head over heels. When he leapt up, the almond leapt up. When he tripped, the almond tripped.

'Help,' screeched the unfortunate fellow, holding his aching stomach. 'Something is trying to kill me!' The magic almond repeated every word.

By then workers from the fields all around were rushing towards him, trying to catch the demented fellow, for they thought he was about to harm somebody. They chased him till the sweat poured from his brow, they chased him till all the laziness and stupidity were sweated out of his head. Sirini then took away the magic spell, and from that day on his lazy brother-in-law was cured. He became as hard working as Sirini himself and he and his wife, Sirini's beautiful sister, lived happily to the end of their days.

But the magic spell has been tucked away somewhere for the others. Do you know how it is done? You take one large almond, the largest one . . . and have a go!

The Red Czar and the Golden-haired Tihota

There once was a mighty czar. His name was the Red Czar. He was red from head to toe. He even wore red sandals with red bobbles.

One day a great disaster struck the czar's country. Dragons stole the czar's sun and moon from the sky. There was such awful darkness both by day and night that people piled the blackness into tubs and emptied it into every river in the land. But even that did not help. No one in all the empire could see an inch in front of him. People slept with their eyes open, walked with their eyes closed. In short, everything was topsy turvy.

The Red Czar promised heaven on earth plus half his empire and his only daughter to anyone who would put the sun and the moon back in the sky. But even the boldest and most reckless men who tried, failed to find the dragons' secret hiding place.

The Red Czar roared in fury and threatened to behead the next person who did not succeed in tracking down the dragons' lair. But how could such an order be carried out when in the pitch dark no heads could be seen? Everyone in that empire grew sadder day by day. The wisest councillor told the czar one day to send for golden-haired Tihota.

'What an excellent idea,' said his royal majesty, 'why did I not think of it before?' And he struck his royal brow with his fist till it rang out like an empty wine barrel.

There was not a soul in the country who had not heard of the golden-haired knight. They said he could break rocks with his bare hands and uproot mighty trees with his little finger.

At once the czar's messengers were despatched to Tihota, carrying with them a sack of gold. When they reached him, Tihota was fast asleep in a meadow, his head in a beehive, his feet in an ant hill.

'Wake up, you lazy loafer,' the czar's men shouted, pricking him with their swords, but Tihota just flicked them aside with his hand as if they were flies. 'His Majesty, the Red Czar, orders you to find the sun and the moon which have been stolen by wicked dragons. If you do not succeed you will lose your head,' they said.

'I will go,' Tihota replied with a yawn. 'I have nothing better to do. But first I have to get even with you, you impudent oafs.' With that he picked up the beehive and poured the whole swarm of bees into the armour of one of the czar's messengers and the whole ant hill into the armour of the other. How those guards ran! How they shouted and screamed with pain and itching. No wonder too, for in their armour they

42

could not reach their tormentors. Tihota laughed so much he thought his sides would split.

At last he set off on his quest and, wherever he went, his golden hair shone so dazzlingly that people ran out of their houses crying, 'Look, look! The sun is coming out!' But who knew where the sun really was! Tihota certainly did not.

Eventually our hero came to the underground dwelling of the greatest blacksmith in the world.

'Thunder and lightning,' roared the blacksmith, his eyes like two bright fires, 'do you want a fight, or shall we drink to brotherhood?' 'If you are a good man, we'll drink to our brotherhood,' was Tihota's reply and he drained a whole barrel of wine in one gulp. The blacksmith liked that.

'You are a good fellow,' he said admiringly, patting Tihota's shoulder. 'I have heard rumours that you are off to the dragons' hiding place to fetch back the stolen sun and moon. The underground springs informed me. If you like, I will show you the way. But first stay a while in my forge and I shall teach you magic which will

help to protect you on your journey.' Tihota was happy to agree. For seven days and nights he dined and wined with the blacksmith and learned some useful sorcery. On the eighth day he was ready to start. Before he left, the blacksmith made a statue of Tihota out of pure iron and placed it in the furnace, so that it would stay red hot.

'Who knows, this statue may save your life one day,' the blacksmith said to Tihota as they parted.

Tihota followed the blacksmith's directions till he reached the end of the world. Here stood

the dragons' palace of black stone. Tihota leapt into the air, turned a cartwheel, and became a white dove. With her beak she tapped at a window of the black palace.

'Let that lovely white dove come in,' said the mother dragon to her two daughters.

But the younger one, who had writhing vipers instead of hair on her head, cried in terror. 'Oh mother no, for this dove has the eyes of the golden-haired Tihota, whom all the world fears. He would slay us!'

Realizing he had not outwitted the dragons, Tihota turned head over heels and next moment

became a tiny golden fly. In this guise he slipped into the room through the keyhole.

'What are you afraid of, you silly creatures,' the old dragoness was saying to her daughters. 'Don't you know we can only die by the magic dragon sword which hangs on that wall? Tihota will never reach it. When your father and your two brothers return from hunting in the Green Forest, we shall set a trap for Tihota and slay him!'

Hearing this, Tihota turned into an eagle and grasping the sword in his talons flew out of the window towards the Green Forest. Once there, he became once again the golden-haired Tihota.

'Come out, brave dragons! I challenge you to a fight,' he called.

At that moment a fierce gale sprang up, jagged lightning shot from the dark sky and the youngest dragon appeared before Tihota.

'Who dares to challenge us!' he stormed, his fiery tongue shooting towards Tihota. But the youth knew what he must do to this monster. Gripping the dragon round his waist, he buried him in the earth up to his neck. Then with one mighty blow of the magic sword he cut off his head. His brother, the second dragon appeared from the forest and shared the same fate. Only the old dragon king remained. The duel was long and fierce but at last the old dragon had to beg Tihota for mercy. He promised to open the black cave where the sun and moon were imprisoned using his little finger as the key. But Tihota did not trust the dragon. He cut off his head and also his little finger. Then he himself went to open the black cave in the Green Forest with the dragon's little finger. Grasping the sun and the moon in his great strong arms, he tossed them into the sky. Immediately the world was a happy place again. The sun shone warmly, people smiled gratefully and waved to the brave hero as he passed by on his way back to the Red Empire.

But on the journey Tihota lost his way. He found himself wandering in a magic garden where grew a golden pear tree heavy with fruit. Tihota's mouth watered at the sight. He was just about to pluck a ripe pear when he noticed that the bees were avoiding the tree. With the magic dragon sword, he cut down the tree at its roots, and as he did so the tree turned into the youngest dragoness with the hair of wirthing vipers. Next moment before Tihota's eyes, her hideous body had burned to a cinder.

Amazed and grateful to have escaped, Tihota wandered on till he saw a well where he might drink. By the well a beautiful rose grew. He

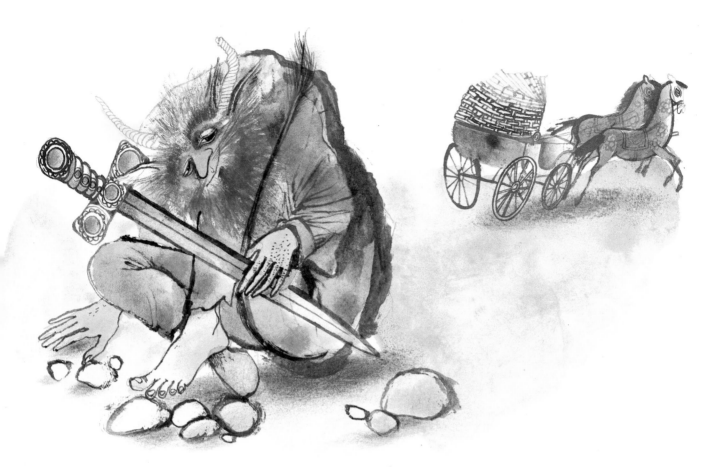

hesitated before he sipped. Not a single fish swam in the clear water, and no butterfly alighted on the lovely rose. Tihota cut through the flower's stem and plunged it into the well. Black blood gushed upwards and it became the body of the second dragoness who had bats instead of hair. Next moment she had disintegrated into evil-smelling black smoke. Tihota's cautiousness had saved him a second time.

Tihota had now used the dragon sword many times and its edge was no longer sharp. So he turned his steps towards the great blacksmith's forge. As he approached it, a black storm cloud appeared in the sky. It was the old dragoness. Her sharp eyes saw that the magic sword had become blunt. With fury in her dragon heart and eager for revenge, she launched herself at Tihota. Just in time he slipped into the forge.

The blacksmith had been watching. With a sudden, swift movement he threw Tihota's red hot statue at the dragoness and shouted, 'You are welcome to Tihota, dragoness, I do not want him here!' And the monster opened her mouth and swallowed the statue as if it had been a raspberry. The dragoness burst like a roasted chestnut and as she cooled, her body turned into a mountain of iron. The blacksmith made an iron carriage and a pair of iron horses out of it. They behaved like real live mounts and when harnessed to the carriage, they carried Tihota to

the beautiful palace of the mighty Red Czar.

But the ungrateful Red Czar was now unwilling to give Tihota his daughter and half his empire, and he sent an old devil to meet him. The sly devil turned into a large boulder blocking the path. When Tihota climbed down from his carriage to push the boulder aside, the old devil seized his chance. As quickly as lightning he became a devil again, took the dragon sword from the carriage and turned back into a boulder before Tihota had noticed.

'Where is the magic dragon sword?' thundered the czar the moment Tihota entered the palace. 'If you cannot produce it as proof, I will have you beheaded.'

Tihota recalled the strange boulder and asked the king to grant him a little time. Returning to the spot, he crushed the devil stone to powder. Tihota found the sword hidden under the crushed devil stone and returned to the palace.

'Here is the dragon sword,' he said, and shook it menacingly before the eyes of the Red Czar. 'Give me your daughter and half of your empire or it is I who will behead you.'

How did it all end? The Red Czar saw that he must agree or die. And so Tihota amidst great festivities married the daughter of the czar and in time the golden-haired hero became ruler not only of half but the whole empire and was loved by all his people.

The Six Fools

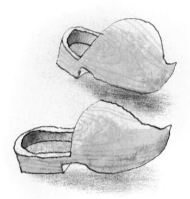

Once long ago there was a miller and his wife who lived comfortably and well. They owned a mill, a fertile field and had a daughter who was as pretty as a picture. Unfortunately, she was as stupid as she was beautiful. It is true, alas, she was sillier than a goose! She could not tell her right hand from her left, went to school on Sunday, said 'good day' to her own shadow and asked the scarecrow in the field to be her partner at the harvest ball. So muddled was she that needless to say young men did not even spare her a glance and her poor parents were worried that she would never be a bride.

And thus one day a poor young traveller passed the mill. His stomach was so empty, it rumbled like thunder and the wind whipped through the holes in his pockets. It so happened that there was a pig roasting in the oven of the mill and the succulent smell drifted out to the wanderer's nose most temptingly.

'Living here would suit me very well,' he thought with longing.

At that moment the miller's pretty daughter had come into the courtyard to draw water from the well. The tattered traveller started to woo her over the garden gate. The minute her parents noticed, they rushed out and began to sing their daughter's praises. They then invited the man to join them at their dinner table. To tempt the stranger further, they sent their daughter to the cellar to fetch a jug of beer.

The girl stood the jug under the tap of the beer barrel, and sat down on the cellar stair and stared into space. Her eye suddenly caught sight of an old rusty axe, wedged into the wooden frame above the door.

'My goodness,' she cried, 'how awful! What if I wed that handsome fellow and what if we have a son! What if he grows up and comes down into this cellar to fetch beer! What if that axe falls down and kills our son! What a disaster that would be!' And the wretched girl began to sob bitterly as if the world was coming to an end.

'What are you gazing at here?' said her mother sharply, coming down to find her. With tears and sobs her simple daughter described the misfortune which would meet her son. And the miller's wife sat down and she too began to cry bitterly. Some time later, the miller, growing impatient, also went down to the cellar to see what was keeping his wife and daughter. When he was told, he too sat down and wept. All three were crying their hearts out when the young traveller appeared. His mouth was so dry that

his tongue felt like cardboard. When he saw the unhappy trio and heard their weeping and wailing and looked at the beer which was spilling all over the floor, his heart almost stopped. 'What is going on here?' he asked. 'Are you trying to drown in beer?'

'Alas, alas,' they wailed in unison. 'Just listen to the calamity that awaits your son.' And they told him. The traveller roared till he nearly choked. He took hold of the axe and tore it out of the wooden frame, threw it into a corner and said, 'I have never met such fools. I would rather go to another house than marry into such a stupid family. But to show there is no ill feeling, I promise to marry your daughter if I come across another three people as stupid as you.' And off he went.

The traveller walked along until he came to a big oak tree. There a strange sight met his eyes. A man was trying to persuade a little pig to climb up into the branches of the tree.

'What do you think you're doing with that animal?' cried the traveller.

'Can't you see for yourself?' snapped the stranger. 'I am teaching it to climb, so that it can pick its own acorns. After all, I can't let it die of hunger.'

'You poor fellow,' laughed the traveller, 'why don't you simply shake the tree and the acorns will fall down?'

'I never thought of that,' said the foolish fellow. 'Thank you for the clever advice! I will do as you suggest.'

The traveller decided it would be hard to find anyone more stupid in the world. But he was wrong! Before the sun went down, he came upon a man who was standing on his head in the middle of the path. His legs were jerking about in the air, as if he wanted to walk upside down.

'My hat has fallen off,' he complained, 'and I simply can't get it back on my head like this. Whenever I try to get on my feet again, the hat falls off my head again.'

'You fool, why don't you put it on with your hands?' laughed the traveller.

'That never occurred to me,' said the stranger, and picking up the hat with his hands, he put it back on his head. 'Thank you for your advice!'

'A greater simpleton I could hardly find,' the traveller muttered. But he was wrong! As dusk was falling, he came to the village of Gotham. The village green was buzzing with activity. Everyone who had a pair of hands was fishing in the local pond, using large ladles, forks, nets, baskets or rods.

'What is this strange fishing contest?' the traveller asked a bystander.

'Great misfortune, dear sir,' the man replied. 'The moon has fallen from the sky right into our pond and we are trying to fish it out.'

'Oh, you fools! Can't you see it is only the moon's reflection,' laughed the traveller, pointing to the sky.

'How dare you insult us and call us names,' the villagers shouted indignantly and chased him with stones out of Gotham.

'Now I know!' cried the traveller, as soon as he got his breath back. 'I am the greatest dunce on earth for trying to advise fools.' And he headed straight back to the mill to marry the miller's daughter.

Tom Thumb

There once stood a cottage in the depths of a forest, where a poor woodcutter lived with his wife. They loved one another dearly, but as they had no children, they were sad and lonely. More than anything they wanted to have a child. Each evening when work was done, the wife would weave in silence, and in silence the husband would carve strange wooden toys — a little horse which neighed and kicked with its hooves, flowers which opened in the sun, sometimes a whole wood full of deer, hares, foxes, gnomes and nymphs. The gnomes frolicked in the glade, the nymphs danced to the chirping of crickets and the twittering of birds. But what was the use, when there was no child to play with them.

'Who is there for me to tell stories to?' sighed the sad wife. 'For whom am I carving all these toys?' sighed the unhappy woodcutter. They both yearned so much to have a son, even if he was tiny, no bigger than a thumb perhaps, so that he would fit into a thimble. As long as they had someone to love and care for they would be completely happy, they told each other.

As they were good, kind people, heaven granted them their wish and before a year passed they had a little son, no bigger than a thumb. And the woodcutter and his wife decided to call him Tom Thumb.

Tom Thumb though small was no weakling. He ate enough for two, had more courage than many a big lad and if he wrestled with a mosquito, he always came out the winner.

But as the years passed, Tom did not grow any bigger. When the family went for a walk in the wood, his father had to carry him in his breast pocket so that he would not get lost among the fir cones, which covered the path. At night his mother put Tom to bed in her work-basket. But young Tom was mischievous and lively. The minute her back was turned, there he was, swinging on the pendulum, or sailing courageously in a saucer in his nutshell boat. Once he even chewed a nice hiding place in their Sunday cake and his father almost swallowed him for tea.

'What a worry you are,' sighed his mother,

shaking her head. 'Whatever will become of you? Always up to mischief, not knowing the meaning of work — it is not right at all!'

Hearing this Tom Thumb blushed with shame, and next time his father was working in the forest, he climbed up to his mother's shoulder and said, 'If you harness the donkey to the cart, I'll take my father his lunch today, and you can rest a little.'

His mother laughed at such a ridiculous idea. 'How could such a shrimp drive a cart?' she asked. But Tom had it all worked out.

'Put me inside the donkey's ear and I'll give him orders from there!' What a sight it was too! The donkey trotting along, braying merrily, while little Tom, snug and warm inside its ear, cracked his tiny whip and shouted, 'Steady on! Turn right! Now left! Faster!'

As they rode along, they passed a couple of suspicious looking travellers. 'What's this?' they cried in amazement. 'A cart without a driver, and yet the donkey is behaving as if someone invisible was holding the reins.' Curious to find out more, they followed to see what would happen to the driverless cart.

When Tom reached the woodland clearing, he shouted for all he was worth, 'Here is your lunch, Father! Come and eat it!' And he dived out of the donkey's ear straight into the open hand of his astonished father. The woodcutter's heart almost burst with pride at the cleverness of his little son, when he heard what he had done. The two hidden onlookers stared in disbelief, their mouths gaping wide.

'That funny little mite could make us a fortune,' they said to each other. 'Just think what a success he would be at fairs and circuses.' So they approached the woodcutter and tried to persuade him to sell them Tom Thumb for a purse of gold.

Of course Tom's father would not hear of it. But his son tugged at his ear and whispered, 'Sell me to them and don't worry. I'll slip away and be back before you've realized I've gone.'

Eventually the woodcutter reluctantly agreed, accepted the purse of gold and set his artful son on the brim of one of the travellers' hats who went happily away.

The two men sauntered along, chuckling and singing happily. They could hardly wait for the money to pour in when Tom appeared at the nearest fair. And Tom was quite content to stroll along the rim of the hat, gazing at the passing countryside.

It was as hot as it often is at harvest time, and the travellers were so thirsty they could have drunk a well dry. So they decided to rest. The minute they stopped and put their hats on the ground, Tom was off. He ran and ran, zigzagging through fields of stubble with the two men in hot pursuit. They almost caught him several times. But at last Tom saw a way of escape. Down a mouse-hole he dived, caught a mouse by her tail and miaowed like a cat into her ear. The mouse was terrified.

'Run for your lives,' she squealed to any other mice who might be listening, 'the tomcat is hot on my tail,' and she ran as fast as her legs would carry her through the underground mouse passage with Tom sitting comfortably on her tail, miaowing for all he was worth. When the petrified mouse brought him out into the sunlight on the far side of the field, Tom let go, curled up in the centre of a yellow bud and fell fast asleep.

Suddenly he was startled by a loud sound buzzing in his ear. An inquisitive bumble bee had landed beside him in the yellow bud.

In a trice, Tom swung himself onto the bumble bee's back, letting out a high pitched scream. The startled bumble bee shot upwards, and flew over a poppy field, over a pond, forest and four more fields before finally coming to rest on a dock leaf.

'I am much nearer home now,' Tom Thumb said to himself. As he stumbled onto the path, he noticed an empty snail shell. That is a nice little house, he thought, and making a bed of soft cobwebs, he was fast asleep before you could have counted up to five.

He was wakened suddenly by the sound of harsh voices. When he peeped out, he saw two evil looking thieves. And he heard them planning to steal the parson's silver.

'I must stop them,' thought Tom Thumb and in his loudest voice he called, 'Kind sirs, put me in your pocket and take me to the vicarage and I will help you to get the silver.'

The thieves were puzzled at first, but when at last they saw tiny Tom they burst out laughing. 'How could a little chap like you help us! Why, you can't even hop over a toadstool!'

'But I can hop through the bars of the vicarage window,' Tom replied. 'Then I can throw the money out to you.'

The thieves liked the idea. They put the lad in their tobacco pouch which made poor Tom sneeze, and off they went.

The moment Tom was inside the vicarage, he shouted in his loudest voice, 'Kind sirs, how much of this silver do you want?' 'Psh...psh..., quiet, stop shouting,' whispered the thieves. But Tom went on crying, louder than ever, till he woke the cook who was sleeping nearby.

'Thieves,' she screamed, picking up a rake and rushing out of the vicarage. The thieves waited no longer, but ran away as fast as their legs would carry them. Tom slipped into the barn and fell fast asleep in a hay stack.

But in the middle of the night the parson's cow felt hungry and started to crunch the very bundle of hay that Tom was sleeping in. Without knowing how, he found himself in the cow's stomach. How dark and stuffy it was! There was so much hay everywhere, he almost choked. 'Stop eating, cow!' he yelled. 'I hate hay!' But the cow took no notice.

Next day when the cook came to milk the cow, she was startled to hear her talking in a human voice. She dropped the pail in fright and ran for the parson. The good man, convinced the animal must be bewitched, had her slain. Unseen by the parson or the cook, Tom climbed out.

But his adventures were not over yet. A hungry wolf was passing by and swallowed Tom in one gulp. 'You silly wolf,' cried Tom, from inside the wolf's stomach. 'Why bother with crumbs like me? I'll take you to a cottage full of delicious food.'

The foolish wolf agreed and Tom directed him to his parents' cottage. There he made the wolf crawl through a narrow window into the pantry. The greedy wolf ate and ate till he was much too fat to squeeze through the window again. It was then that the woodcutter found him and cut off the wolf's head with his axe. Suddenly, to his surprise, from inside the dead animal there came faint cries, 'Mother, father, let me out!'

Taking his knife, the woodcutter carefully slit open the wolf and out stepped Tom. What a reunion they had! Mother, Father and Tom Thumb talked all night and far into the morning. And the woodcutter never sold Tom Thumb again. He would not have parted with him for all the riches in the world.

The Devil
and
the Old Hag

There was once an old hag who dealt in rags. She was dusty and musty, ugly and nasty, with a tongue that stung like a bee. No wonder everyone gave her a wide berth, just like the devil does a cross. This story tells what happened when the devil himself met that old hag, whose tongue never ceased to wag.

One sunny day this ogress with her bag of rags was bound for the town. As she stumbled along, her barbed tongue never ceased muttering and cursing. A brook lay in her path. Flood waters had swallowed the little bridge which was the only means of crossing the brook and the fast current had carried it away. The old hag stuck her thumb into the water and began to shake all over, like a wet dog. The water was so cold, it pierced her skin, like the edge of a razor. Bracing herself the hag gathered up her skirts and prepared to wade through the icy water.

'I wouldn't care if the devil himself carried me across,' she grumbled, 'if I could remain dry.' The words had scarcely left her lips when the devil himself was standing before her. He lifted the old hag on his horns and in a trice he had crossed the brook and was hastening, not towards the town, but straight down to hell.

'I bring you an old hag, devil brothers,' he called gaily.

'She can oil our devil fur skins, shoe our hooves and keep the fires of hell burning.' And turning to the old woman, he ordered her to start work.

The old hag did not move. Comfortably wedged between the devil's horns she held his ears as in a vice, giving him now and then a nip so vicious that the creature howled with pain. He twisted and turned like a demon possessed, but no matter how he kicked and bucked, the old hag could not be shaken from her perch. As if that were not enough, she started to scream so piercingly that the eardrums of every demon in hell nearly burst. The noise was so unbearable that the devil was at last forced to take the old hag back to earth. But all the way she held on with all her might, riding the devil as if he were a horse and at the same time pulling his ears and screeching and shrieking like a demented being. The devil was at his wits' end.

Suddenly he came upon a potmaker who was taking his wares to town. 'Rid me of this hag,' begged the panting devil, 'and I will repay you well.' The potmaker knew the old hag all too well. He took out his whip and struck her smartly across the back. Such treatment the old woman understood. She immediately released her grip on the devil's horns and took to her heels.

The devil was so grateful to be free that he at once told the potmaker how he would be rewarded.

'Tomorrow,' he said, 'the king's daughter will fall gravely ill. She will be possessed by the devil — that is, myself. Go and tell the king you can cure her for a handsome reward. When you enter her bedroom, crack the whip above her once and whisper, "It is I, my devil friend." Immediately the princess will be cured, but only for a short time. It happens that she is spoiled and wilful, so I shall return into her body and carry her to hell. But I must warn you. Do not think of trying to cure the princess a second time!'

The potmaker agreed. Then he continued on his way into the town, sold all his pots and pans and spent the night with his friend, the cobbler.

The next morning he was wakened by cries in the street. 'The king's daughter is gravely ill! She is possessed by the devil!' the citizens were saying. The potmaker rose at once and went to beg an audience of the king.

'If you cure my daughter, you will have a sack of gold,' the king promised the potmaker, and led the way up a staircase leading to the princess's bedroom.

The wretched princess was writhing and rolling about on the floor, her eyes wild and full of pain. The potmaker approached the princess and cracking the whip above her head, he whispered, 'It is I, my devil friend.'

'Good,' the devil replied. 'Now I have kept my promise. If you value your life, take the gold and never return to this place.'

The princess was cured, as if by magic. The potmaker took the sack of gold from her grateful father, shared some with his friend, the cobbler, and left the next day for his own village. But before he had reached the town gate, armed guards caught up with him.

'Stop,' they cried. 'Our princess is once again possessed by the devil. Come back again with us and cure her, or the king will have your head.'

What a choice for the potmaker! On the one hand he was to lose his head, on the other, he would land in hell!

When the potmaker reappeared in the princess's chamber, the devil hissed in fury. 'You fool! I warned you never to return.'

But the crafty potmaker had an answer ready. 'I would not dream of meddling in your devilry, brother devil,' he said softly. 'I have come only to tell you that down in the square the old hag is waiting. She is marching along, heading this way. It seems she wants to talk to you.'

The devil waited to hear no more. In the princess's chamber the chimney rumbled as he scrambled back to hell. Never again would he encounter the hideous old hag, he promised himself.

As for the potmaker! It was not long before he had married the wilful princess. And when, now and again, she seemed possessed a little by the devil, all her husband had to do was crack the whip above her head and she was cured.

Jose
and Princess
Florabella

The old folk say that once upon a time two brothers lived in a village in Spain — Jose the older and Juan who was young and spoiled. No one knows why their parents idolized the spoiled Juan, who was selfish and a miser as well! Who knows why good, kind Jose was ignored, criticised and unloved!

There came a day, however, when Jose was so miserable with his life of injustices, jeers and sneers, that he enlisted in the army and went to serve far away beyond the sea. He was a good soldier and served well and loyally for many years.

When at last he returned to his native village, he was told that his parents had died. Sadly, he prayed at their graveside and went to seek out his younger brother, Juan, to claim his share of the inheritance.

Juan, the miser, had taken everything and did not mean to part with the smallest coin.

'What inheritance?' he sneered. 'Up in the bedroom you will find an empty old chest; that is all our father left us. You are welcome to take it away,' he told his brother.

'It may come in handy for firewood,' said the kind Jose, never questioning his brother's lies.

And he proceeded to chop up the old chest. Suddenly out of a crack there rolled a magnificent jewel. Such a valuable jewel few human eyes have seen.

Overnight Jose became the richest man in the district. He sold the jewel to the king himself, and with the money decided to buy land and a nice house for himself. But on the way home he met a woman who was weeping bitterly.

'My husband has died,' she sobbed. 'He left

me with many children and I do not even have a copper to pay for his funeral!' Jose was filled with pity for the poor woman and he gave her husband a splendid funeral, built a house large enough for her and her many children and made sure they all had enough money to live in comfort. When all this had been paid for there was nothing left in his pocket.

'What will be, will be,' he said to cheer himself, and as he did not know where to go, he asked the king to take him into his service. The king was surprised at the request, for had not this man only recently been paid handsomely for his precious jewel! But he asked no ques-

tions and took Jose into his service. And as always Jose served well and faithfully and in time the old king appointed him his chief courtier.

In the meantime the younger brother squandered his inheritance on drinking. His house burned to the ground and his wife and children ran away from him. For a time Juan kept alive by begging, then he turned for help to his brother Jose. Jose, filled with brotherly love, persuaded the king to take him also into his service. But Juan was so filled with spite and envy that he wanted only to harm his brother.

One day Juan heard that the king once long ago had loved the beautiful Princess Florabella. She had not, however, returned the king's love and had run away to hide from him in a dense forest.

This was the information the wicked Juan was waiting for and he decided to use it to harm his brother. He went to the king and told him that Jose knew where the princess was, but refused to reveal her hiding place. The king was furious, and told Jose that if he did not bring Florabella to the palace immediately, he would lose his head.

What could Jose do? Sadly he went to the stable to saddle a horse. Putting his arms round the neck of the first grey horse he came to, he burst into tears. To his astonishment the grey spoke soothingly in a human voice.

'Do not weep, kind Jose,' he said. 'Mount me and I shall take you to Princess Florabella. Do not worry that I am all skin and bone; together we shall find her!'

The astonished Jose was happy to accept the horse's offer. 'At least there will be someone to talk to on the way,' he thought, as they rode off. Soon they entered a dense forest where the ground was alive with huge ants.

'Let them have the loaf of bread which you brought with you,' said the grey horse. Jose obeyed, and the ants thanked him in tiny ant voices.

On the far side of the forest they sighted an eagle trapped in a hunter's net. Acting on the horse's advice, Jose quickly set it free. Shortly afterwards they saw a little fish struggling in a puddle.

'Take it and throw it into a river,' said the grey. The moment this was done, another dark forest rose before them. In the depths of this forest stood Princess Florabella's palace.

'When the princess comes out on the lawn, I will start to buck and kick in such a comical way that she will laugh and ask to ride me,' said

These words angered the king and he sent Jose to find the princess's lost possessions.

'Oh, how unfortunate I am,' Jose lamented. 'How can I find things I did not even know were lost? Surely nothing but death awaits me.'

But the grey horse cheered him. 'Do not complain, Jose, for nothing is lost. Now that you need help, seek it from those to whom you have shown kindness.'

Then Jose remembered the ants in the deep forest whom he had given the loaf of bread.

'Ants, my good friends,' he cried, 'find me whatever Princess Florabella has lost.' Before he could even look round, the ants were piling the little gold beads in the high grass.

'Ask the eagle whose life you have saved for help,' advised the last ant. And Jose did so. The eagle appeared as soon as he was called, circled overhead, then soared to the peak of the highest mountain and brought back the lost scarf.

'Go and see the little fish who owes you its life,' the eagle called, flapping his gigantic wings in farewell. And Jose called the little fish from the riverbank. The water bubbled and broke, and from the bottom of the deepest pool the little fish appeared, holding in its mouth the princess's gold ring.

'What a kind little fish you are,' cried the happy Jose, but the little fish replied, 'It is not I you should thank, but your own good heart.' With that it disappeared.

When Florabella heard from the king that

the grey horse. 'As soon as she mounts, I will start to rear as if I wanted to throw her. Hold my reins and pretend to calm me. Swing into the saddle behind her and I shall carry you both to the king's palace.'

Everything went according to plan. Soon the happy Jose was galloping through the forest, heedless of the cries of the unhappy Princess Florabella.

As they waded across the river, the princess dropped her ring where the water was deepest. Later she dropped her scarf and the wind caught it and took it to the top of a high mountain. When they rode through the ant forest, she broke her necklace of tiny gold beads and scattered them in the grass. Jose noticed nothing.

The king was overjoyed to see the beautiful Florabella in his palace, but the unhappy princess locked herself in one of the rooms and wept bitterly. In vain the king tried to persuade her to let him in.

'I shall not unlock the door till everything I lost on the way is returned to me,' she cried.

Jose had returned with all her lost possessions, she wept even more bitterly than before. 'I shall not open this door until that scoundrel who abducted me from my palace has been thrown into boiling oil,' she cried.

The ungrateful king did not even hesitate. Ordering his servants to fill the largest barrel they could find with boiling oil, he told Jose to jump into it of his own free will!

'Do not be afraid,' whispered the grey horse. 'Canter on my back once round the courtyard, then smear yourself with my sweat and plunge without fear into the barrel.' Jose had so much faith in the little horse that he did as he was told. And lo and behold! When Jose plunged into the boiling oil, he came to no harm, but stepped out of the barrel looking so handsome that Princess Florabella fell in love with him instantly. And the old king and Juan, the evil brother, envying Jose's good looks, without hesitation also dived into the boiling oil. There was a cloud of smoke and neither was ever seen again.

The brave and handsome Jose married the lovely princess and became ruler of the kingdom. When with tears in his eyes he thanked the little grey horse for its loyal help, the horse replied, 'Do not thank me, but thank your own kind heart. I am the one to whom you have shown the greatest kindness. Do you recall the poor man whose burial you arranged when his wife and children could not even buy a crust of bread? I am that man. My soul entered the body of a grey horse so that I could repay you.' The little horse then turned into a puff of grey smoke and no one ever saw or heard of him again.

But King Jose and Queen Florabella tell their children about him still and teach them to show at all times kindness and love to all people.

East of the Sun, West of the Moon

(The Tales of the South Wind)

The East Wind had finished telling his stories, and the young woman, who had wandered to the cottage belonging to the aged mother of the four winds, sighed, 'How beautiful it was!' Then her eyes clouded again. In none of the stories was there a single mention of the mysterious palace drifting on an island in a distant sea, east of the sun and west of the moon. The prince must be waiting for her, pining for her.

'Do not be sad, my dear,' said the mother of the four winds, stroking her hair. 'All will be well.' The East Wind then clapped his butterfly wings, pecked at a few golden grains and soared off towards the sun.

'Goodbye! Have a safe and successful journey!' he cried. 'I see my brother is returning, flying in from the south. Perhaps he can help you to find your prince.'

Suddenly a large golden bloom fluttered from the sky onto the old woman's lap. Out of it peeped a merry young man. A garland of wild flowers circled his brow. He stretched out shining bee wings, waved bee-like feelers and played a gay tune on his willow whistle. All of the flowers in the meadow turned their heads to listen, and the long grass swayed back and forth like a green sea in time to the music.

'Where have you been all this time, my handsome son,' his mother chided. And she gave him a drink of honey and said, 'South Wind, my son, tell us the secret way to the castle in the transparent sea which lies to the east of the sun and west of the moon. There the wicked stepmother is imprisoning the handsome prince.'

'I roam the world close to the sun and the stars, but I know of no such place,' replied the South Wind. 'Perhaps West Wind, my brother, could tell you more. In the meantime I shall, if you will listen, tell you stories which I have gathered on my journey.'

Cinderella

Once long ago there was a widower who had an only daughter. He had lost his wife when the girl was only a child, so she became his only joy. How lovely she was! Her face shone like the morning sun, and when she laughed, the sound was like little bells tinkling with happiness.

Father and daughter loved each other dearly and with love they remembered the mother, who had died. But as time passed by and his daughter grew up the widower could not help looking round and wondering who would help to care for his household in his old age.

One day he brought a stepmother for his daughter, and two stepsisters as well who were as ugly as his own daughter was beautiful. Their thoughts were ugly too. They were spoiled and conceited into the bargain. They were also lazy and malicious.

The poor, lovely daughter was miserable. Each day she wept. Her wicked stepmother never threw her a kind word or a kind glance, but scolded her from morning till night, giving her the roughest work to do, whilst her stepsisters showered her with abuse, jealous because she was so beautiful.

The poor, unhappy father! A bad choice he had made! He tried to make amends, he argued and pleaded with his wife, but it was no use. The malicious tongues of the three women always silenced him. He worried so much that he fell ill and before long he was buried beside his first dear wife. Harder times than ever were in store for the orphaned girl. From sunrise to sunset she was forced to toil in the house to serve her stepmother and stepsisters without a single word of encouragement, without a single word of kindness ever spoken to her.

One evening, when worn out, she sank to a chair by the table, the stepmother turned on her. 'What are you doing here, you ragamuffin? Your place is among the cinders and ashes in the chimney corner. There you can stay! And keep out of the way of my noble daughters!' What could the poor girl do but obey? After that she would sit in her corner when her work was done, shelling peas and talking to the fire about the happy bygone days with her mother and father. And as she always looked dirty from crouching among the ashes and cinders, her stepmother and stepsisters started to call her Cinderella.

'Tie my shoe, Cinderella! Powder my nose, Cinderella! Change the hay in the sty, Cinderella! Sweep the chimney, Cinderella! Make haste, Cinderella!' That was all she heard from morning till night. Yet, no matter how badly she was treated, Cinderella grew more and more beautiful. She was a hundred times, no, a thousand times lovelier than her witchlike stepsisters

with their long pointed noses and beady eyes. In her humble rags she looked like a bewitched princess from a wonderful fairy story.

It happened that the king of that kingdom was holding a ball, hoping that his son the prince would choose a bride. What excitement that was for the stepmother and her hideous daughters!

'Surely, dear girls, you come from one of the best families!' said the stepmother. 'Surely you are rich enough for the king's son! We shall see.' And she swelled with pride. They searched for the finest silks, laces and veils. Merchants from all corners of the land met one another at their door, offering scented ointments, pearls and diamonds, sashes of gold and silver, slippers of finest and softest leather. While the sisters dressed up in their new finery, Cinderella had to work harder than ever. At last came the day of the ball. What commotion there was in the house then!

'Tie my shoe, Cinderella! Powder my nose, Cinderella! Starch my cap, tighten my corset, brush my hair! Make haste, Cinderella! shouted the sisters, encouraged by their mother. When at last they were dressed and brushed and powdered and scented, they paraded in front of the mirror, admiring themselves, preening themselves, curtseying to themselves, till poor, tired Cinderella could not help laughing at all their antics. This made her sisters angry.

'What are you laughing at, you slut?' they cried. 'You are jealous that you are not coming to the ball! What would they want with someone like you! Why, even a scarecrow would be ashamed to be seen with you!'

Alone at last, Cinderella huddled in her corner by the hearth, biting back the tears, dreaming of the handsome prince she would never, never meet. 'Oh, my darling mother, my kind father, if only you would take me to be with you in heaven,' she sobbed.

Suddenly someone gently opened the door and an old lady stood in the room, her hair like the head of a dandelion. She was Cinderella's fairy godmother, but this the girl did not know.

'Do not be sad, my child,' the old lady whispered. 'Before this day ends you will dance with the prince in the royal palace. Look what I have brought you!' the old woman said, taking from her apron three hazelnuts and passed them to Cinderella.

'How kind of you!,' said the girl, smiling through her tears. 'It is so long since anyone has given me a present. But how could I go to the palace dressed in these rags?'

'You have a good heart, Cinderella. You were pleased even with this humble gift,' remarked the old lady, nodding in approval.

'So that you know goodness is repaid with goodness in this world, you shall crack one of these nuts I have given you.'

Cinderella obeyed. She could hardly believe her eyes — the little shell contained the most beautiful gown. It was fashioned from a rainbow, was as light as air and strewn with sparkling dew drops and little wild flowers. Round the flowers fluttered rainbow-coloured butterflies, and they held with their feelers the most delicate veil of gossamer. On top of the lovely robe sat a pair of glass slippers, so tiny that only Cinderella's little feet could have slid into them.

As soon as Cinderella had dressed, the room became bright with rainbow light. 'Fetch me a pumpkin from the garden,' the old woman said, and in the yard she sliced the pumpkin in two and with a touch of her wand it became a fine coach, glittering with silver and gold. 'Now bring the mouse traps from the pantry,' the old woman told Cinderella, who soon came back with four live grey mice in the traps. A tap with the magic wand turned the mice into fine horses with golden hooves before Cinderella's astonished eyes. At that moment a fat rat peeped out of a hole in the floor, and in an instant was turned into a bewhiskered coachman in grand livery. Cinderella then found six green lizards in the garden, and they became slim footmen dressed in gold.

'God be with you, Cinderella, when you reach the royal palace,' the good fairy cried, as she bade her goodbye. 'But remember one thing: before midnight strikes, you must part from the prince. You must not remain in the palace one second after twelve o'clock. Do not let anything keep you in the palace longer than that.'

Cinderella promised to obey her godmother and off she rode to the royal palace. As she neared it, a magnificent rainbow gate opened before her, the blare of trumpets sounded from the palace walls and grooms carried her in their arms to the courtyard, so that she would not soil her lovely glass slippers.

As she walked into the ballroom, everyone gasped at her beauty. The prince himself knelt before her, begging her to do him the honour of sitting by his side.

'Oh, how lovely she is,' the noble ladies present murmured with envy, whilst the court gentlemen crowded round to pay Cinderella compliments.

Her stepmother and the two ugly sisters almost burst with envy. They did not know this lovely girl was poor Cinderella whom they had left at home among the ashes.

No one spared the sour-faced sisters even a passing glance, but the handsome prince never let Cinderella out of his sight or out of his arms on the ballroom floor.

As midnight approached, Cinderella looked at him sadly and whispered, 'Now I must leave you, dear prince.'

In vain he begged her to stay. But, like a bird she flew from the palace, and with a crack of the golden whip the carriage was gone. But as it vanished from sight, a shining rainbow appeared across the dark midnight sky.

The moment Cinderella reached home, the carriage disappeared, as did the team of horses, the coachman and the footmen. All she could see were little grey mice running across the floor, and one fat, whiskery rat diving into a hole. The green lizards scattered in the garden. Her beautiful dress had turned into rags and when her stepmother returned with the sisters, they found Cinderella as they had left her sitting in the corner of the hearth.

What a lot they had to talk about! The sisters vied with each other in describing the beauty of

the palace; they boasted about the suitors they would have danced with if only their slippers had not pinched their feet, if only their heads had not ached. Above all they talked with admiration of the mysterious princess, whose beauty surpassed anyone's present. Cinderella listened, not uttering a word, only smiling to herself.

Before long another ball was to be held at the palace, and again the stepmother and her ugly daughters were to attend.

As soon as they were gone, Cinderella cracked the second hazelnut. Inside she found an even more magnificent robe than the first. It was made of moonbeams and there was a head-band of stars and a necklace of glowing fireflies.

Again a pair of beautiful glass slippers lay on top. Thus once again, aided by her fairy god-mother, Cinderella went to the palace ball, and once again she disappeared before the stroke of midnight. And once again the ugly sisters found on their return only a dusty Cinderella sitting by the hearth.

The prince, in the meantime, walked about as if in a dream, feeling as if his heart would burst with longing. The king, to cheer him, invited the most beautiful princesses from all over the world to attend another ball. But though the musicians played merry tunes, the prince remained sad, his thoughts with the lovely unknown princess who had not appeared.

Suddenly there was the sound of a carriage in the courtyard, and there was Cinderella, dressed in a robe of sunbeams. The lovesick prince looked into her eyes and whispered, 'Be my wife! Do not leave me again!' Cinderella placed a finger on his mouth to stifle his words. And they danced and danced, forgetting the time, until suddenly midnight began to strike.

Cinderella, dismayed, slipped from the prince's arms and fled to her coach, leaving behind one glass slipper as she ran. Before she reached the courtyard, the last stroke of midnight had sounded. The golden coach turned into an empty pumpkin shell, and instead of horses, coachman and footmen a few little pests scuffled away into the night. The robe of sunbeams turned into rags, and poor Cinderella ran in bare feet all the way home.

'Has a beautiful princess passed this way?' the prince asked the guards, to be told that only a beggar girl had sped through the palace gates. All that was left of the unknown princess was one tiny glass slipper.

Next day the king ordered his heralds to search for a maiden whose foot would slide into the glass slipper. But it was too small for all who tried it. One day the heralds came to Cinderella's house. Try as they might, the ugly sisters could not force their huge feet into the glass slipper. One of the heralds noticed the humble Cinderella by the hearth and suggested that she too might try it on. The stepmother and the sisters laughed at such an idea, but their laughter turned to amazement when they saw it fitted perfectly. A moment later their wonder was even greater, for Cinderella brought out the second glass slipper, which her fairy godmother had allowed her to keep.

Then Cinderella's wicked stepmother and her ugly stepsisters fell to their knees, begging her forgiveness. Do you think she forgave them? Of course she did! For her beauty sprang from the goodness of her heart. The happy prince drove Cinderella to his palace and soon a magnificent wedding took place, so splendid indeed that people still speak of it to this day.

The Haunted Well

Two men were once travelling over the desert, bound for far-off Cairo. So that they would not suffer hunger and thirst on the way, each man carried a sack of flour and a jug of water. One traveller was called Sly, the other Softie, though their real names were Musa and Muhsin, but nobody ever called them by their real names. They were both as poor as the hungry sand fleas of the desert but each had different ideas about dealing with poverty. Sly liked to get the better of people by swindling and robbing them whenever he could. He did not care if he caused others to suffer. He did not listen to Allah and was unmoved by people's sorrow and sadness. But Softie trusted the human heart above everything and found happiness in the happiness of others.

Both men were hot and weary that day in the desert so they squatted on the sand and each from his own sack of flour made on a flat stone enough dough for a meagre flourcake.

'Listen Softie,' Sly said, as they sat by the fire sipping from their water jugs after their humble meal. 'Why should we both take a drop of water and a pinch of flour from our own jugs and sacks? We have a long way to go and you are weaker than I. Let us first use up your water and your flour, then you won't have so much to carry. When your supplies have gone, I will share mine with you.'

The trusting Softie thanked him heartily and agreed gladly. As his burden grew lighter, he walked more easily and was grateful for Sly's thoughtfulness. Soon Softie's sack and jug were quite empty.

'Give me some of your flour and water now that I have shared mine with you,' he said to his companion.

But Sly just roared with laughter at Softie's misery.

'I will give you half of my flourcake and a sip of water in exchange for one eye!' Sly said curtly. 'Have I not toiled harder than you by carrying a heavier load?'

Softie had never paid such a price. When all his pleas were ignored and he was almost dead with hunger and thirst, he had at last to agree to let the cruel Sly stab him in one eye for a morsel of food.

But hunger and thirst will always return. And when Softie's stomach was again as empty as

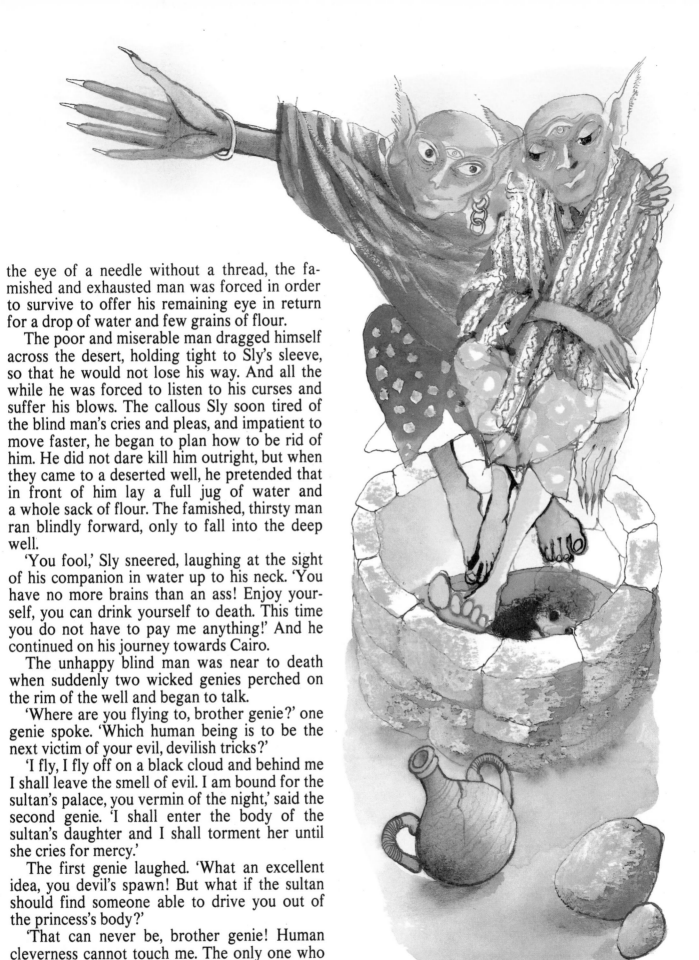

the eye of a needle without a thread, the famished and exhausted man was forced in order to survive to offer his remaining eye in return for a drop of water and few grains of flour.

The poor and miserable man dragged himself across the desert, holding tight to Sly's sleeve, so that he would not lose his way. And all the while he was forced to listen to his curses and suffer his blows. The callous Sly soon tired of the blind man's cries and pleas, and impatient to move faster, he began to plan how to be rid of him. He did not dare kill him outright, but when they came to a deserted well, he pretended that in front of him lay a full jug of water and a whole sack of flour. The famished, thirsty man ran blindly forward, only to fall into the deep well.

'You fool,' Sly sneered, laughing at the sight of his companion in water up to his neck. 'You have no more brains than an ass! Enjoy yourself, you can drink yourself to death. This time you do not have to pay me anything!' And he continued on his journey towards Cairo.

The unhappy blind man was near to death when suddenly two wicked genies perched on the rim of the well and began to talk.

'Where are you flying to, brother genie?' one genie spoke. 'Which human being is to be the next victim of your evil, devilish tricks?'

'I fly, I fly off on a black cloud and behind me I shall leave the smell of evil. I am bound for the sultan's palace, you vermin of the night,' said the second genie. 'I shall enter the body of the sultan's daughter and I shall torment her until she cries for mercy.'

The first genie laughed. 'What an excellent idea, you devil's spawn! But what if the sultan should find someone able to drive you out of the princess's body?'

'That can never be, brother genie! Human cleverness cannot touch me. The only one who could pluck the sultan's daughter from my power would first have to lose his sight, then regain it. He would have to stand up to his neck in water in this very well for a whole day and a whole night, then at dawn of the day following the night of the full moon he would have to sprinkle the sultan's daughter with the blood of the black cockerel. You surely do not think such a man could be found! Human people are not as clever as that, my infernal friend.'

'You are right, my fellow fiend. Men are stupid. Look how many of them are blind in Cairo, and not one of them knows that all he needs to get back his sight is to cover his eyes with a leaf of the bush which grows by this well. Farewell, brother genie. May the devil's fortune shine on your venture! We shall meet again one day.' With that the two genies parted, each to his own devilish purpose.

The blind man in the well had not missed a word of their conversation. But how was he to escape from the well! For the whole night and the whole of the next day he stood up to his neck in the icy water, shaking with cold. But the following evening a caravan stopped by the well. Travellers lowered a bucket for water. Softie gripped the rope and he was pulled out. 'If there is a bush growing near this well, please lead me to it,' he said. And when they had taken him, he placed two leaves on his

blind eyes. With that his sight was miraculously restored. Thanking his rescuers the joyful Softie set off for Cairo. With him he took an armful of leaves from the magic bush.

In Cairo, he found a shady spot in the market place and the blind people of the city came to him and he cured them with the magic leaves. He accepted no payment, only food and words of gratitude, for, unlike Sly, Softie's happiness lay in the happiness of others. The fame of the miraculous physician spread far and wide, and crowds of unfortunates came to be healed. Softie never refused to help.

One day the sultan himself heard about his uncommon skill. His only daughter had only recently lost her reason and his learned counsellors said that she was possessed by an evil spirit. Wasting no time, the sultan hastened to find Softie.

'If your power is not of evil origin, please help my only daughter,' he implored. 'She has fallen under the spell of a wicked genie.' Softie then recalled the genie's words at the well.

'I shall come at dawn on the day following the night of the full moon,' he promised. 'I cannot help your daughter before that.'

'If you cure my daughter, you shall be her husband,' the sultan announced. 'Meantime, take this bag of gold with my gratitude.'

But Softie said, 'All I want from you is a black cockerel. Give the gold to the poor of the city.' And this was done.

The day following the night of the full moon dawned and Softie with the black cockerel under his arm entered the sultan's palace. Long before he reached her he could hear the cries of the unfortunate princess. When he entered her bedroom he found the unhappy girl twisting and turning on the floor, as if whipped by fiery, stinging lashes. In her distress she had torn her garments to tattered shreds and if anyone dared to approach her, she spat like a wild thing. All the servants were terrified of her and ran from her chamber.

Softie wasted no time, but cut the cockerel's black throat and sprinkled its blood on the princess. Immediately a black cloud rose up from her head, spitting and cursing, then it dissolved and vanished. The evil genie was gone from her and the grateful princess knelt before Softie.

The mighty sultan kept his promise and Softie and his daughter amidst great rejoicings were married. When later the sultan died, Muhsin, who never again was called Softie, became ruler of the land. He often walked among his subjects and told the tale of the well where his happiness had begun.

One day many years later the tale was heard by an old beggar, Musa, whom people called Sly. Since the time he had treated Softie so cruelly, he himself had fallen on hard times. To his fury he now heard that his wicked deeds had helped Softie to fame and riches.

'Why shouldn't I too seek happiness and good fortune in the well,' he now mused, and set off across the desert. The minute he jumped into the well, the wicked genies squatted on its rim again.

'Life is hard, brother genie,' grumbled the first, and he told how Softie had driven him out of the body of the sultan's daughter. 'Since that day I have failed in all my evil plans.'

'Do you think someone that day could have been eavesdropping in the well?' the second genie suggested.

'You might be right, my evil-spirited brother,' said the first. 'Let us fill in this cursed well!' Whereupon the wicked genies gathered rocks and stones and piled them on the head of the cruel Sly till he was completely buried.

Since then people have avoided the well. They say it is haunted and that at night an imploring human voice cries, 'I want my happiness! Give me my happiness!'

Stumpy

There was once a poor cottager and his wife. They were so poor that even on Sundays they had very little to eat and it was a miracle that they stayed alive. Despite their misery, the wife longed for a little son, so much so that she would even have accepted one from the devil.

'Do not blaspheme, dear wife,' her husband warned her. 'It is not good to go against Heaven.' But she paid him no heed.

The husband, trying to please her, one day brought home a tree stump from the forest. It was shaped like a baby, and all he needed to do was cut out the legs and scoop out little holes for the eyes and it became almost as lifelike as a real little boy.

The wife wrapped him lovingly in a shawl, rocked him in her arms and sang to him, 'Sleep, sleep, my little toy, sleep sweetly, my wooden boy. And I shall call you Stumpy.'

All of a sudden Stumpy wriggled in her arms, opened his eyes and cried, 'I am so hungry, Mother!' Oh what joy! At first the astonished man and his wife did not know what to do. Then quickly the woman warmed some milk in saucepan and Stumpy drank thirstily. Not only that, he next gobbled up the saucepan and the spoon before their eyes. And before they had recovered from their amazement, Stumpy was crying again. 'I am hungry, Mother!'

What were they to do? There was not a morsel of food in the cottage. The poor woman ran to beg from her neighbour, and after much pleading, she was lent a jug of milk and a loaf of bread.

The moment she put them down on the table, Stumpy's mouth opened from ear to ear and in a few seconds there was not a trace of the bread, the milk or the jug!

'Lord have mercy on us,' muttered the now frightened woman. 'Surely Stumpy did not eat all that!' 'I did!' Stumpy replied. 'I was hungry and I am still hungry, so now I am going to eat you!' And Stumpy had opened his mouth wide and swallowed her.

Just then her husband came in from the yard.

'Oh Father, I am so hungry,' Stumpy wailed. The man could not believe his eyes. There was his wooden son, his stomach like a barrel, his mouth like the entrance to a forge.

'Lord protect us from all evil!' whispered the man, making the sign of the cross. 'Where is your mother, Stumpy?'

'I have eaten her,' Stumpy replied, 'and now I am going to eat you too!' And in one gulp his father disappeared down Stumpy's throat.

Now that there was nothing left in the cottage for Stumpy to eat, he staggered off to the village square. A dairymaid was pushing a wheelbarrow across the square when he appeared.

'You are a fine, fat, overfed fellow,' she cried. 'What have you got in that gigantic stomach of yours?'

'All sorts of things,' Stumpy replied. 'Bread,

milk, a saucepan, a spoon, a jug and a mother and a father. Now I shall have you too.'

And next moment, she — and her wheelbarrow — were swallowed by Stumpy.

Stumpy rolled on, out of the square, down the hill and did not stop till he met a farmer with a cart heaped with hay.

'What an enormous stomach you have,' the farmer exclaimed. 'What is in it?'

'All sorts of things,' Stumpy said. 'Bread, milk, a saucepan, a spoon, a jug, a mother and a father too, a dairymaid and a wheelbarrow — and now — you!'

Before the farmer knew what was happening, he was swallowed whole, together with his horse and his cartful of hay. Not even his whip remained. And Stumpy rolled on.

A shepherd was driving his sheep from pasture, their bells tinkling merrily. And as he went, he played a gay little tune on his whistle.

'Well!' he cried, when he saw Stumpy. 'What things are rolling about in your massive belly?'

'All sorts of things,' Stumpy replied. 'Bread, milk, a saucepan, a jug, a mother and a father, a dairymaid, a wheelbarrow, a farmer with his cart of hay, now, if I may, I shall eat you too!' And in a flash, the shepherd and his herd were in the belly of the ever greedy Stumpy.

How dark it was inside Stumpy. The shepherd could not even count his sheep. Then the smallest lamb, only a few weeks old, baaed.

'Baa, we have forgotten my sister Cherub. She is still in the meadow. The wolf will get her!'

When the old ram, who was father of the flock, heard this, he reared up, and lowering his head, flung himself full tilt at the wall of Stumpy's stomach. His horns pierced it as though it had been a rotten barrel and Stumpy sank slowly to the ground.

Out came the shepherd with his herd, blowing his whistle and counting his sheep at the same time. Out came the farmer driving his cart and cracking his whip, followed by the dairymaid and her wheelbarrow, followed by the mother and the father running for their lives, chased by the borrowed loaf of bread, an empty jug, a saucepan and a spoon. The milk had spilled and was quickly licked up by the smallest lamb.

Thankfully the cottager and his wife returned to their poor cottage and never, never again was the wife tempted to call upon the devil to give them a child. She and her husband were content to wait for Heaven to answer their prayers. And as they loved one another dearly, their prayers were answered at last and they were given their long-awaited son.

Czarina Frog

Beyond the copper forest, beyond the iron mountain, beyond the stony river there once lived a mighty czar. He had three handsome sons, who could fight like falcons. There was no one who could match their strength, nor their courage. The two eldest sons were stiff and proud, but the youngest czarevitch, Ivan, was loved by all for his goodness and kindness.

One day the czar said to his sons, 'Take your bows, my sons, and each of you shoot an arrow towards the horizon. The maiden at whose feet your arrow falls, shall be your bride.'

The eldest czarevitch was the first to shoot. His arrow flew through the air and came to rest at the feet of the beautiful daughter of a prince. The eldest son brought her home as his bride with great ceremony. The old czar was content, honouring and praising his new daughter.

Then came the turn of the middle son, who was fortunate enough to send his arrow to the doorstep of the daughter of the richest merchant in the land. The czar was again full of praise and admiration.

It was now the turn of Ivan, the czar's youngest son. Far away towards the horizon the arrow sped, and mounting his horse the czarevitch went in search of it.

He rode farther and farther, vainly asking everyone he met if they had seen where his arrow had landed. Many days had passed since he started his search, when at last he came to a deep bog in a dark forest. The czarevitch dismounted, so that his horse would be lighter. Suddenly he caught sight of an ugly frog perched on a stone. In its webbed foot it held his arrow.

'Welcome, Czarevitch Ivan, my husband to be,' it croaked. Ivan recoiled in dismay and was about to turn tail and flee, when the frog said, 'Stop! You are the czar's son, and you have given your word! The one who found the arrow has the right to be your wife.' Czarevitch Ivan was deeply ashamed that he had been about to break his word to his father. He put the frog in his linen handkerchief, tied it in a knot and with a heavy heart, set off homewards with his bride. Many people were on the look-out for his arrival and they were surprised to see him returning alone.

'Where is your bride, brother Ivan?' asked his curious brothers. When the czarevitch untied his handkerchief they gasped with horror.

'Throw out that ugly creature, kill the hideous pest!' they shouted one after the other. As for his father, the czar, his brow creased in a deep frown and he had no words of praise for his son.

Then Ivan noticed that the little frog was weeping tears of fear and sorrow. His heart melted and he said, 'You must not harm my bride! This is the will of destiny, so I will marry the frog.'

So the frog remained in the palace. No one wanted to touch it, even the servants avoided it, but Ivan was always polite and civil and treated the little creature with kindness.

One day the czar said, 'Before giving my permission for a wedding to take place, I want you my sons, to tell your brides to bake white bread. I want to see what sort of housewives they will make!'

Hearing this, Ivan sadly sought his little frog, for he had grown fond of it in a very short time. 'I have bad news my frog bride! My father has ordered all three brides to bake white bread. How can you achieve such a thing?'

But the frog calmed him. 'Tomorrow is wiser than today, Czarevitch Ivan! Sleep soundly, and you will see.'

The other two brides, however, did not take the czar's request so calmly. At home they had never lifted a finger to help, even with the lightest tasks. They had no idea how to mix or even light a stove. They therefore sent the maid to spy on the frog, so that they might learn how to make bread. The maid did not have to be asked twice, and was happy to tell them what she had seen.

'All that the frog did,' she said, 'was to pour flour into a pail of water and then put the dough straight into the oven.'

The brides tried this, but the wet dough ran out of the oven into the fireplace and mixed with the ashes. By the time the brides managed to bake a couple of loaves, the bread was as black as a boot and as hard as iron.

But at midnight the frog bride cried from her window, 'Sisters, my dearest, maids and servants loyal and faithful, come and bake the white bread that the czar has ordered!' And from the pools, the bogs and the marshes frogs hopped to her aid. Before her they changed into beautiful maidens who baked loaves as white as fresh snow with crusts of golden brown.

The next morning, when the astonished Ivan took the loaf to his father, the czar was lavish in his praises. 'It tastes even better than the cakes baked by your mother, the czarina,' he commented, licking his lips.

But the brides of the elder brothers were dismissed with scorn. 'Your bread is fit only for swine,' said the czar, and ordered the brides to weave a rug for his throne by the next day.

The brides of the two elder brothers had no idea what to do. So again they sent the maid to spy on the frog. 'All the frog did was to cut the yarn up into pieces and throw them into the grass,' the maid reported.

The two brides tried it, but the pieces lay there uselessly. There was nothing to do but gather up the yarn and somehow sew them together before morning. But the rug of the frog bride was a sight to behold! The colours shimmered like the sunlit sky, and the czar could not take his eyes off it. No wonder too, for once again the little frog had been helped by its frog maidens.

The third order of the czar was to his sons. 'Invite guests from all over Russia to our table. The husband of the bride they like best will become czar after my death,' he said.

Ivan was sad. How could anyone like his frog bride? But the frog comforted him, 'Do not worry, Czarevitch Ivan; sit with your brothers at the oak table among your guests. When the time comes, you will find at your side the most beautiful bride.'

From far and wide the guests gathered at the czar's palace and their eyes were quite dazzled by the beauty of the brides of the two elder sons. It was indeed difficult for them to decide which was the most beautiful. 'What about you, Czarevitch Ivan,' they asked. 'Where is your frog bride?'

Suddenly a carriage made of mother-of-pearl drove into the courtyard. In it sat a maiden who was a joy to behold. On her brow shimmered a tiny moon, on the crown of her head a band of shining stars and on each silky hair hung a rainbow coloured pearl.

'I am Vasilisa, the frog princess, the bride of Czarevitch Ivan,' she announced.

Everyone was struck dumb with amazement but when at last they regained their composure, a great cry went up. 'Long live Czarevitch Ivan, the future ruler of our land!'

But Ivan slipped away and hurried to the chamber of his frog bride. There on the white bed lay the ugly frog skin. Czarevitch Ivan did not hesitate. Snatching it up he threw it onto the fire which burned in the hearth. There was a crash of thunder in the sky, and Vasilisa and her carriage burst into the room.

'Alas, alas!' she cried, 'if only you had waited till morning, I would have been your wife forever. But now, thanks to your hasty act I must return to the palace of the mighty magician, Skeleton Eternal, who turned me into a frog.' And with that she disappeared.

Ivan with a heavy heart but full of love for Vasilisa, saddled his horse and set out to search for his frog princess. In the depths of a forest he came to a strange cottage made of moss! It seemed to spin on a human foot and its windows were shaped like human skulls. This was the home of an old witch called Jag. She had bony feet and iron teeth and was the ugliest hag Ivan had ever seen. She was standing by the stove, cursing the magician Skeleton Eternal, because he was chopping down her birch trees.

'I know why you are here,' she croaked. 'Here is a ball of wool, made from rats' fur. It will lead you to Skeleton's palace. Before it grows an oak tree which is so tall that you cannot see its crown. In the topmost branches you will find a copper chest, inside is a silver duck with a golden egg and inside the egg is a rusty needle. Break off the eye and Skeleton Eternal will die.'

The czarevitch thanked the old hag and followed the ball of rat fur. On a river bank he came upon a bear and an eagle fighting over a pike. 'Stop!' he cried, 'I have food enough for all!' Sharing out the food he had brought with him he let the pike slide back into the water.

'You have acted kindly and wisely,' said the animals. 'When you are in need, we will come and help you.'

Ivan walked on until at last he reached Skeleton Eternal's palace. High in the clouds, in the crown of the oak hung the copper chest, suspended on seven chains. Ivan could not uproot

the oak. 'If only that strong bear were here,' he sighed, and in an instant the bear was at his side. He charged only once, and the oak tree came crashing down. The copper chest burst open, and the silver duck flew out over the sea.

'Help me, friend eagle!' Ivan cried, and in an instant the eagle had landed at his feet, the duck in its talons.

But the duck had laid its egg in the bottomless ocean.

'If only the pike were here,' Ivan thought, and there was the pike, the golden egg shining in its mouth. Quickly Ivan broke the egg and snapped off the eye of the rusty needle.

With a crash of thunder the palace crumbled to dust and with it the magician. And suddenly Vasilisa stood before him in all her beauty. Joyfully she fell into Ivan's arms and he carried her home, his heart full of love.

There was a magnificent wedding at the czar's palace which lasted for seven days and seven nights and Ivan and his bride danced and danced for joy till their shoes were quite worn out. And on the eighth day the proud and happy czar embraced his youngest son and proclaimed him his heir and everyone rejoiced at the news.

The Emperor's New Clothes

There once lived an emperor who loved new clothes. He spent all his days dressing up, admiring himself in the mirror, telling himself how elegant he looked. He was such a dandy, with thoughts for nothing but his appearance that his minister had to put a notice on the palace door each morning, which read, 'As new clothes are being tried on, the emperor will not rule at present.'

Consequently there was great disorder in that empire!

One day two tricksters wandered into the city. They happened to pass the emperor's palace where they read the notice. Roaring with laughter, one of them had a brainwave.

'My good man,' he called loudly to a passing servant, 'please inform His Royal Highness that we are weavers from a distant land and that we can weave robes of unimaginable magnificence.'

The servant was lazy and paid no attention, but the emperor himself heard the man's words for he was just then preening himself like a proud peacock at the open window of his chamber. He ordered the two men to be brought to him.

'Your Highness,' the swindlers said with a bow, 'the materials we weave are the finest and richest on earth and, furthermore, they have magic power. Garments made from them are invisible to any person who is lazy or stupid. You will not be sorry if you let us make you a suit of new clothes.'

'What a stroke of good fortune,' the emperor said to himself. 'Not only will I have the finest garments in the world, but I will be able to discover all the stupid, incompetent and lazy people in my palace, and indeed in all my empire!'

And he ordered a workroom to be prepared immediately for the imposters and that it was to be filled with gold, silver, jewels and anything else the most honoured weavers might require. The tricksters rubbed their hands in glee. The valuables sent by the emperor they hid in sacks, then sat down by the empty looms and pretended to be hard at work.

'We need more gold! More jewels!' one commanded.

'Bring pearls and silks,' the other cried. 'The emperor's treasurer will surely not grudge us that when he sees the robes we are weaving.'

The servants hastily obeyed every command and fetched the best of everything. Before long the emperor's coffers were almost empty, and the swindlers' sacks were filled with riches.

On the two weavers worked. Day and night the rattle of the empty looms could be heard. Now and then there were cries of satisfaction from the weavers. 'Oh look, just look at our splendid work!' And, 'What brilliance! What excellence! Such patterns!'

The emperor was agog with curiosity and excitement. He would have liked to look at these wonders, but dared not.

'What if he proved to be a fool! What if he had no right to sit on the throne!'

With that fear in mind, he sent his oldest and wisest minister to see how the work was progressing. 'That man is my best and most dependable adviser,' the king said to himself. 'He will surely be able to see the magic robes.'

The minister found the two swindlers working hard at the empty looms.

'Please, step nearer, most honourable Prime Minister,' cried the weavers. 'Do you not agree that this cloth is beautiful? Feel its fineness! Note the shimmer! Nowhere could you find material to match this.'

The poor minister stood dumbfounded. 'I cannot see anything on these looms,' he muttered to himself unhappily. 'Am I such a fool, or am I unfit for my office?' he lamented silently. But aloud he began to praise the invisible cloth, and when he returned to his emperor, he described the magnificence of the cloth with enthusiasm.

The second, the third and the fourth minister sent by the emperor returned also to describe the material in glowing terms.

At last the swindlers announced that the cloth was finished and they were about to fashion a suit which would be so beautiful it would astound the emperor. They cut the air with their scissors, sewed with threadless needles, and when their work was done, they proudly marched to the emperor, their arms stretched out in front of them as if holding the precious garments.

'Goodness me, I cannot see a thing! Am I such a fool? Should I not be sitting on the throne?' thought the horrified emperor. But he dared not mutter a single word aloud.

The tricksters bowed deeply and said, 'Most honourable Emperor, please allow us to dress you personally in these magnificent garments.'

Permission was granted and the two men pretended to pull on breeches, a shirt, a waistcoat and a flowing cloak, with frilled sleeves.

'Look! What a wondrous suit of clothes! Such colours! Such a splendid cut! How well it fits! And those patterns...' cried the emperor's counsellors, ministers and servants, while the bewildered emperor preened himself, twisting and turning, bowing to his naked image in the mirror, admiring his imaginary clothes.

At last he was ready to face his subjects. He would walk through the streets of the city and show off his finery to his loyal people.

With a satisfied look on his face, he stepped under the purple canopy which was to be carried over him. His chamberlain lifted the invisible train, his servants smoothed the invisible frills and lace, and followed by ministers, coun-sellors, servants, the ceremonial procession marched through the city.

The streets were lined with people, for the news had flown from mouth to mouth and no one wanted to miss seeing their emperor in his magnificent new clothes.

People stood on tiptoe, pushing, jostling, craning their necks to catch a glimpse. At the sight which met their eyes they were struck dumb.

'Are we such fools? We do not see a thing,' they thought to themselves. But recovering quickly the citizens cried aloud, 'Oh, what splen-dour! Those colours! Such richness! Look at the brilliance of those magnificent robes! Long live our emperor!'

Suddenly the voice of a child cried out, 'But Mother, Father, the emperor hasn't got anything on!'

These innocent, truthful words made even the biggest fools see clearly. Everyone started to laugh. They laughed till tears poured from every eye. Then they began to shout to each other, 'Look! Look! Our emperor hasn't a stitch on! He is quite naked!'

The conceited emperor pretended not to hear, but marched proudly back to his palace. Once there he roared and thundered with rage. He commanded that the swindlers be caught and brought before him. But who knows where they were! They had disappeared without trace from the city, from the empire. Perhaps in some other land they are weaving invisible clothes for foolish people willing to be convinced that they can see the invisible.

The Doll in the Grass

Once upon a time there was a king who had twelve sons. One day he sent them out into the wide world to find brides.

'But I tell you this,' said their father, 'do not bring any girl who cannot spin, weave and sew a shirt in one night.'

So the brothers set out, but they did not take the youngest one, whom they called Softy. 'Where would a milksop such as you find a bride,' they mocked.

The unhappy Prince Softy sat down in the tall grass of a meadow feeling lonely and miserable.

A daisy growing nearby suddenly moved and opened, and a tiny maiden so minute he could barely see her stepped out. She sparkled like a dewdrop and to the surprise of the young man, she spoke.

'Do not be sad, Prince Softy. I will take you to

our Doll in the Grass. She will make you happy again, I am sure.'

The prince followed her until she stopped at a little chair carved out of a gold nut. In the chair sat a little doll as fresh and as white as a daisy.

She asked why the prince was sad. When he told her she said encouragingly, 'Do not worry. By the morning I shall sew you a shirt that will be the envy of everyone. But then you will have to marry me.'

She was as good as her word. Though the shirt was as small as the Doll in the Grass, the

no longer as tiny as a daisy but the same size as other maidens, though much lovelier. The old king when he saw her was so enchanted by his son's bride that he could hardly take his eyes of her and without further ado he set Softy on his throne.

As for the eleven brothers who had set out in search of brides, not one had found a beautiful maiden who could spin, weave and sew a shirt in one night. And each of them had to be content with a wife who was so ugly, that their father shuddering at the sight of so many witches, banished them all from his palace.

king when he saw it admired and praised it. 'Go and marry your Doll in the Grass,' he told his son.

Softy mounted his horse and rode back to the meadow. He wanted to set the Doll in the Grass in the saddle beside him, but she said she had her own carriage.

And she hopped onto a silver spoon which was pulled by two white mice with a gold harness. As they were crossing a foot-bridge, Softy's horse suddenly neighed, the mice took fright and the spoon carriage topped over, throwing the Doll in Grass down into the waters of the the brook below.

Softy leapt from his horse, fearing he would never see his bride again. But a water sprite rose from the brook and helped his dear little doll onto the bank. And lo and behold, she was

79

The Little Girl Who Wanted Everything Back

There was once a little girl who found a melon. She took it to her mother, who was eating a potato cake. 'Why are you eating that potato cake, Mother?' she said. 'Why don't you ask me for my sweet melon? Or do you think I am too selfish to give it to you?'

So her mother took the melon and ate it straight away.

Later the little girl came back to her mother and whined. 'I want my melon, Mother!' Her mother told her that she had eaten it, and the little girl flew into a temper. Stamping her feet, she cried, 'How could you eat the melon I found?' To calm the screaming child, the mother gave her a needle.

The little girl went to her father who was sewing a strap with a bone. 'Why are you toiling away with a blunt bone, Father? Why don't you ask me for my needle? Or do you think I am selfish?' she asked. The father took the needle and sewed on, but the needle broke.

A little later the child came back and begged. 'Father, give me back the needle Mother gave me in return for the melon I found!' When the father told her that the needle was broken, the little girl flew into a rage. To pacify her, the father gave her a knife with a steel blade.

The little girl went to her brothers in the forest. They were using a stone knife to scoop out a bees' nest from a tree. 'Why don't you ask me for the knife with the steel blade? Or do you think me selfish?' she snapped. And so they borrowed the knife. Before long the knife struck against something hard and broke.

Later the little girl returned to her brothers. 'Give me back the knife Father gave me, when I gave him the needle Mother gave me when I gave her the melon I'd found!'

The brothers explained that the knife had broken and with that the little girl flew into a temper and wailed. To quieten her, they gave her a honeycomb.

On her way home the little girl met an old woman, who was chewing bark.

'Why are you chewing hard bark, old woman? Why don't you ask me for some honey? Or do you think me selfish?'

So the old woman asked for the honey and enjoyed it very much. When she had eaten it all, the little girl returned.

'Old woman, give me the honey my brothers gave me when I gave them the knife which my Father gave me, when I gave him the needle my Mother gave me, when I gave her the melon I'd found!'

When the old woman told her that she had eaten all the honey, the little girl started to scream and stamp her feet. To pacify her, the old woman gave her a handful of corn.

Some time later the little girl met some pheasants. 'Why don't you ask me for some corn?' she said, 'or do you think me miserly?' So the pheasants took the corn and gobbled up every grain. The little girl was soon back, demanding the corn. When told it was all gone, she started to scream and rage. To quieten her, the pheasants gave her lovely colourful feathers from their tails.

The little girl offered the feathers to some children so that they would not think she was selfish. When the children lost the feathers, the bad-tempered little girl asked for them back. So that they would not have to listen to her screams, the children gave her a saucer of milk.

The little girl was carrying the milk when she met a cat who was gnawing at some bones. 'Why don't you ask me for this saucer of milk?' she asked with a frown. 'Or are you afraid I won't give it to you?' So the cat asked, and licked the saucer dry.

Soon the little girl was back. 'Pussycat hurry, hurry!' she cried. 'Give me back the milk the children gave me, when I gave them the feathers the pheasants gave me, when I gave them the grain the old woman gave me, when I gave her the honey my brothers gave me, when I gave

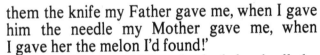

them the knife my Father gave me, when I gave him the needle my Mother gave me, when I gave her the melon I'd found!'

When the cat told her she had drunk all the milk, the little girl stamped her feet, and demanded something in return. But the cat gave her nothing. She just hissed and spat, and took to her heels, with the little girl in hot pursuit.

What a chase it was too! The cat in a bush, the little girl in the bush! The cat in the mud, the little girl in the mud! The cat up a tree, the little girl up the tree! The cat down the tree, but the little girl did not jump down after her. Her head was spinning round at that height, and she was afraid to climb down!

And there she sat for the rest of the day crying and shouting for help. She had been such a nuisance that everybody decided to teach her a lesson. So they let her stay in the tree till she promised to be good. And under a nearby bush the clever cat yawned, stretched and fell asleep.

81

The Crystal Sisters

Long, long ago when the world was still young, Nartu, the keeper of dreams would sit from dusk till dawn in his cave. Night after night he stayed awake by the fire watching over the slumbering sun maiden Yhi, and making sure she did not oversleep. As each night ended, and the eyes of men were opening from sleep, Nartu took away the dreams from the sun maiden's head, opened her eyelids, and said, 'Go on your journey from horizon to horizon, shine upon and warm the earth, for it is time for light and for hunting!' Hearing these words, the sun maiden shook her golden locks and strode into the sky.

Long, long ago, when Nartu, the keeper of dreams was rousing the sun maiden from sleep, two brothers were born. They were inseparable, never parting from one another. Together they played and spent their days and as time passed and they grew to manhood, together they hunted, venturing farther and farther away from home. Though they had become men, everyone called them berai-berai, which means youths.

Once they were hunting red kangaroos. For a long time they followed the trail of the beasts while behind them the hot wind covered their steps with dust so that the youths could not find their way back. The sun maiden Yhi was already slipping back to earth. Nartu, the keeper of dreams, was preparing to wrap the earth in darkness, and still the youths searched for a path which would lead them home. Suddenly they noticed a flickering glow beyond a hill.

'That must be a fire; there we shall spend the

night, until the sun maiden Yhi lights up a new day,' the youths said to each other. They climbed the hill and were amazed at what they saw. Round the fire were seven maidens and they were of pure crystal. Their transparent locks fell to their waists, their bodies glittered with hoarfrost and icicles like stars in dewdrops. The glow from the seven maidens shone

not want to part from the crystal sisters, or see no more the glow of their transparent hair.

When they fell asleep, Nartu, the keeper of dreams, placed dreams of the lovely maidens inside their heads. They slept well and in the morning, when the sun maiden, Yhi, stepped into the sky, the sisters were already far away. The youths followed their tracks and when

brighter than the flames and they were lovelier far than other maidens.

The brothers spoke. 'We are berai-berai,' they said quietly, 'which means youths. Who are you?'

The maidens were about to flee, but fear gripped their feet. So they answered, 'We are maja-maji, the crystal sisters. Please do not harm us! Our mother and father live on a distant mountain, and they never climb down. We hunt alone. We do not follow the tracks of men. Warm yourselves by our fire, if you wish, eat our food, sleep on the furs of the oppossum we have caught. But promise that when the sun maiden, Yhi, rises, you will leave us and follow your own path.'

The youths were sad. Aloud they said 'yes', but their hearts whispered a silent 'no'. They did

these grew faint, they were led on by the glow above the sisters' heads. They travelled along a path never before used by men and each night they lit a fire within sight of the maidens' fire.

When the sun maiden, Yhi, fell into a deep sleep in the cave of the keeper of dreams, the young men crept into the camp of the slumbering maidens and placed gifts by their heads— seed cakes made from grass seed, colourful stones or a shell of crystal clear water. But the sisters never once glanced behind as they travelled on. Berai-berai walked on alone.

On the path untrodden by men, they met an odd creature digging up a nest of bees. Though he had a face, he had no eyes, and a sharp axe served as a forehead. 'I am of a race which sees through the nose,' he explained, and to quieten their fear, he handed them a dish carved bark filled with honey. And the youths continued on the trail of the crystal sisters. Next morning when the maidens awoke they found the dish of sweet honey by their heads.

The path led the brothers into bushes alive with mosquitoes and flies. They wanted to break branches from a tree to protect themselves, but the trees started to move and come towards them. These were no trees, but people overgrown with bark and leaves, with glaring sunken eyes. The youths took to their heels and

fled from the mosquitoes, flies and living forest.

They came to a blue lake. It gave them water and fish. They lit a fire to cook the fish, and when they looked round, the lake had vanished. Only a stony plain remained.

'I am astonished at the strange things that are happening,' said one of the brothers. 'A man without eyes can see. A man has bark instead of skin. The lake has water, which we have both drunk and which also gave us fish, yet the lake is no longer here!'

The next morning the maidens found baked fish by their heads. The youths followed their tracks, but maja-maji did not glance behind.

Then the man named Wurrun who was of the same race as turkeys wandered into the maidens camp. He walked not the path of men, for he had harmed them many times and feared their revenge. The sisters gave him food and water, and sent him on his way. When he was out of sight, he hid and waited for one of the sisters to lag behind. Wurrun was tired of travelling on his own and wanted companionship.

Berai-berai, however, learned from the tracks that Wurrun was slithering behind the sisters like a snake, and they wished to warn them. So the maidens found a snake by their heads the next day. But they ignored the warning and walked on.

Eventually two of the maidens wishing to dig up sweet herbs from the earth fell behind their sisters. Wurrun pounced upon them from behind the bushes and grasped them firmly round the waist. The sisters cried for help, but no. one heard them, for the other maja-maji were a long way ahead and berai-berai were too far behind.

The two sisters had to walk in the footsteps of the wicked Wurrun, who threatened them if they tried to escape. He was afraid that the glow from the two crystal sisters would bring the rest of the maja-maji.

'You are all shimmer and light; I must get rid of the hoarfrost and icicles,' he said, and lighting a fire, he pushed them into the flames. But the fire died. Wurrun grew angry and ordered the sisters to cut bark from the pine trees to relight the fire.

'The crystal sisters must not cut the bark of pines. If we do, your eyes will never see us again,' they warned him.

But when the terrible Wurrun threatened them with his heavy club, they obeyed and with their stone axes they cut deep into the bark of the trees.

'Birrah, birrah, ohey, birrah!' they cried loudly, and the pines began to grow, higher and higher,

carrying the crystal sisters up into the sky. And Wurrun was afraid.

Suddenly the youths ran out of the thicket, for they had heard the cries. Wurrun cursed and turning into a turkey, for he was of the same race as they he flew away. Berai-berai gazed upwards at the growing pines carrying the two sisters. When their crowns were touching the heavens, the five remaining sisters leaned down from above and helped them into the heavens.

Now, for the first time the crystal sisters looked at berai-berai with a sad smile. 'When the sun maiden, Yhi, rises, maja-maji will not find our gifts by their heads,' the youths sighed.

An old man suddenly appeared. 'I am Nartu, the keeper of dreams,' he said. 'I see grief in your eyes and know that your hearts are heavy. I will help you. You must follow the path the sun maiden travels to earth, for as many days as there are fingers on one hand. You will come to a scorched land licked by the sun's flame, and there you will find my cave in which the sun

maiden sleeps. Wait till she is high in the sky, then toss two lighted sticks into the black hole she passes through. Then flee for your life, as if birds had lent you wings.'

Berai-berai did as Nartu told them. And as they fled, as if birds had lent them wings, the mountain trembled, boulders burst with fiery heat and water springs shot high in the air before them. The youths were suddenly trapped by a whirl wind of hot breath and steam, and carried high into the sky. There they were met by the crystal sisters and the eyes of the brothers were filled with joy. When the sun maiden rose in the morning, maja-maji found a smooth red stone from Nartu's cave by their heads.

Time has passed. Maja-maji and berai-berai are constantly together. Men think they are stars, and call them the Pleiades. But we know they are youths and maidens. The youths dance, while the maidens sing. And when in the morning the sun maiden, Yhi, rises, we shall find a fairy story by our heads.

The Witty Joker

Everyone knew Nasreddin, the roguish clown. Tales of him spread through the sunny countryside, to the land of snowflakes and to the kingdom of night. Even the birds, the fish and the flowers knew and passed on stories about him. In short, he was the greatest jester in the world. Worry was not for him, as for other people; he preferred to think up ways of making people laugh and he loved to play practical jokes. One day he borrowed an old pot from a neighbour, a solid round pot it was too! The next day, when he returned it, there was a smaller pot inside, a solid round pot it was too!

'Just look, neighbour,' Nasreddin stammered, looking stunned. 'That pot of yours had a baby in the night!'

The greedy neighbour thought that Nasreddin must be very stupid, but he thanked him cordially and gladly accepted the pot-child. He was laughing under his whiskers at outdoing Nasreddin.

Some time later he returned and said, 'Listen, young fellow! I could do with another little pot, but that old pot of mine simply refuses to have another baby. Keep it with you, then perhaps it will oblige for you!' The miserly neighbour thought that with a little flattery Nasreddin would put another little pot in the big round pot, to prove what a good magician he was. Nasreddin took the pot, but the days passed and he did not return it.

The impatient neighbour called on him and asked, 'What is wrong with my pot? Has it not had another child yet?'

Nasreddin sobbed, 'Courage, my friend. I have bad news for you. Your old pot has died. I buried it yesterday. May it ease your sorrow that death came quickly, without suffering. It simply seezed, and that was the end!'

'Stop jesting with me!' the neighbour cried angrily. 'Who has ever seen a pot die?'

Nasreddin looked most hurt. 'But neighbour! If a pot can have a child, surely it can also die?'

The grasping neighbour did not want to accept such an explanation, so he called all the neighbours together to drink tea at the tea house and decide the question. How they all laughed when they heard the tale! They all agreed that by right the pot belonged to Nasreddin and the oldest of the neighbours added, 'If a pot can give birth to a child, why should a fool argue that it cannot die?'

'That is true, that is true,' the others muttered, while with a smile on their lips they sipped their tea.

Some time later the neighbour met Nasreddin

again. 'Why do you frown at me, my friend? Let us forgive and forget what has happened!' Nasreddin said, 'I have an idea. Let us have a wager! If you manage to drink from our river, I shall return your pot. If you do not, then you will have to give me your little pot.'

'What an easy task,' thought the neighbour. 'That Nasreddin really must be a fool.' He accepted the wager, for it did not occur to him that he could possibly lose again.

They set off for the river nearby. The greedy neighbour was just about to lean over and drink, when the foxy young man said.

'Just one moment, neighbour, who knows what is up your sleeve! We had better fetch some witnesses. What if you did not take even a sip, but insisted afterwards that you had fulfilled the wager.'

'Whatever you think,' the foolish man agreed, and returned to the tea house with Nasreddin.

'Well?' cried the curious men. 'Did you, or did you not have a drink from that river?'

The miser then realized he had lost the wager with Nasreddin. There was nothing else for it, but to return the little pot to the young joker.

Nasreddin still drinks from it today, sipping his tea, smiling and thinking up new practical jokes. For in the land where pots give birth to babies, there are many more fools to be hoodwinked.

Aladdin and his Magic Lamp

Once upon a time a mighty magician lived in the depths of Africa, and he owned a magic ring. Whenever he twisted the ring thrice, a powerful genie appeared in a cloud of smoke from the kingdom of spirits.

Always the genie bowed and said, 'I am the slave of the ring, Master! I shall obey your every command.' As soon as the magician spoke his wish, the genie carried it out. One day the old magician asked the slave of the ring who was the most powerful person in the world.

The spirit replied, 'Far to the east, where the sun rises, an ancient lamp burns in a magnificent underground garden. Whoever rubs it, will become the master of my brother, the slave of the lamp. He is the most powerful genie of all. But it is written in the stars that only Aladdin, who lives with his poor widowed mother in that distant eastern country, will be allowed to enter the buried garden. If he discovers this secret,

and brings out the magic lamp, he will rule with supreme power. But on his journey underground he must wear your magic ring for protection.'

On hearing this strange tale, the magician ordered the genie of the ring to take him to the distant eastern country, to the town where Aladdin lived. There he straightaway sought out his mother.

'I am the brother of your deceased husband,' he lied. 'While I journeyed through the world, I heard that your husband had died. I have come to help you in your poverty, as it is only right that I should. Let me train your son Aladdin and I shall make him rich.'

Aladdin's mother was most surprised, for she had never heard her husband talk of a brother. But when the magician bought expensive clothes for the boy, she was convinced and told her son to accompany his so-called uncle on his travels. The artful magician's intention was, of course, to lay his hands on the magic lamp with Aladdin's help. And so he took the lad on a journey according to the instructions of the slave of the ring. When they came to the foot of black mountains, the magician scribbled secret signs in the air, and muttered a secret spell. In a trice with a noise like thunder, an enormous boulder with an iron ring in its centre appeared before them. But try as he might the magician could not move the boulder. But when the terrified Aladdin grasped the iron ring, the boulder rolled away quite easily uncovering a dark staircase which led down to the very heart of the earth.

'You must descend at once, Aladdin, and bring me the lamp which burns in the magic garden,' the magician said. 'If you value your life, do not touch anything else. Take my ring; it will protect you against the powers of darkness.'

Aladdin obeyed with fear in his heart, but he dared not refuse his strange uncle. Once at the foot of the dark staircase, he ran through three halls filled with untold treasures, until he came at last to a wondrous garden. Gold trees and bushes were laden with the strangest fruits for they were not fruits at all, but precious stones. Under the rainbow-coloured vines hung clusters of grapelike pearls and in the grass diamond nuts opened their shells. Aladdin could not resist picking a handful of shimmering fruit and stuffing them in his shirt. Then, taking down the ugly old lamp which was blinking in a niche, he ran back to join his uncle. But the opening was too high. From the top step he could not pull himself up.

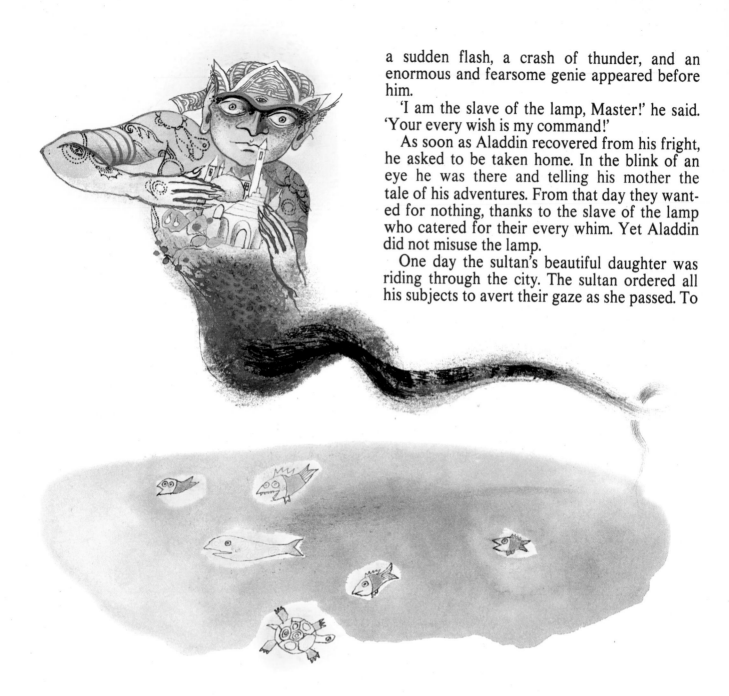

a sudden flash, a crash of thunder, and an enormous and fearsome genie appeared before him.

'I am the slave of the lamp, Master!' he said. 'Your every wish is my command!'

As soon as Aladdin recovered from his fright, he asked to be taken home. In the blink of an eye he was there and telling his mother the tale of his adventures. From that day they wanted for nothing, thanks to the slave of the lamp who catered for their every whim. Yet Aladdin did not misuse the lamp.

One day the sultan's beautiful daughter was riding through the city. The sultan ordered all his subjects to avert their gaze as she passed. To

'Give me your hand, Uncle,' Aladdin cried, 'and help me to climb out.'

'First pass me the lamp!' the magician called, for he meant to leave Aladdin forever underground just as soon as he had the lamp. But Aladdin refused, and although his uncle threatened and pleaded and raged and pleaded again, Aladdin stubbornly held on to the lamp. The magician flew into a towering rage.

Defeated by Aladdin, he pushed the boulder back over the opening, and like a black thundercloud flew back to Africa.

Poor Aladdin! He sank down on the steps of his subterranean prison and burst into tears. Tears as big as peas fell from his eyes on to the dusty lamp, and the boy absentmindedly began to wipe them off with his hand. There was

disobey meant certain death. But Aladdin, hidden behind a window, did not avert his eyes and when the breeze slightly lifted the corner of her veil, his heart was filled with her incredible loveliness.

'She must one day be my bride,' he vowed. Then he remembered the precious fruit he had picked in the underground garden. He set about persuading his mother to take it as a gift to the palace. 'When the sultan accepts it, you must then tell him that your son desires the hand of his daughter,' said Aladdin.

In vain, his mother tried to change his mind and in the end she went, fear in her heart to the palace.

When however the sultan saw the jewels, he grew pale with envy. Why, one of those stones was more valuable than any treasure in his kingdom. He asked Aladdin to come to court.

Learning this, Aladdin ordered the slave of the lamp to conjure up an endless procession of slaves, carrying gold and jewels. Clad in a magnificent robe he rode at its head, dazzling the sultan and his daughter with his handsomeness and wealth. The young princess was happy to consent at once to become his wife.

But the envious vizier, who was the sultan's adviser, wanted her for himself. He advised the sultan not to promise his daughter to Aladdin, until a palace of gold and jewels had been built for her. Aladdin laughed at such a wish. The slave of the lamp carried out the sultan's order in one night. By daybreak a magnificent palace stood in the gardens near the sultan's own palace. It glittered like the morning sun and without further hesitation the sultan gave his daughter to the happy Aladdin.

...But one day the old magician in darkest

Africa heard that thanks to the magic lamp Aladdin had not perished in the depths of the earth, and that he had now become the sultan's son-in-law and heir. Without wasting a minute, he flew in a black cloud to the eastern kingdom, determined to seize the magic lamp.

One day when Aladdin was out hunting, the magician placed beautiful new lamps under the palace windows and cried, 'New lamps for old, new lamps for old!' Aladdin's wife heard his cry and remembered the ugly old lamp hanging in a corner. A maid was sent at once to exchange it for a new one.

The moment the magician had the lamp in his hand, he laughed horribly. Calling the genie to his aid, he ordered him to transport the gold palace and the unsuspecting princess to his African home. No sooner had he spoken than the palace dissolved in a puff of smoke. The furious sultan had Aladdin brought before him.

'You have three days only to bring back my daughter, or you will lose your head,' he threatened. And calling his guards he had the young man thrown into prison.

What was Aladdin to do? Without thinking he twisted the ring the magician had given him. And behold! The genie of the ring appeared in a cloud of smoke, and said, 'I am the slave of the ring, Master! Your wish is my command!'

Aladdin was overjoyed, and ordered the gold palace and his wife to be returned at once. But the spirit said that such a feat could be accomplished only by his brother, the slave of the lamp, which was in the magician's possession.

'I will take you to the evil magician in Africa,' said the genie. 'He carries the lamp round his neck.' And in a trice Aladdin found himself in the golden palace, embracing his lovely wife, who swooned with joy at seeing him.

'Promise to become the magician's wife,' Aladdin said, 'if he drinks a goblet of wine in your honour. Before he does so, pour into the goblet this magic powder given to me by the slave of the ring.'

The princess did what Aladdin told her. She made sure that the magician drank from the goblet of poisoned wine. In a few seconds he had fallen to the floor and next moment he had disappeared forever in a cloud of black smoke. At the spot where he vanished there now stood an old ugly lamp.

Aladdin wasted no time, but rubbed it with the palm of his hand and asked the genie, who instantly appeared, to transport his princess, himself and their golden palace back home. And there they lived happily to the end of their days.

The Dewdrop Tiara

In a distant kingdom there reigned a mighty emperor who had a beautiful daughter. Tales of her loveliness spread far and wide, but at the same time there were rumours that she was proud and vain. She wore only the finest robes embroidered with pearls and jewels, golden dragons and purple skies with white clouds floating on patches of blue. Jewellers from all over the world brought her priceless treasures, and poor fishermen had to dive to the sea bed for the biggest and most colourful pearls. But all the wealth in the world did not satisfy the proud princess. She envied flowers their beauty, she longed to sparkle like the stars; she wanted to glow like flames of fire.

One night the princess, consumed with desire for new jewels, found herself unable to sleep, so barefoot she ran from the palace and wandered through the gardens till daybreak. Then, when the sun swung into the sky was the time its beams shone on every dewdrop strewn on grass, petals and leaves. Never before had the princess seen the sparkle of dawn. It was so breathtaking that her head spun round. Even the birds stopped singing for a moment in wonder. Then their song burst from their throats again as they welcomed the sun, the noblest, most beautiful maiden in all the world.

'Oh, what magnificence,' the princess sighed, and ran to her father.

'Father, father,' she insisted, 'I must have a tiara made of dewdrops, otherwise I shall die with longing!'

The old emperor could deny nothing to his spoiled daughter. So he called together all the jewellers in his empire and ordered them to carry out his daughter's wish by next morning; otherwise they would be put to death.

The unfortunate men left the palace with heavy hearts, hastening to their families to bid them goodbye and to prepare for death. It was beyond human power to fashion such a tiara. All that night sounds of sorrow and weeping echoed over the city.

When morning came, the jewellers walked sadly back to the palace, their hands empty.

'Do you bring the dewdrop tiara?' stormed the emperor.

'Have mercy, Master,' cried the unhappy men, 'we cannot make such a jewel with our hands.'

The princess was frowning angrily and the emperor was about to hand the jewellers to the executioner, when suddenly an old, unknown man spoke from a corner by the door. Nobody had seen him enter, yet he looked as if he had been standing there always.

'I shall give your daughter what she yearns for, my most noble Emperor,' he said in a shaky voice. 'But she must herself pick the finest dewdrops; then she will have a gem of her very own choice.'

The princess was delighted by these words, and rushed into the garden to collect the biggest, shiniest dewdrops, but as soon as she touched them, they melted under her hand, their glitter dying like an extinguished candle. The maiden went over the whole garden, leaned

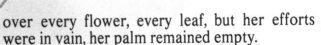

over every flower, every leaf, but her efforts were in vain, her palm remained empty.

The proud princess sat down and cried and cried. All of a sudden she noticed the old jeweller smiling at her strangely.

'Hurry with the drops of dew, Princess, so that I can start working. If you collect a handful, I will make you a tiara such as even the nymphs in heaven do not possess.'

'I cannot gather the dewdrops. They dissolve the moment I touch them,' the princess complained.

The old man stopped smiling and said sternly, 'Then return to the palace and tell your father to have you beheaded too when the jewellers are executed. You yourself have not managed even in part what you demand of others under sentence of death.'

The princess turned scarlet with shame, and as her colour deepened more and more, the aged man gradually began to dissolve in the glow of the sun.

'I no longer want the dewdrop tiara,' the princess whispered. 'I was foolish to ask!' The disappearing old man smiled kindly at her once more, stroked her hair, and was gone.

And the proud, vain princess? She was no longer proud, nor vain. Her vanity had dissolved with the morning dew.

The Bride from Bird Island

Once upon a time there was a young hunter who lived on a small island. More than anything else he loved to listen to the song of birds. One day he built a stout boat from a tree trunk and set out across the sea to Bird Island, hoping to catch a singing bird with his net. He sailed for two days and nights till the silent darkness was broken by the twitter of awakening birds. Now he knew he was nearing Bird Island.

Pulling his boat onto the beach, he secured his net and waited quietly under a tree. Suddenly he heard the sound of weeping. Parting the bushes, he saw that he had trapped a beautiful silver bird in his net. Round its head was a golden ribbon, round its foot a coconut ring. 'Do not harm me,' it pleaded, 'and I will teach you my song.'

'Very well,' the hunter agreed, 'but bird songs are difficult for a man to learn. I will take you home with me.' The hunter then tied the bird to a lock of his own long hair and set it on his shoulder, and they sailed away in the boat to his little island. On the way the silver bird begged, 'Please take off my coconut ring, my foot hurts.'

The moment the youth obliged, the silver bird turned into a lovely silver maiden. Round her head she wore a golden ribbon. 'Who are you?' asked the hunter in wonder. 'I am the daughter of the chieftain of birds from Bird Island. I am allowed to marry the man who takes the coconut ring from my foot.'

'My name is Manimporock,' the youth replied. 'As it was I who took the coconut ring off your foot, I shall now take you for my wife.'

94

'Manimporock?' laughed the girl, her voice like the twitter of a bird. 'That is a strange name. I shall call you Coconut Ring.'

Manimporock agreed, and led the silver maiden to his parents' hut. Then he loaded his boat with simple gifts and set out again across the sea to Bird Island. He would offer these gifts to the chieftain of birds in exchange for his daughter. As he sailed along, he met Mololewo, the blacksmith from a nearby island, whose boat was so heavily laden with rich gifts that it was nearly sinking.

'What is your destination, blacksmith?' Coconut Ring called out.

Mololewo replied that he was on his way to Bird Island to see the chieftain of birds, for he desired to marry his beautiful daughter.

'Return to your forge, blacksmith,' Coconut Ring cried. 'You are late! The bird daughter is my wife, and she lives in the hut of my parents.'

But the blacksmith refused to be persuaded to turn back, and when the two of them had placed their gifts at the foot of the tree of the chieftain of birds, he asked him to settle their dispute.

'My daughter belongs to the man who pulled the coconut ring off her foot,' chirped the chieftain. Hearing this, the blacksmith scowled threateningly and vowed he would revenge himself on Coconut Ring and his bird bride.

Manimporock was afraid. To be threatened by blacksmith Mololewo was not a thing to be ignored. Everyone knew he dabbled in magic, and the old people said he was on friendly terms with demons and forest spirits. But when Coconut Ring returned home, he was relieved to see all was well, and soon he forgot the blacksmith's threat.

There came the day of the great hunt. All the men from the village went into the jungle, and there was a great noise of spears and knives being struck against shields as the frightened beasts were flushed from the bushes. Coconut Ring was in luck; he slew a wild boar and several other beasts. But in the thicket he heard the song of the little hermit bird, who foretells unhappiness to men.

Coconut Ring called out, 'Little bird, your song I have heard. Which of us is the unlucky one? Who will lose a wife, a daughter, a son?'

'For you only I sing, to you sorrow I bring,' replied the bird. Coconut Ring was frightened.

95

He recalled the threat of blacksmith Mololewo and fearfully he hastened home. In his hut he found only a dead fire, his mother bitterly weeping by the ashes.

'Alas, my son,' she cried. 'The wicked Mololewo has taken your bird bride to his island. All those who tried to stop him, were slain. Who knows, perhaps he was aided by evil spirits from the dark jungle.'

Hearing this, Coconut Ring tore a root of curcuma from the ground, and whistled in bird language to his friend the parrot, whom he had tamed many years before. 'Brother bird, take this intoxicating root to my wife Moon Nymph, who has been kidnapped by our enemy. Tell her to give it to blacksmith Mololewo to chew; it will put him to sleep.'

As soon as the parrot had flown off, Coconut Ring lowered his boat onto the sea and sped with the wind to help Moon Nymph. From a distance he could see the wicked Mololewo hammering with one great arm red hot iron. With the other he held Moon Nymph to make sure she would not run away. Fragments of burning metal flew from his anvil, often striking the poor maiden's face, marring her beauty and causing her pain, but the cruel Mololewo paid no attention.

From the bushes Coconut Ring signalled to his wife in bird language.

When Moon Nymph heard him, she pleaded, 'My back is aching, Mololewo! Please chew and soften this root of healing curcuma, which my brother the parrot brought me. Then I can put it on the places which hurt.'

Mololewo reluctantly agreed and soon his head dropped to his chest and he began to snore. Coconut Ring and Moon Nymph did not wait but sped home across the sea.

When the blacksmith awoke from his deep sleep, he vainly searched for Moon Nymph. Blowing angrily into the lukewarm ashes, he asked, 'Tell me, little blue flame, where has Moon Nymph gone?' Sparks jumped from the fire and blew towards the sea, in the same direction Coconut Ring's boat had taken. Mololewo wasted no time, but picked up the red hot cinders with his hands and threw them onto the surface of the water. It hissed and it spat, and a fiery canoe emerged from the deep. With Mololewo aboard like a ravenous shark it raced after the fugitives.

'Oh, Coconut Ring, what shall we do? The cruel Mololewo is catching us up,' cried the bird princess, when she saw the dazzling glow on the sea.

But Coconut Ring threw his ivory-handled knife into the air as a gift to the god of the wind, and cried, 'Mighty god of the wind, I beg you for a favourable voyage!'

No sooner had he spoken than a fierce gale blew up, gathering the fugitives' boat in its arms and hurling it across the sea like an arrow.

The blacksmith, seeing this, roared with rage, till even the sun trembled, and tossed into the air an axe with a haft of rosewood. 'Noble demon of storms, do not turn your back on me. Let the hurricane give my canoe wings! It is I, blacksmith Mololewo, who calls you!'

The demon of storms, content with the gift, granted his request.

When Coconut Ring saw that Mololewo was catching up with them again, he asked the god of the mountains to come to his aid. And the god split a towering rock in two, making a bar-rier across the straits between the islands. But the blacksmith, aided by the hurricane, sailed round the islands and was again gaining on Coconut Ring.

'Mysterious god of the jungle, save us!' Coconut Ring cried. And the god of the jungle answered his call and ordered the jungle to crash into the sea and bar Mololewo's way.

But Mololewo summoned the forest spirits and fought his way through the densest bushes.

His hands were reaching out for Moon Nymph, when Coconut Ring called in desperation upon the god of the seas, but he was fast asleep and did not hear his cry.

Moon Nymph then sang a bird song, 'Good god of the seas, I shall teach you the lullaby you listened to on the shores of my island. It is I, the daughter of the chieftain of the Island of Birds who calls you. Save us from wicked Mololewo!'

The god of the seas awoke and lifted the blacksmith's boat from the ocean and the blacksmith and the fiery canoe were never seen again. And Moon Nymph then taught the god of the sea her lullaby. At night if you listen you can hear the lullaby of the sea which was learned from Moon Nymph so long ago.

Giufo's Debts

Once there was a rascal called Giufo and he was one of the most artful rogues who ever lived. He walked about barefoot, his trousers full of holes, but he held his head high and despite his crafty tricks, he was not disliked by his neighbours.

One day he said to himself, 'I am tired of poverty. Am I wearing trousers just for the wind to whip through the holes? Why do I have to use my own skin to walk on?' And off he went to the market to see a tailor.

'Listen, Needle my friend, I have been invited to visit some very noble people tomorrow. Sell me fine suit. I will pay for it as soon as I return, when those noble people have settled what they owe me.'

'Who has invited you, Giufo?' the tailor asked, but Giufo's face took on a mysterious look, and he pointed to the sky. The tailor, quite dumbfounded, bowed to the ground before him.

'Here, Giufo, take my very best suit. And please be kind enough to speak on my behalf up there; let all my sins be forgiven,' he begged. Giufo gave his promise, took the offered suit with a smile, and turned towards the cobbler's shop.

Before reaching it, all the market was astir. Everyone knew that Giufo was preparing to visit Heaven. You should have seen them making up to that rascal! The cobbler selected a pair of shoes fine enough for a ball, the sock-maker collected a mountain of socks to choose from, the capmaker tried one beret after another, and the barber used his finest razor to shave his chin. When Giufo apologized that he had no money that day, they all simply waved their hands and said, 'No matter, you shall settle up when Heaven returns what it owes you. But don't forget to put in a good word for us!'

Giufo promised anything, everything, and why not? When dressed so splendidly he felt he was walking on a heavenly cloud.

Some days passed and Giufo's creditors started to approach him. 'Hello there, Giufo! Are you back? When will you repay your debt?' They hammered at his door, till Giufo did not know what to do except to feign death. So, when the neighbours peered through the window, they saw Giufo stretched out on the bed, his eyes closed, and in his clasped hands a cross.

'What fools we were to let him have our goods on trust,' the tailor lamented. 'It should have occurred to us that people do not come back to earth from such a visit!'

'Poor Giufo! So Heaven has repaid you what

it owed you. It was death they owed,' muttered the cobbler sadly. And they all agreed.

'What is gone, is gone! We forgive you your debts, unfortunate Giufo!' said the capmaker. 'After all, that visit of yours cost you more than it cost us, don't you think so, friends?'

They nodded, made the sign of a cross, and carried Giufo straight to the chapel. As was the custom, there he was to rest till morning in an open coffin. Brr, how cold it was there! Giufo trembled like a rain-soaked hen and waited impatiently for dusk to fall, so that he could take to his heels.

But as the shadows lengthened, thieves crept into the chapel, and began to divide amongst themselves the money they had stolen. But no matter how often they counted it, they could not

agree, for there was one gold coin to spare. They argued, they quarreled; they were almost at each other's throats.

It was then that poor, shivering Giufo sneezed, and it was a sneeze as loud as a shot from a pistol.

'Look at that corpse,' thundered the leader of the robbers, 'he dares to sneeze in the house of God even when dead! I tell you what: the one who from the distance of ten paces can hit his nose with a shot from his pistol shall have the odd gold coin!'

Giufo turned as white as death. But he was not known to be the most artful rascal in the land for nothing.

To the thieves' horror, he sat up in his coffin, stretched out his hands and cried in a terrible voice, 'Rise, oh dead people, rise and come to my aid!'

The terrified robbers leapt to their feet, and leaving the money scattered on the floor, they fled in all directions. In fact one frightened thief left his wooden leg behind, and for the rest of his days had to hop around the world on one foot.

The crafty Giufo collected all the gold, missing not a single coin, and went home. The next morning he repaid all his debts to his astonished creditors. But the robber's wooden leg he kept as a memento of his little adventure.

Snow White
and the
Seven Dwarfs

Once upon a time there reigned a powerful king, who loved dearly his good and lovely wife. With all his heart he longed for her to give him a daughter equally lovely and equally good, but his hopes seemed in vain.

One winter day, as the queen sat embroidering at her window, she gazed out at the snow-covered coutryside above which a flock of crows was hovering. Deep in thought, she pricked her finger with the golden needle, and three scarlet drops of blood fell on the white linen.

All at once she heard a bird cawing, 'Brother crow! Do you know that the queen will soon give birth to a baby girl with skin as white as snow, with cheeks as scarlet as these three drops of blood that have fallen and with hair as black as a crow's feathers?' 'Good news indeed, good news indeed,' crowed the other bird, circling the castle tower. Then they both flew after

the rest of the flock. The queen was overjoyed, for she longed for a daughter just as the crows had described, and she hastened to tell the king to prepare for the christening.

The crows' predictions came true. Before the year ended, the queen was nursing in her arms a baby girl as white as a snowflake, with cheeks blood red and hair as black as crow's feathers. They named her Snow White and there was much rejoicing throughout the kingdom.

But the royal parents were not destined to enjoy their happiness for long. One day the queen fell gravely ill, and before very long had closed her eyes for ever. The king was beside himself with grief, unable to forget his kind and lovely wife. But as he watched Snow White grow, more and more he thought that she should have a mother's love and care. One day he brought a stepmother to the castle.

No other woman in the land was the new queen's equal in beauty, but simple folks whispered that she was a proud witch, who dabbled in evil magic and had tricked the king into marrying her. They said she had a lump of ice for a heart and snow crystals for eyes. Certainly she had a magic mirror in her chamber, which she would sometimes ask, 'Mirror, mirror on the wall, tell me, who is the fairest of us all?'

The mirror always answered, 'Lovely mistress mine, no one has beauty to outshine thine.'

The queen was happy, but not for long. Little Snow White was becoming as beautiful as an opening rose bud, and tales of her loveliness spread far beyond the kingdom's borders. The stepmother hated her stepdaughter with all her heart. One day she put on her loveliest robe

and, standing before the magic mirror, she asked, 'Mirror, mirror on the wall, tell me, who is the fairest of us all?'

The mirror replied, 'Lovely mistress mine, Snow White's beauty does now outshine thine.'

Hearing this, the queen fell into a rage of temper. In a fit of anger she smashed the magic mirror, till cracks ran from edge to edge like a cobweb. Then she summoned the royal huntsman and said, 'You are to lead Snow White secretly into the depths of the forest and kill her there. Tell the king that she has been torn by wild beasts. If you disobey, I shall feed you to your own dogs!'

The terrified huntsman dared not refuse to carry out the order of his cruel mistress, for he feared for his life. And he lured Snow White into the forest by promising to show her the nest of the golden bird. Once there, he drew his knife and was about to obey the queen's command when Snow White cried, 'Dear huntsman, do not kill the golden bird.'

Turning red with shame, the huntsman threw his knife away and fled from the heart of the forest, leaving Snow White quite alone.

'Perhaps she will be found by someone before wild beasts devour her,' he thought.

Snow White wandered through the thicket,

till her legs grew so tired they could hardly carry her. All round her she could hear the roar of wild beasts and see in the dusk the shining eyes of poisonous snakes. But nothing harmed her, and it seemed as if she was being watched over by good fairies.

When she could not walk a step further, an old crow flew into the crown of a tree and crowed, 'Crah, crah, Snow White, I am the king of all the black crows. Because your hair is as black as our feathers, I shall help you. Follow the black feather I shall throw down to you. It will lead you from here!'

This was the very same crow who, years before, had told the queen of the forthcoming birth of her daughter. Now he plucked a feather from his plumage and threw it into the air. It fluttered above the ground and led Snow White to a small clearing in the forest. A strange little cottage stood there, built of moss and pine cones. Its roof was made of toadstools, and the door from nut shells. And wherever one's eyes fell, jewels shimmered like drops of dew. Snow

White knocked shyly on the door, and when no one answered, she turned the knob and stepped inside. She could hardly believe her eyes! The room was as tiny as a cage, with seven little beds lined against the wall, a firefly instead of a lamp shining above each one. In the centre was a little table and round it seven little chairs. On the table were seven tiny plates, seven tiny mugs, seven tiny knives and forks and seven tiny loaves. But what untidiness there was in that little room! Mice were playing round the stove, spiders running from cobweb to cobweb along the ceiling, and everywhere there was dust.

Snow White thought what a nice little house it was if only it were clean. So she picked up the broom and then the mop, and she brushed, polished and scrubbed till everything shone with cleanliness. Such hard work made her hungry, so she took a little bread from each plate, and a little sip from each mug, and as by then she was terribly sleepy, she chose the largest of the little beds, fell into it and slept and slept.

Suddenly there was the sound of a merry song from the forest. It was sung by the seven little dwarfs who were the owners of the cottage and who were now returning home. Each morning they left to go to work in the mines, searching for gold and precious stones, returning at night to the cottage, their little sacks filled with gems. They always looked forward to their supper and their rest.

When they entered the cottage, the first dwarf cried, 'What has happened, brothers? Someone has taken a bite of my loaf!'

'And someone has helped himself to a piece of my bread!' cried the second.

'Who has taken a sip from my mug?' wondered the third.

'Who has been sitting on my chair?' thundered the fourth.

'My knife has been used! My fork has been licked!' cried the fifth and the sixth dwarfs angrily shaking their fists.

There was a sudden, terrified squeal from the seventh dwarf. 'Who is that sleeping in my bed?'

The dwarfs crowded round and gazed in wonder at the sleeping Snow White.

'Oh, how beautiful she is!' they whispered. 'Keep quiet, brothers, we must not wake her!' And the kind little dwarfs crept away on tiptoe and snuggled into their beds, hardly daring to breathe. The seventh dwarf settled down on the stove, where he was very comfy.

When in the morning Snow White opened her eyes, there were seven little men, hardly taller than a fir cone, staring at her. Losing all fear, she greeted them nicely and begged to be allowed to stay, so that her wicked stepmother would not harm her.

'Stay by all means,' the dwarfs gladly agreed. 'It will be lovely to have you.'

'Just think how clean our cottage will be,' chirped the smallest. 'You can cook us lovely puddings! And tell us fairy tales!' shouted the dwarfs, one after the other.

'But promise to open the door to no one!' the eldest warned. Snow White promised and waved them off to work.

In the meantime sadness reigned in the royal palace. The huntsman told the king that his dearest daughter had been devoured by wild beasts in the forest. Everyone in the kingdom wore black and went about with downcast eyes. The king was beside himself with grief, but the wicked stepmother rushed to her mirror and asked, 'Mirror, mirror on the wall, tell me, who is the fairest of us all?'

The cracked mirror frowned and replied,

'Mistress mine, Snow White's beauty outshines thine! She hides from your anger and hate in the dwarfs' cottage, where she was led by fate.'

The queen was so angry that sparks flew from her eyes, and she vowed a terrible revenge on the wretched huntsman who had not carried out her order. Disguised as an old pedlar woman, she set out immediately for the dwarfs' cottage, following the directions given by the magic mirror. Once there, she tapped lightly on the door, calling in a sweet voice, 'Come outside, lovely maiden, I have a basket laden with pretty things!'

The unsuspecting Snow White stepped outside when she saw that it was only an old pedlar woman at the door. She chose a lovely bodice, and asked the old woman to tie it up for her. The wicked stepmother laced it up so tightly, that she squeezed the breath out of Snow White's body, and the poor maiden fell to the ground senseless.

How lucky it was that the kind dwarfs were already on their way home from the mines. They quickly cut the laces and brought Snow White back to life. 'Did we not tell you to be careful?' they scolded. Snow White promised that she would not make a mistake again.

The queen, meanwhile, sure of her victory, addressed the magic mirror in the palace again, but it answered her curtly, 'Mistress mine, Snow White's beauty still outshines thine!'

The queen fumed and raged till the walls trembled. Turning into an old gipsy, she made her way back next morning to the forest cottage. This time she took from her basket a comb which was poisoned.

'On your door I knock, so that you can buy a silver comb for your crow-black hair,' the gipsy cried. She was so persuasive, that Snow White opened the door and took the comb, but as soon as it touched her hair, she sank lifeless to the ground.

That evening the dwarfs returned home, they could not bring Snow White back to life again. But as they sobbed and stroked her silky hair, the poisonous comb fell out and Snow White slowly sat up.

'Never will I open the door again, no matter who comes,' she vowed.

The wicked stepmother soon found out from her magic mirror that Snow White was still alive. Her evil heart nearly burst with rage. She picked the loveliest apple from the royal garden and filled half of it with a terrible poison she had brewed. This time she disguised herself as a fruitseller and knocked the window.

'An apple I bring, so red, so sweet, a special treat for you to eat,' she cried. Snow White surely would not be tempted. But when her stepmother bit into the healthy side of the apple, she could not resist taking a bite from the poisoned half. The moment she tasted it, she fell down dead.

Upon her return, the stepmother again spoke to her mirror. And this time she was given the answer she longed to hear. 'Lovely mistress mine, no one has beauty to outshine thine.'

In the cottage in the forest, the dwarfs in vain tried to revive Snow White. They sobbed, they

wept, they smeared her with healing ointments, but it was all to no avail. So they placed her in a glass coffin, and this they put in the scented heather, so that the forest birds could sing her favourite songs for the very last time. Snow White looked as if she slept.

It happened that a prince from a foreign

kingdom rode by. At the sight of the lovely maiden, his heart nearly burst with love and sorrow. He begged the dwarfs to allow him to take Snow White home to his palace. He pleaded until at last the dwarfs yielded. Lifting the glass coffin all seven carried it behind the prince.

Suddenly one clumsy dwarf tripped over a tree root and the coffin fell to the ground. The lid flew off and the jerk shook the piece of poisoned apple out of Snow White's throat. Sleepy-eyed, she sat up in her coffin, rubbed her eyes, then smiled brilliantly at everyone.

What joy there was! What rejoicing! The happy prince took Snow White to his palace and soon a great wedding was held. And the

seven little dwarfs sat in the seats of honour at the banqueting table.

Soon the wicked stepmother heard of the lovely princess. Filled with envy, she quickly asked her mirror, 'Mirror, mirror on the wall, who is the fairest of us all?' The mirror frowned and said, 'Wherever the sun directs its light, there is none as lovely as Snow White.' The mirror then broke into a thousand fragments. The evil queen turned into a black crow and flew away, cawing loudly.

And when the king, her father, found out his beautiful daughter was still alive, he hastened to her side. He did not return to his castle where he had been so sad, but lived happily with her and her prince till the end of his days.

The Magic Bag

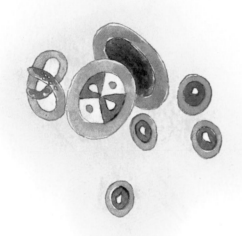

Once there was a poor peasant who owned a field not much bigger than his fist. Need and poverty stuck to him like glue, and just to make sure he had everything to make him unhappy, fate provided him with a wife who had a whip for a tongue and a heart full of greed. One day the peasant sowed millet in his poor field. It grew so well that the neighbours envied him.

'Is it not wonderful,' the peasant said to his wife. 'We will have as much sweet millet porridge all the year round as we need.'

'Keep your porridge, you fool! You call that good living?' snapped the wife. 'If only the wind would scatter that cursed millet, if only the sparrows would gobble it up!'

No sooner had she spoken than an impudent wind blew across the field, shaking all the millet seeds out. The sparrows swooped down at once and scooped up every single grain.

'Oh, you idiot! Why did you not gather the millet before now?' screeched his wife. 'What shall I cook in my pot now?' And she ordered her husband to seek out the mother of the four winds to ask for something in return. 'Don't dare to return empty-handed,' she rattled on, 'or you'll be put in the sty with the swine!' To make sure he remembered her words, she gave his back a thump to send him on his way.

The peasant walked till he came to the cottage belonging to the mother of the four winds. He called from under the window, 'My good woman, will you pay for the damage your son has done. He has robbed us of all our millet, and my wife sobs at home.'

A frail old woman came out of the cottage. She smiled and nodded her head, 'Very well, young man, I shall pay for the damage. But what good would my money be to you, when it is made only of wind? As soon as you blow, the money is gone. I shall give you a magic bag instead. All you have to do is to say "Little bag, little bag, open wide," and you will have as

much food as you desire. When your hunger has left you, then say, "Little bag, little bag, close up tight!" and everything will be cleared from your table.'

The peasant took the bag, thanked the old woman and turned towards home. His wife welcomed him with biting words. 'So you bring an old bag instead of cash!' And she stormed and raved till his ear drums nearly burst. But when he fed her lavishly out of the magic bag, she forgave him. After that day every meal was a feast, and they ate and drank whatever they fancied. The silly woman, however, could not keep her tongue to herself, and bragged to people about their good fortune.

And so it was that their wealthy and miserly neighbour heard about the magic bag. He paid the couple a visit, and waited till they gave him a taste of the delicacies which poured out of the bag. Then he offered the peasant ten sheep, including a ram in exchange for the magic bag.

The peasant stood his ground, but his ever greedy wife wiped the stubborness from his head with a blow from her broom. Then she gave the neighbour the magic bag, taking the sheep and the ram in exchange.

When at the end of the next day the ram was leading the sheep from pasture, instead of turning to its new home, it made for the rich neighbour's shed, as was its custom. The poor peasant vainly demanded for his little flock to be returned. The wealthy farmer only laughed and kept the ram and the sheep.

'Oh, you fool,' grumbled the wife, 'go and sow some millet seed, so that at least we shall have some porridge to eat.'

The peasant sowed the seed, and it grew and grew, till it was a sight to behold. The husband hastened to boast to his wife, but she snapped, 'Oh, that millet of yours! It tastes like soil and sticks to your mouth like glue. If only the wind would take it!'

No sooner had she spoken than the impudent wind blew across the field, shaking the seeds out, and the sparrows gobbled it up. The angry wife sent the peasant back to the mother of the four winds.

'Very well, I will pay for the damage to your field,' the old woman agreed. 'Here is another bag. When you say, "Little bag, open wide," there will be an unforgettable treat for you.'

The peasant rushed away and ordered the bag to open. A whip jumped out, and treated him to a thrashing. Luckily the peasant remembered to cry "Little bag, close up tight!" Then he ran home, black and blue all over.

'There is a treat in store for you in this little bag,' he said to his greedy wife. Next moment the whip was out of the bag, lashing and thrashing. When the peasant thought his greedy wife had learned a lesson, he sent her to the rich neighbour to exchange the bag for a flock of sheep.

The miserly farmer was only too pleased to seal the bargain. As soon as the woman left, he told the bag to open. The whip jumped out of the bag and began to beat the miserly farmer till he ran for his life. And as far as anyone knows, he is probably running still!

East of the Sun, West of the Moon

(The Tales of the West Wind)

'You rascal,' scolded the mother of the four winds, pretending to be cross, when the South Wind had told his last story. 'That was not a true fairy tale. I remember that magic bag of mine very well. And I also know,' she added, wagging her finger at him, 'that you were the rogue who scattered the millet all over that peasant's field!'

The South Wind laughed impishly, played a tune on his whistle and cried, 'I can see the West Wind returning. Dear sister from the world of men, who knows, perhaps he may be able to tell you something of your lost prince. I must now return to work.'

So saying, he curled up in his golden flower, fluttered his bee wings and was gone.

Suddenly dark blue clouds raced across the sky. They brought sounds of thunder and flashes of lightning. But these were not ordinary clouds. They were the enormous wings of a handsome man with flowing hair of grass and seaweed. His transparent eyes were filled with tears. As he hovered above the cottage, raindrops fell and a rainbow shone in the sky.

'Welcome, my son, the West Wind,' cried the old woman, stretching her arms towards him. 'I see you bring showery weather. I noticed that the frogs today crawled from the brooks, as they always do before rain. Tell me, do you know the secret way to the castle in the transparent sea, which lies to the east of the sun and west of the moon? The wicked stepmother keeps the handsome prince a prisoner there. His unhappy wife is searching for him.'

'I roam the world close to the sun and the stars, but I do not know the way. But do not lose heart, perhaps it lies in a fairy story! Just listen while I tell you a tale or two.'

Red Riding Hood

Once upon a time a little girl lived with her mother at the edge of a forest. She wore a red cloak and hood which her grandmother had made for her and she looked so pretty that everyone called her Red Riding Hood.

One day her mother tied some cakes in a bundle, added a pot of butter and said, 'Go through the forest and take these to your grandmother, for she is poorly and must stay in bed. Do not stop on the way and do not talk to anyone in the forest,' she warned.

Red Riding Hood promised to go straight to her grandmother's cottage. As she walked along the forest path, a wicked wolf watched her from the bushes. He would have liked to pounce on Red Riding Hood and have her for his dinner. But he did not dare do so, for there were woodcutters working nearby, and they would have made him pay dearly. So the wolf greeted her politely though his tongue curled greedily in the corner of his mouth. He asked Red Riding Hood where she was going. And the little girl, forgetting about her mother's advice, told the wolf that she was going to visit her grandmother who was poorly.

'I tell you what,' said the wolf, 'let us see which of us will get there first. I too happen to be on my way to your grandmother's. I was just going to pick some flowers for her to cheer her up. You go to the left through the forest, I will take the path to the right.' And the wolf raced away as fast as his legs would carry him. Red Riding Hood was also in a hurry, but there was so much to look at on the way. There were birds to listen to, butterflies to chase.

The wolf, in the meantime, had reached the cottage. He knocked on the door, he scratched at the door, and he whispered in a small voice, 'It is I, Grandmother, your granddaughter.'

'Come in, come in, the door is open,' the grandmother cried happily. She was rather deaf and did not recognize the wolf's voice. The wolf bounded through the doorway, and with one leap was by the bed. In one gulp he had swallowed Red Riding Hood's grandmother. He did not even lick his lips. Next he put on her cap, stretched out under the covers, pulling them right up to his chin so that his whiskers were hidden. And he waited for Red Riding Hood.

'So I can eat you better, my child,' growled the wolf, and swallowed poor Red Riding Hood, bundle and all. Then he stretched out on the bed and snored loudly.

The gamekeeper was passing by, and was surprised to hear the noisy snores. Without hesitation he burst into the cottage, and as soon as his eyes fell on the bed, he guessed what had happened. Next moment he had slit open the wolf's stomach with his sharp knife.

Red Riding Hood was first out; behind her came Grandmother, clutching the bundle of cakes. With tears in their eyes they thanked the brave gamekeeper, and Red Riding Hood vowed that in future she would always do what her mother told her.

'I was so afraid, Grandmother. It was so dark inside the wolf. I could not see a thing,' she cried.

Then the gamekeeper brought a huge stone, which he sewed inside the wolf's stomach, and threw him out of the cottage. When the wolf woke up, he was thirsty. He crawled to the brook, and when he leaned over to drink the heavy stone inside pulled him into the deep water and the villain drowned.

Soon there was a tap, tap on the door. Red Riding Hood was knocking with her little finger. 'It is I, Grandmother, Red Riding Hood! I am bringing you something nice to eat!'

'How kind of you to come! Come in, come in, my child, the door is open,' the wolf whined. Red Riding Hood thought the voice sounded very strange, but she remembered her grandmother had a bad cold, so she did not worry but stepped over to the bedside. But what was this? Her grandmother did look very odd. Had the illness changed her so? Red Riding Hood's eyes brimmed over with tears.

'Oh, what large hands you have, Grandmother!' she cried, when the impatient wolf stretched his paws towards her.

'All the better to embrace you with, my child! Come nearer, don't be afraid,' the wolf drawled.

'Oh, what big eyes you have, Grandmother,' cried the frightened Red Riding Hood.

'All the better to see you with, my child!'

'Oh, what big ears you have, Grandmother.'

'All the better to hear you with, my child.'

'Grandmother! Why are your teeth so big?' Red Riding Hood cried.

The Cat Palace

In the land where the sun rises there once lived a beautiful and high-born lady. But she was as wicked as she was beautiful, and this story tells how she paid a high price for her wickedness.

In the house of this beautiful, but evil-hearted lady lived a poor servant and her cat. The maid's name was Jukiko. Jukiko was unlucky from the day she was born. Her parents died when she was still little, and now her mistress, who employed her, treated her shamefully. Poor Jukiko had no one but her cat to talk to and listen to her woes. She loved her like a real sister. But her haughty, wicked mistress objected to Jukiko's friendship with her cat and ill-treated the animal on purpose, to hurt Jukiko. Then one day the little cat disappeared without a trace.

In vain Jukiko wept, in vain she searched for her little friend. Her heart was heavy with grief when, one day a seer came by, and, noticing her sorrow, told the maid that her cat had gone to the cat palace which stood high on the cat mountain on the cat island. Jukiko immediately begged her mistress to allow her to visit her cat friend.

'Very well,' said the woman without a heart, thinking that the maid would suffer many hardships on the journey, and such a thought pleased her greatly. 'But you will have to work as many nights as the days you will take for the journey,' she said.

Jukiko gladly promised and left. She travelled for many days until at last she came within sight of the cat island. She asked a fisherman to row her over and the kind man warned her that she would be torn apart by wildcats on that island. But when the maid insisted he rowed her across the straits.

Jukiko started to climb the mountain in search of the cat palace. Her feet were blood-stained and torn when at last a strange building came into view on the highest peak. The roof was shaped like a cat's back. At the windows beautiful cats sunned themselves, their eyes shining, their mouths purring, their little pink tongues now and then licking their sleek bodies. Suddenly a black beauty came out of the palace.

Jukiko bowed deeply and said, 'I am searching for my lost cat sister. Do you know where I shall find her?'

The black beauty stuck out her long claws and said, 'Come in! You are just in time for supper. In fact you will be our supper!' Just then a strange old woman with cat ears appeared. She chased away the black beauty and led the maid into a lovely room.

'As you love your little cat so much and you dared to enter the cat kingdom, I shall allow you to meet your friend.' The old woman then clapped her paws and a slim maiden entered. She had a human body, but the head of a cat, and the astonished Jukiko realized that this was her lost friend. How happy they both were to see each other again. Then the cat made Jukiko sit by a small table and kneeling down, she treated her as an honoured guest.

'You are in the cat palace,' she said. 'When cats grow old and are ready to die, they come here. I had to come here too. But if you value your life, do not stay long, for after dark my sisters would tear you apart. I want to give you a present as a keepsake, but do not look at it until you are home. If my wild sisters attack you on the way back, just shake this little parcel before their eyes, and do not be afraid!'

Jukiko thanked her cat friend and set out for home. In the dark forest she was attacked by wild cats, their green eyes gleaming, their mouths spitting. But when Jukiko shook the little parcel, they ran for their lives. The fisherman's boat was waiting on the shore and she was soon rowed to safety.

At home her wicked mistress gave the maid an icy welcome, and demanded to see the present given to her by the little cat. Inside, to their astonishment they found a picture of a dog with bared teeth. But whenever they looked at him, he barked and a gold coin fell from his mouth.

The mistress listened with envy to the maid's tales of the cat paradise, and she too yearned to be given such a valuable present. So one day she set sail in a fine boat for the cat island. She did not climb the mountain on foot, but was carried in a sedan chair to the very gates of the cat palace.

There she called haughtily, 'I came to you, my servant cat, to collect my reward for taking care of you.'

No sooner had she spoken, than wild cats rushed at her from all sides, and that was the end of the beautiful but evil-hearted woman.

The Good Girl
and
the Bad Girl

Once there was a widow with two daughters. The elder one was the apple of her eye. She had only the choicest food to eat, and the prettiest clothes to wear. But for the younger daughter the widow had no love and grudged her every morsel that she ate. It made the poor maiden terribly sad. She tried to earn the affection of her mother and sister by doing good deeds, but it was no use. No matter how kind she was, she got no kindness in return.

One day the good daughter went to the forest to pick wild strawberries, and she lost her way. It was a desolate place, and darkness was falling. The maiden, frightened and lonely, started to weep bitterly. As she wept, she upset the cup of strawberries, and they rolled everywhere. Suddenly a strange old woman appeared. She was dressed entirely in black, with white hair flowing to the ground.

'Why are you crying, dear maiden?' asked the old woman.

The girl told her how she had lost her way, how all the strawberries had scattered, and that even if she knew her way home, she was afraid to return, because she would surely be beaten.

'If you are afraid of your own mother, then come and serve me. You will not regret it,' the old woman offered. The miserable maiden agreed.

They wandered through the wood, till they came to a brook. 'Carry me to the other side, dear girl. I am old and frail, and the water would take me away,' the woman begged. 'Of course I will,' the girl assured her, though she worried in case the old woman was too heavy for her. But she proved to be as light as birds' feathers, and the maiden carried her to the other side. Before long they came to the cottage where the old woman lived. There was not

114

a soul about, except for two dogs and two cats. 'You will look after the house and care for my animals,' said the old lady. 'If you work well, you will be amply rewarded.'

The maiden gladly set to work. It was a very strange household. The old woman talked to her animals in her human voice, and the dogs and cats answered her also in human voices. If she needed them for anything, she would ring a little flower bell and say, 'Dogs and cats, pets of mine, pass me my stick! Open the window! Scrub the floor!' Not once did she glance even out of the corner of her eye at the young girl.

But the latter, of course, jumped to her feet at once and carried out all the work given to the animals. And she made sure that the little dogs and the little cats lacked for nothing. The maiden combed and brushed their furry coats, pulled thorns from their paws, played little games with them. When it was time for the stove to be lit, the old woman would give the obedient girl a grain of barley and a pea, and would say, 'Cook a meal for us all, and divide the food fairly, so that everything is equal.'

The girl would shake her head, wondering how two grains could be expected to feed so many hungry mouths, but she never said a word, and began to cook. And wonder of wonders, there must have been a magic spell in that pot, for as soon as she put the pea and barley in it, it started to bubble and rise and soon there was food enough for an army. The young girl divided it all fairly, not robbing anyone of a single spoonful, and the old lady thanked her warmly for being so helpful.

So it went on, day after day, week after week, month after month. When one day was left to complete a whole year service, the old woman said to the girl, 'You have been my right hand, for you have been endowed with a kindly heart. I shall reward you well. When you get up in the morning, choose any chest you fancy from the room at the back of my cottage. Then you can return home with God's blessing.' The maiden thanked her and went to bed. The animals rubbed themselves against her legs, and one of the cats purred, 'You have been kind to us, so you deserve the very best present.'

'The old woman has some fine chests in the back room, some are nicer than others,' continued the second cat, and one of the little dogs added. 'They are beautifully made, some are inlaid, others edged with gold, or finely carved, with lovely paintings, so I am told!'

'Oh, my dear little pets, I shall be satisfied with just a simple chest to carry my few pieces of clothing,' replied the modest girl, stroking the animals gently. 'Think it over, you don't want to be too humble,' the other little dog advised. But the maiden acted as she said she would. When the next morning the old lady led her into the back room, she chose the most ordinary chest out of all the magnificent ones. It truly was an old, shabby chest, hardly good for anything but the fire. A strange smile spread across the old lady's face, and she praised the girl. 'You have chosen wisely, my child. But wait a moment, for the chest is heavy. It would be too much of a burden to carry. But I know what to do.' So saying, the aged woman harnessed the two little

dogs and the two little cats to the chest, sat the maiden upon it, gave her a little gold whip, and soon the pets were trotting merrily towards her home. What a happy journey that was! Many travellers joined the strange procession, so the maiden was never lonely on the way.

Their arrival was something to behold! Her mother and her wicked sister thought that the younger girl had died somewhere in the forest. They did not mourn, they did not miss her. Yet the moment she set foot over the threshold, they rushed to the chest to see what nice things she had brought them. When it was opened, they were agog with astonishment and envy. No wonder too! That chest was filled to the brim with gold and jewels. The moment the greedy pair thrust their hands into the chest, a young, handsome prince jumped out of it, embraced the youngest daughter and said, 'You must be my wife! There is no other on this earth for me!' And all the travellers, who had accompanied the strange procession, cheered loudly. They

were all the prince's servants. The old mother and her wicked daughter nearly died with envy and ill temper. Eventually the mother persuaded her elder daughter also to go into the forest to seek her fortune with the strange old woman they had been told about.

The moment the girl reached the deepest part of the forest, she sank into the grass and began to weep and wail so loudly that even the forest bears ran away. Then the old woman, all in black, with white, flowing hair, appeared again.

'Take me into service,' commanded the girl. 'I want the same reward as my younger sister had!' The old woman had no objection. But when they came to the deep water, it did not occur to the selfish girl to help the aged woman across. 'Do you want me to drown on your account?' she snapped, as she waded in. The old lady only smiled, and walked across, her feet dry.

Once in the cottage, she gave the girl a pea and a grain of barley, and asked her to prepare a meal for them all. The girl just laughed, and cooked pea soup out of a whole sack of peas. And wherever she could, she stole a spoonful or two from the animals. She never cared for the pets, ignoring cats and dogs alike, and when the old woman gave them a task to do, she never attempted to give a helping hand. Soon the animals were thin and wretched, thorns and dirt sticking to their coats. So it continued, day in, day out, week in, week out, month after month. When the new year met the old, the woman offered the girl a chest for her services. The greedy girl chose at once the most beautiful one, rimmed with gold, inlaid with jewels. The old lady smiled, harnessed her pets to the chest as she had done before, set the haughty girl on

top and sent them off home. What a journey it was! The cruel daughter struck the unhappy pets with the gold whip, till the fur flew from their back. Snakes, lizards and all types of vermin slithered along behind the strange procession.

At home the mother and her greedy daughter quickly opened the chest. Curled up inside was an ugly old snake. Rearing up, it cried, 'You must be my wife! There is no other on this earth for me!' Hearing this, the snakes and lizards who had travelled with them, pounced on both the wicked women and carried them off. And they were never seen again.

The Little Mermaid

Far out in the sea the water is as blue as the petals of the cornflower and as clear as the purest crystal. Yet it is impossible to see the sea bed with the human eye...

In the farthest depths the most wondrous land is hidden. It is full of multi-coloured blooms, bushes and trees, with bright little fishes darting through their branches like birds. The plants and the underwater meadows stir silkily from side to side with the movement of the water, like grass dancing in the breeze. But the flowers have no scent, the leaves do not hum, the fish are silent. Yet from the depth of the transparent waves beautiful songs are now and then heard sung by sea creatures who resemble men. From the waist down their bodies are covered in fish scales, and they have tails instead of legs. They live happily in the blue glow of the sea, and when the time comes, they dissolve into wisps of salty foam. Peacefully then they float on the sea surface, warmed by the sun, silently they float, without memories. They feel no pain or joy, they are only dead white foam, rocked by the waves in their everlasting sleep.

In the deepest part of the sea stands the palace of the sea king. The walls are of coral, the pointed windows of the clearest amber and the roof is made of mussel shells, which open and close with the movement of water. In each shell sparkles a beautiful pearl.

Many years ago the sea king had six lovely mermaid daughters. One day their mother peacefully dissolved into white sea foam, and from then on their grandmother, the king's mother, looked after them. She was a most honourable and proud lady of the sea, who wore twelve oysters on her tail, to mark her noble birth. She was wiser than anyone else in the whole wide sea world. Whenever the little mermaids returned home from their games with shoals of frolicking fish, or from the secret cabins of sunken wrecks, the old queen told them tales of the strange world of men. And the little princesses would listen entranced. The youngest looked forward to her grandmother's stories more than anyone; she was a tiny mermaid with deep, thoughtful eyes and a melodious voice, which haunted the sailors who sailed the wide seas.

The youngest mermaid was different from her sisters. While the others amused themselves by dressing up in the strange objects they found on wrecked ships, she would sit in silence in her little garden by the statue of a handsome youth carved from white stone. It had sunk to the sea bed during a terrible storm, together with the bodies of the shipwrecked crew. The little mermaid was the first of the sisters to realize that men could not live in their silent underwater kingdom, and it saddened her. So she planted a rose-coloured weeping willow by the statue of the youth, and gazed longingly through its swaying branches up to the sun, whose rays shone through the water like an enormous rose.

One day the old queen told all of her granddaughters a secret. 'When you are fifteen years old you may rise to the surface to sit in the moonlight on the rocks and watch the big ships sail by. You will see the starlit sky, dark forests and bright cities. You will see the world of people!'

The little mermaid grew quieter still after this. How she yearned to see real birds twittering in the sky, smell the scent of flowers, gaze on beings resembling her lovely marble statue. But she was the youngest of all the sisters, and had to wait six long years for her turn to come. If mermaids could cry she would surely have wept bitter tears.

Every year it was the turn of one of the sisters to enter the world of men. They returned to the underwater palace with shining eyes which were filled with wonder at all they had seen. They told of the sky, which arches above like a huge glass bell, of scarlet and purple clouds which sail along the sky like majestic vessels, of beautiful swans flying towards the dying sun. They whispered about the glow of the sun, the sparkle of the stars, merry dolphins and whales which shoot water upwards through their nostrils, and look like hundreds of fountains. They talked of fine ships, their sails flapping like the wings of seagulls, of warm, incoming tides on sandy beaches and of the wintry dark green sea, scattered with icebergs like big shining pearls. The little mermaid liked best of all to listen to the stories about cities which light up the dark sky at night, and about flower-strewn meadows, ripening fields and little human children, who can swim without fins.

Sometimes when a tempest was brewing, the older sisters would swim to the surface, dance round the ships and tempt the sailors with their sweet singing voices into the deep, to visit their wondrous underwater kingdom. But the sailors were terrified by their song, for they believed it was the voice of the tempest calling, and they made the sign of the cross to ward off danger.

One day, when a ship was wrecked and had sunk slowly and silently to the sea bed, the little mermaid asked her grandmother. 'If men are not drowned in the sea, do they live for ever? Or do they too dissolve into sea foam?'

'Men die before we do, but unlike us, they have an immortal soul,' the wise old queen replied. 'When their time has come, the soul leaves the body and rises into the heavens above. While we float after death with the waves as dead white foam, without feeling, without memory, their soul lives on in a kingdom of happiness and peace.' 'How I wish I could have an immortal soul,' the little mermaid cried, and the wise queen smiled sadly.

'We live according to the laws of our kingdom, my child,' she sighed. 'You cannot have an immortal soul, unless a man loved you so much that you would mean more to him than mother and father. Then his soul would enter your body. But that cannot happen. Look at your fish tail! To be beautiful in the eyes of men, you have to have legs instead of your magnificent tail!'

After this conversation, the little mermaid was even more silent, gazing with even greater yearning at the distant sun. 'I shall be rid of my fish tail, I shall have an immortal human soul,' she promised herself. But the time passed so slowly.

At last she was fifteen! The old queen gave her a garland of pearls and fastened eight gold shells to her tail in honour of her high rank. 'Goodbye!' cried the little mermaid, rising upwards like a clear, light bubble of air.

The sun had just gone down and a white ship was floating on the rose-tinted sea. The mermaid floated by the ship's side with the tide, when suddenly a wave lifted her high and she saw through a round cabin window the most handsome young prince. He was as beautiful as

her marble statue under the sea. His eyes were as black as the starless sky and as deep as the deepest sea. He was smiling.

The ship was just then preparing to celebrate the prince's sixteenth birthday. As darkness descended, the ship looked like a flaming torch with its coloured lanterns and the fireworks which burst into a million lights. Though the little mermaid had never seen anything so beautiful, she could not take her eyes off the young prince.

'If only he would give me his soul!' she breathed longingly. Suddenly the sea began to froth and foam, and the waves rose higher and higher. A storm was approaching fast.

The little mermaid started to sing, wishing to warn the men, but they listened in terror and made signs of the cross. Soon the ship was dancing on the waves like a helpless shell, and before very long the lashing hurricane had torn it to pieces as if it was a little house built of cards.

The little mermaid searched among the wreckage and the drowning men for her prince. At last she saw him, unconscious, sinking to the sea bed. Taking his limp body in her arms, she gently rose with him to the surface and swam to a nearby sandy beach. There she laid him on the warm sand, then hid herself in sea foam and waited for dawn.

When daylight came, a lovely maiden stepped out of a nearby church and ran towards the prince's still body. She leaned over him, and the prince opened his eyes and looked at her gratefully. The smile stabbed the little mermaid's

dry land will hurt as if you were treading on sharp knives. And if another captures the prince's heart, you will turn into dead sea foam without a memory.'

The little mermaid stood firm, so the witch cut out her tongue, then brewed up a potion from her own blood. 'Drink this at sunrise near the prince's palace,' she said, and disappeared.

The little princess then silently bade goodbye to her father and her sisters who accompanied her to the shore. At sunrise, when the mermaid drank the magic potion, she was so overcome by pain that she fainted.

When she awoke, the black-eyed prince was leaning over her; he had been called by the sad song of the sisters. The little mermaid saw to her astonishment that she had two slim legs instead of a tail. The prince asked who she was and what she was doing alone on the beach, but the maiden only shook her head and pointed to her mouth. The prince, filled with compassion, took her by the hand and led her to the palace. Every painful step was an ordeal, yet she bore it with a smile on her lips. And, when later on, the prince asked her to dance, the princess danced like no other, as if she wanted with her elegant movements to make up for her lack of voice.

The prince fell in love with the little mermaid. He never left her side and told her all his secrets. 'You are as beautiful as the maiden who once saved my life. But she disappeared, I do not know where. If I could forget her, I would marry you,' he often said. The little mermaid only smiled sadly, for she was unable to shed tears.

'He will never know that it was I who saved him from the sea,' she thought bitterly.

One day the old king selected from a neighbouring kingdom a bride for his son.

'I will not marry this princess,' the prince promised. 'I would much rather stay with you, my lovely dumb creature! You resemble so closely the one I lost!' And the little mermaid then forgot her suffering. But before long an imposing ship sailed into port and out of it stepped a princess so beautiful, that everyone gasped in astonishment. The moment the prince saw her, he cried, 'It is she! The maiden who found me on the sea shore!'

His happiness knew no bounds. He proudly led his bride to the palace, then hastened to share the good news with the little mermaid.

'I know my joy will be your joy, for you love me best in all the world.' And the little mermaid kissed his hand, though her heart was breaking, but she had no tears.

heart. Then she remembered the old sea witch, and dived under the surface, and made her way through a forest of twisting octopus and vicious vipers to the witch's ugly house.

'Please take away my fish tail and make me into a human being, so that I can have an immortal soul,' the little mermaid begged.

The witch laughed harshly. 'I shall grant your foolish wish, if you give me your beautiful voice in return. But remember, each step you take on

It was the day of the wedding and after they were married, the prince and his bride accompanied by the little mermaid, boarded the ship.

The little mermaid thought of the coming night, knowing that at daybreak she must die, dreading the moment when her body would turn into white sea foam without a memory.

As darkness fell and the ship was aglow with hundreds of lights, as on that fateful day when the prince had come into her life, the little mermaid's sisters suddenly rose from the sea, and called, 'We bring a magic knife, for which we have paid the sea witch with our beautiful hair. Before the sun rises, you must use it to pierce the prince's heart. When drops of his blood trickle on to your legs, they will grow together again into a fish tail, and you will be one of us again.'

The princess took the knife and waited. With the approach of dawn she entered the prince's cabin. The lovely head of his bride lay on his chest and the prince wore a happy smile. The little mermaid leaned over him and kissed him on the lips. The knife she tossed into the sea. Then she plunged into the waves. She did not feel herself dying. The sun rose, and in its glow it seemed thousands of transparent forms were flying. She thought they were talking to her. 'Who calls me?' she asked, astonished that she could hear her own beautiful voice.

'We are the daughters of the air,' they replied.

'We also do not have an immortal soul, but we can get one through doing good deeds. As you have a kind heart, you are to become one of us!'

The little mermaid felt herself soaring high towards the sun. For the last time she glanced at the prince's ship. She no longer felt pain nor sorrow, but for the first time she felt the relief which comes with tears.

The Bride from Heaven

In the high mountains of a distant land there once lived a mother and father with their son. Kechua was his name. One morning the father told his son to go to a nearby field for potatoes. Kechua obeyed. But to his amazement half the field had been dug up and not a potato in that half remained. Someone had stolen them.

'Just wait, thieves. You will pay for this!' Kechua vowed, and when evening came, he squatted down in the middle of the field and kept guard. But there was not a sign of the thieves. Towards morning Kechua felt very drowsy. His eyelids dropped for only a moment, yet when he opened his eyes again, the field was in a worse state than the day before. So it continued for several more nights. While Kechua kept guard, the thieves kept away. The moment he closed his eyes, they came and helped themselves to more potatoes. 'I'll catch you yet, you villains!' Kechua promised. One night he stretched out in the grass and pretended to sleep. Suddenly all the stars from the sky started to fall on the field. The moment they hit the ground, they turned into lovely golden-haired maidens dressed in glowing silver robes.

'Oh, you thieving stars,' cried Kechua. 'Are you not ashamed to rob paupers? I'll give you something to remember!' But before he could rise to his feet, the stars scattered and rose into the sky all except for the youngest sparkling star who tripped in her flight over a large potato. Kechua caught and held her. But she was so beautiful and she wept so piteously, that Kechua fell in love with her and straightaway asked her to be his wife. 'I like being on earth,' the star replied, 'but while I am clad in my silver robe, I cannot remain with you. It would carry me back into the sky.'

'That can easily be overcome,' Kechua said, and when they arrived home, he asked his mother to hide the starry robe at the bottom of a chest. Kechua then married his star.

They would still be living happily today, if the star had not one day looked into that old chest. It was so long since she had worn her starry robe that she put it on out of curiosity. Next

moment she rose like a feather up to the stars. Kechua saw her flying off from a distance, and in despair he raced for the highest mountain, hoping to pull her back to earth. But no matter how high he climbed, he could not reach the sky. Suddenly a shadow passed over him. It was a condor, a giant bird, the king of the mountains. 'Stop lamenting, Kechua! If you catch two llamas for me I will take you on my wings to your star,' the bird promised. Kechua hurried off, and soon returned with the beasts. The giant bird ate, then strengthened by the meal, placed Kechua and the remaining meat on its back, and soared into the sky. They flew day and night, and whenever the condor was tiring, it asked Kechua to give it meat. This renewed its strength. Many days passed when at last they saw in the distance an endless blue lake, in the middle of which stood a magnificent golden palace built on high terraces. 'That is the temple of the sun,' the condor said. 'All the stars assemble there each evening. But if you do not give me more meat, we shall not reach it and I shall crash to the ground.' Kechua was afraid, for there was no meat left. Then without hesitation, he offered his arm to the bird. The condor pierced it with its beak, drank Kechua's blood, and reached the blue lake without difficulty. The moment Kechua had bathed his wound in its waters, his arm was miraculously healed. 'Hasten to the temple,' the bird advised. 'When the stars assemble, take the last one in your

arms, for that will be your wife. Then hurry back to me. But do not look back, either of you, or you will be parted for ever.'

When the evening came, the silver stars flew to the temple. They were all identical, but Kechua, hidden nearby, grasped the last one round her waist and hastened to the condor. 'Don't look back,' he begged her, 'or else we shall never meet again.'

The condor was waiting, its wings spread out, when the other stars began to cry, 'Do not desert us, sister!'

Kechua's wife could not help it. She looked back, and turned immediately into a star. The condor gripped the unhappy Kechua with its claws and together they fell like a stone to the ground. 'Do not be unhappy, Kechua,' the condor tried to cheer him. 'Though you will never see your wife again, she will shine night after night above your house to ease your sorrow!' The bird was right. When darkness fell, a bright star appeared above Kechua's house which had never shone there before.

The Little Shepherdess and the English Prince

There was once a little shepherdess whose name was Mette. She took her lambs to graze in the hills, valleys and plains, and though she was as poor as a church mouse, she loved the world and every day she sang from morning till night.

At that time a handsome young prince of England set out to roam the world to find a bride. But he would not wed just any maiden. As pretty as a picture she must be, with a heart of gold, of noble family, modest, hard working and sincere she also had to be. No lesser bride would do! To find her was no easy task. There were many princesses the English prince could woo, but not one suited his needs. Nevertheless the prince set sail with his favourite horse across the sea to seek his perfect bride.

On and on he rode until one day he met Mette, the shepherdess. Clad in tattered rags, a garland of wild flowers in her hair, she was tending her lambs. The prince said with pity in his voice, 'Lord be with you, little Mette, for your life must surely be hard.'

But Mette chirped merrily, 'I love my life as it is, and soon I shall be your wife!'

'That can never be, sweet maiden,' laughed the prince.

'Yes it can and it will, my handsome prince,' laughed Mette.

The prince rode on till he came to a rich kingdom where lived the most beautiful princess. She told so many people how modest she was that they all believed her. The prince too was taken in by her honey-like voice, and he asked the king for her hand. But he insisted that before their wedding she must visit him in England.

The princess at the head of a splendid cavalcade set out to visit the prince. On and on they rode, till they met the little shepherdess Mette. 'Lord be with you, little Mette,' the princess called proudly. 'How is the English prince?'

'Very well,' Mette replied. 'He is waiting for his bride. But beware, lovely lady. By the prince's threshold lies a magic stone. This stone describes every person who steps on it.'

'And what of that?' the princess said. 'I am, after all, as pretty as a picture, and a modest creature too. What have I to fear?'

But the moment she stepped on the stone by the prince's threshold, a voice boomed, 'Go home, princess, your modesty is but a lie! You may not be vain, but you are stupid and lazy.'

When the prince heard this, he did not even open his door, and the princess had to turn unhappily away from the palace gates.

The prince set out once more to seek a bride.

On and on he rode, till he met the shepherdess Mette. 'May the Lord help you, poor little Mette! How hard your life must be!' he said pityingly. But little Mette laughed merrily.

'I may look like a church mouse, but when I am your wife, I shall be a sight to behold, for you will dress me in gold!'

'Oh, foolish girl, that can never be!' said the prince. 'It can and it will!' said little Mette. And so they parted.

The prince rode on and on, till he heard of a lovely princess who told everyone how hard working she was. Nobody had ever seen her do anything, but they all believed her. Soon the English prince was asking the king for her hand, but once again he insisted that before their wedding she must visit him in England.

The princess set out on her journey to the prince's palace. Her servants and ladies-in-waiting attended to her every wish and she did not once lift a finger to help herself. On and on she rode, scolding the servants, shouting at the ladies-in-waiting, till she met Mette, the shepherdess with her little herd of sheep. 'God be with you, Mette. Lace up my shoe!' the proud princess snapped. Then she asked, 'How is the English prince?'

'Very well,' Mette replied. 'He is waiting for his bride. But beware, lovely lady! By the prince's threshold lies a magic stone. This stone describes every person who steps upon it.'

'What of that?' the princess said. 'Everyone says how beautiful and hardworking I am. You will not find anyone better.'

When she came to the palace, she stamped her feet proudly on the magic stone. What a surprise she had! 'Fie, fie! You hardworking?' the voice boomed. 'Conceited, stupid and lazy are you. Turn on your heel and go home!' And the princess, moaning and groaning, turned away from the palace gate.

So the prince set off into the world for the third time. On and on he rode, humming sadly, till he came to little Mette with her sheep. Her little skirt was damp, creased and torn, her little shoes muddy and worn.

'God be with you, little Mette,' the prince said pityingly. 'I can see life is not easy for you.'

But Mette smiled happily and cried, 'What does it matter that I wear a ragged old skirt? When I am your wife, we shall have a son dressed in gold.'

'Foolish maiden. How many times must I tell you that this can never be?' laughed the prince.

'Yes it can, and it will,' Mette insisted, laughing too. And so they parted once more.

A long time passed before the prince found another lovely princess. But she was one of the most untruthful princesses who ever lived. When she told everyone how honest she was, of course, everyone believed her because she was a princess.

The prince invited her to visit him in his palace. And on the way the third princess too was warned by little Mette. But as liars often do, she thought Mette could not be telling the truth.

As she stepped on the magic stone, the voice boomed. 'Hear this, oh prince! Her voice is like honey, but her words are untrue. A liar she is, and lazy too.' The princess was furious.

The prince was near despair. Was there nowhere a princess who was good, honest and true? Then one day he heard that in a distant eastern land there was a princess as lovely as a dream, as good as a good fairy, modest, hard working and true. Once more the prince set out on his travels.

Again he met little Mette, tending her sheep, clad in rags even more tattered and old. Again he pitied her and again she smilingly brushed his words aside. 'Before long now I will be your bride!' And the prince gently shook his head at her foolish words and hurried on.

The foreign princess proved to be more beautiful than all the others, and it gave the prince much pleasure to ask her to visit him in his palace before their wedding.

Soon the foreign princess was on her way to the English land. She rode and rode, till she met the little shepherdess Mette.

'God be with you, Mette. How fares the English prince?' she asked proudly.

'He fares well, and he is waiting for his bride. But you would be well advised, lovely lady, to turn back now. The prince has a magic stone by his threshold, which tells the truth about anyone who stands on it.'

This frightened the lovely princess, for she knew that she always pretended to be better than she was. So she asked little Mette to put on her robe and go to the palace in her place. 'The magic stone will hardly be able to speak against such a good soul,' the princess thought. Mette gladly agreed.

When she stepped on the stone, the voice cried. 'This is the one! Lovely, modest and good, marry her you should.' The delighted prince embraced the beautiful maiden and promised to come and fetch her from her home very soon. As a keepsake he wove a golden headband into her hair. Little Mette then hastened back to her lambs. The lovely Eastern princess was waiting. Mette gave back the robe and put on her old rags, but she kept the gold headband. And the foreign princess hurried back to her kingdom to wait for her bridegroom.

A few days later the English prince followed. On and on he rode, till he met little Mette and her lambs.

'God be with you, Mette! Is life still treating you unkindly, my poor little maiden?' But Mette's laugh rang out like a little gold bell. 'Have you not heard how lovely the world is? When I am the prince's bride, poverty will never touch me again.'

'Oh, my dear little fool, that can never be,' smiled the prince.

'It can and it will!' smiled little Mette. As she bent her head, the gold headband glistened in her hair. And the prince then knew that little Mette was his beautiful, good and honest bride.

Even today people still talk of their wedding.

As for the foreign princess she is probably still waiting for her bridegroom.

And the magic stone?

Since that day it has spoken not a word.

King the Liar
and
Liar the King

In a certain kingdom there ruled a king who could lie so well that he himself could hardly tell truth from a lie. This was why his counsellors always had to feel the tip of his nose to see if it was soft, for in that kingdom that was how to find out if people were telling the truth.

'Your Royal Highness,' the counsellors would say, bowing to the ground, 'your noble royal nose is like an overcooked potato!'

'Are you trying to say I am lying?,' the king would thunder.

'Oh no, Your Excellence, we simply wish to state that according to your nose you are not quite speaking the truth,' the terrified counsellors would say, while the king patted his enormous stomach and roared with laughter. This king had a handsome daughter. Her face was so freckled that she looked as if she had sunbathed under a sieve, and her hair was the colour of a rusty nail. She was indeed beautiful! He decided to give his daughter in marriage to the man, who could think up such a monstrous lie that the king would have to say to him, 'You are lying!' Hearing this message, his envoys sped to all corners of the world.

A certain poor youth in Ireland heard the proclamation and deciding to try his fortune he set off for the kingdom of lies.

'Do you dare think, young man, that you can tell such a monstrous lie that even I shall not believe it?' the King said in greeting, when they brought the youth before the throne. 'That will not be easy, you know. I myself am an experienced, cunning liar, but I have yet to come upon a lie which could not be the truth. But if you are confident, you may now begin. And if you do not force me to call you a liar, you will be shorter by a head!'

Gazing out of the window, the young man said,' 'I see you have a fair-sized herd, Your Majesty. But it is nothing compared to my Mother's herd. She has so many cows that when there is a drought and the river waters fall low, we use their milk to work all the mill wheels in the country...'

'And so on, and so on,' remarked the bored king with a groan and a yawn. 'That could easily be the truth. I myself own such an enormous cabbage...'

'That is nothing,' the youth interrupted, 'our cabbage is so large, that during festivals the whole village can dance under a single leaf...'

'It could be so,' smiled the king. 'We have such gigantic beans, that in battle we fire cannons with them...' The youth pulled a face. 'As to your beans! If only you could see mine! Once, when they were ripe, I was going to pick a few and I had to climb right up to the clouds. Those clouds were so solid that I banged my head and it swelled up like an egg. Feel here, Your Highness, it is the gospel truth!'

The king touched the young man's head, and said, 'And so on, and so on! It is an old story. It could be true, like this bump on your head.'

'I haven't finished yet,' the youth continued curtly. 'When I climbed to the top, I remembered I had nothing to put the pods into. Then a flea nipped me under my shirt. I killed the pest with my shoe, and skinned the flea. From its skin I made nine sacks and seven leather jackets. I filled them all with pods and started to climb down. But by then Autumn had come and the leaves on the bean plants were dry and brittle. Believe it or not, I fell from that height, and it took ten days in all for me to reach the ground. I landed on solid rock, and was stuck in it up to my neck. What now? I took my penknife out of my pocket, cut off my head and sent it to fetch help. But an old fox suddenly appeared and got to it first. He grabbed my head between his teeth and raced off into the wood. This made me so angry, that even the solid rock could not hold me. I jumped out and raced after that thief and I cut off his tail. Guess, My King, what was written on that tail!'

'Gracious me, how should I know?' the king protested.

'I read,' said the youth with a smile, 'that your father was a cowherd working for my father.' 'That is a vicious lie,' cried the king furiously and the youth clapped his hands with glee.

'You have lost, My King! Go and make arrangements for my wedding! And if you want to see whether I have lied, feel my nose!'

Do you think the King dared to feel it? Certainly not. What, if after all, it proved what the fellow said was true...? And so the liar married the princess and became the king.

The Golden Fish, the Wicked Sisters and the Good Forgetta

Seven sisters there were: the first was pretty, the second prettier and the third prettiest of all. The fourth could walk on air, the fifth could balance on a pear, the sixth had jet black hair. As for the seventh, the other six conceited sisters did not care about her at all.

The name of the seventh sister who was the youngest, smallest and shortest was Forgetta. She was called Forgetta not because she forgot things, not because she had a bad memory, but because she was always being forgotten. When their mother had boiled rice, all the sisters swooped on it like hungry sparrows, picking and pecking till there was not a grain left. All that remained for Forgetta was the dirty dish.

It was worse for Forgetta when her mother

and her father died. The elder sisters quickly married the young men of the village, and there was not a single one left for poor little Forgetta. How sad she was!

The elder sisters prospered. They had able husbands, comfortable huts and sacks full of rice. But poor Forgetta had not even a roof over her head. She slept in the long grass and used the wind for a cover.

One day her sisters sent for Forgetta to thresh the rice. From morning till night the poor maiden slaved, and when at last her work was

done, she begged her sisters to give her at least a handful of rice. She should not have asked! The miserly sisters called her a beggar and turned her out empty-handed.

Forgetta, crying bitterly, stumbled off, not caring where she went. After a time she came upon an old fisherman who had just caught a little fish with his rod. It was so tiny that it could hardly be seen. Yet how beautiful that little fish was! It glistened and glittered like gold.

Forgetta felt so sorry for the tiny creature. 'Fisherman, please give me your little fish,' she pleaded. And as the fisherman had a kind heart, he did not refuse her. Forgetta in all her life had never been so happy. This was the first time anyone had given her anything. Quickly she filled a coconut shell with water and slipped the little fish into it. She named it Leungli, which means precious. Forgetta hardly had a bite to eat, but when kind people gave her a little rice because they were sorry for her, she would share it with her little fish. And Leungli grew and grew till it outgrew the coconut shell. Forgetta then let it out into a little lake near the wood.

'Leungli, my friend, you can have a feast,' she would call to the fish when she managed to get something to eat. So that Leungli would always know it was she who called, Forgetta composed a little song, 'Swim to me, little fish, I will grant you your wish, a grain of rice for you, and the NOTHING we'll share too, and no one will ever dare to part us two.'

Hearing the song, Leungli always swam to the shore of the lake and took the food from her hand. Then he would let Forgetta tickle his golden scales. Before long Leungli was almost as big as a human baby, and one day he turned into a beautiful golden carp, whose scales tinkled like a pocketful of gold coins.

The envious sisters soon found out that Forgetta often talked to a golden fish in the little lake, and they tried to persuade her to catch the golden carp.

'Don't you know, silly girl, how tasty a fish cooked on a spit can be?' they cried, licking their lips greedily. But Forgetta would not listen. How could she harm her beloved little fish!

Her elder sisters were furious. 'Just you wait, we'll show her!' they said to each other, and when one day Forgetta had left the lake to earn a little money to buy rice, they set out to catch the golden carp.

But Leungli never appeared near the surface unless he heard Forgetta's song. The sisters did not know this, and they tried in vain to tempt him to the shore in order to catch him.

Then one evening the eldest of the sisters hid in the bushes nearby, and she heard Forgetta singing, and learned the song by heart. The next morning, when Forgetta had gone into the vil-

lage to work, the sisters took a net, sharpened a knife and sat on the bank, while the eldest sang in a sweet voice, 'Swim to me, little fish, I will grant you your wish, a grain of rice for you, and the NOTHING we'll share too, and no one will ever dare to part us two.'

When the golden carp heard the song, he sped, open-mouthed, towards the shore. The sisters scooped him into the net, lifted him from the water and slit his throat. At home they divided up the flesh, and each of the greedy thieves cooked her share the way she liked best. Not one of them wanted the fish's head, so for the moment they left it on a shelf above the fire.

That evening, when Forgetta called her darling, there was not a ripple on the lake. 'Have you forgotten me too, my little brother carp?' she cried. Suddenly, through her tears she saw a patch of blood in the grass. And she guessed what had happened. She sped to her wicked sisters and cried, 'What have you done with my little brother, the golden carp?'

The sisters turned on her, 'Do you take us for thieves? Take a look round our huts, you will not find a trace of your carp.' Forgetta searched and searched, but she found nothing.

Suddenly a hen clucked from the yard, 'Whoever heard that the shelf above the fire is a place for a fish's head?'

The sisters hastily hid the head among the pots, but the hen cackled again more loudly, 'Whoever heard of a fish's head being put among the pots?'

The sisters now did not know what to do, so they threw the head into the oven and covered it with a baking dish.

And the hen crowed again. 'An oven is no place for a fish's head, but for baking bread!'

The wicked sisters were so angry with the little hen, that they stoned her to death. Then they tossed the fish's head into the yard, and snarled at Forgetta, 'Go on, take the head of your precious fish; it is no good for anything now.'

Poor little Forgetta could scarcely see where she was going for tears. In her hands she nursed the head of her beloved Leungli, as she stumbled to the lake shore. There she buried the head.

But her tears had magic power. A most unusual bush grew on the little grave. Its leaves were shaped like fish scales, and they were of pure gold. On the little branches silver flowers opened, and as they bloomed and lost their leaves, miraculous fruit appeared — diamonds, emeralds, and other precious stones, all of them

as big as a fish's head. How beautifully that little bush glittered in the sunlight!

One day a young king rode by. He saw the miraculous bush and stopped to wonder at its beauty. Just then a lovely, sad maiden stepped out of the wood and told him the story of Leungli and the wicked sisters. It was Forgetta. The king fell in love with her at once and carried her off to his palace. The little grave of her golden fish was dug up and taken with the magic bush to the royal garden. Forgetta visited the little grave each night, watering the bush with her magic tears, so that it grew bigger and stronger and yielded more and more precious jewels. And their kingdom became one of the richest in the world.

But a terrible drought struck her homeland. Men and beasts roamed the countryside, searching for a trickle of water. The jungle turned grey and withered like an old cobweb. The rice was as dry as husks, the buffalo perished with hunger and thirst.

Forgetta's sisters fared badly too, for they had not a morsel of food. They knew that Forgetta was a powerful queen now, but so far they had not dared to visit her, for they feared she would punish them for their wickedness. But when their children were crying with hunger, they went to see their youngest sister to beg for help. Queen Forgetta could not, however, forget their cruelty, and she turned them away three times from her door. In vain her sisters begged and pleaded and cried.

One night, when Forgetta was weeping again over the little grave of her beloved Leungli, the magic bush suddenly shone even more brightly, and the golden fish scales rang out, 'A golden bush grows over an old wrong. Let it stay buried! Cruel is he who does not forgive, Forgetta!' Forgetta felt ashamed and she forgave her sisters with all her heart, and forgot the wrongs they had done her. And the sisters were ashamed too, and from that day they forgot to be wicked and lived happily for the rest of their lives.

Puss
in Boots

There was once a miller who had nothing to leave to his sons but his mill, his ass and his cat.

'Share them out justly,' he said on his death bed, before his eyes closed for ever. The two elder brothers carried out his instructions as they saw fit. The eldest kept the mill, the second the ass, whilst the youngest had nothing. So that he would not pity himself too much, his brothers gave him the cat. Needless to say he did not think highly of their sense of fairness.

'It's all very well for you, brothers,' he said in reproach, 'you can put your possessions together and live well, but what about me? When I have eaten my cat, all I'll have left will be his hide for a beret. How am I to survive?' At this the crafty brothers only shrugged their shoulders.

The cat heard these words too, and he did not like them at all. What a fine thing that would be, to end up in his master's stomach. So he exclaimed, 'Stop complaining, master! Buy me a fine pair of boots with spurs, a hat with a big feather and a strong sack! Then I will prove how useful I can be!'

The miller's son laughed at the idea. Fancy the cat wanting to play games when he was so miserable! But then he recalled all the wily things his cat had done in the past, as he lay in wait for rats and mice in the mill. How he hid in the flour, pretending to be dead, hung upside down from the rafters, as if all there was left of him was his own hide and head. All this to outwit the silly mice.

'There is no harm in trying it,' the youth thought. With borrowed money he bought the cat what he wanted, and when he was dressed he looked as smart as a bridegroom. Then the cat slung the sack over his shoulder and went to a large field which he knew was alive with plump rabbits. In his sack he had some bran and lettuce stalks.

Lying down in the grass, he pretended to be dead. The sack lay open beside him. Before very long an inquisitive rabbit hopped along and sniffing the food, hopped into the sack to have a feast. Up jumped the cat, pulled tight the strings round the sack, and sped to the king!

'My master and my lord, the noble Marquis of Hereandthere sends his loyal greetings and a present of this fine rabbit to Your Majesty,' said Puss in Boots, when he was admitted to the royal chamber.

'Well, well, what an unusual guest you are,' said the king. 'But I do happen to be very partial to a tasty rabbit.' And he thanked the cat and returned greetings to his master.

Not long afterwards Puss in Boots caught a brace of young partridge in his sack, and again he went to the king with the present from his master, the Marquis of Hereandthere. The king was delighted, enquired about the marquis's health, and gave the cat a handful of gold coins for his trouble. That was the end of poverty for the miller's son and his cat.

Naturally the king often wondered who this noble Marquis of Hereandthere was, who so often presented him with fresh game, but he preferred not to ask the cat any questions, in case he would offend the generous marquis by his ignorance.

One day Puss in Boots heard that the king was about to take a drive with his daughter by the river. Racing home, he said to his master, 'You can see it was no mistake to keep me. We have enough money and enough to eat. If you listen to me again you will not be sorry.'

The cat then told the miller's son to go down to the river to bathe. His master gladly obeyed and took off his shabby old clothes. Before long the royal carriage approached, and Puss in Boots cried with all his might, 'Help! Help! My lord and master, the Marquis of Hereandthere is drowning!'

It happened that the king looked out of the window, and recognized the cat who kept him well supplied with game, he ordered his footmen to help. The clever cat, who had hidden his master's old clothes, stepped up to the royal carriage and whispered into the king's ear, secretly of course, that some robbers had stolen all his master's clothes, though he had cried for all he was worth, 'Robbers, thieves!' 'So, if you will pardon him, my lord, the Marquis of Hereandthere is covered only in his bare skin!'

The king, sorry for the marquis's misfortune, quickly sent back to the palace for the best suit of clothes once worn by the royal great-grandfather. When the Marquis of Hereandthere put them on, he bowed charmingly to the king, and smiled dazzlingly at the princess, his daughter, who sat in the coach and she fell in love with him then and there. So handsome and noble did he look, she thought. And as regal as her great-grandfather in his portrait.

The king was also charmed by the handsome youth's appearance, and invited him to ride with them in the royal carriage. That was exactly what the scheming Puss in Boots had in mind. Running ahead, he came to some farm labourers, who were raking hay in the field.

Standing before them, his spurs gleaming in the sunshine, his whiskers curling, he cried, 'Listen, my good people! The king is coming this way. When he asks who this fine field belongs to, you must say that it is the property of the Marquis of Hereandthere, or you will all be thrown into jail!'

The farmhands, terrified by the words of such a noble feline gentleman, obediently replied to the questions of the king when he stopped to admire the field and the hay, 'It belongs to our lord, the Marquis of Hereandthere!'

The king praised the young man for having such fine property, and whilst the two discussed what a good income it brought, the cat sped on as fast as his legs would carry him till he came upon farmhands gathering the harvest.

'Listen, my good people,' he cried, his paws stuck into his belt. 'When the king drives past, be sure to say that these fine fields belong to the Marquis of Hereandthere, or you will all be thrown into jail.'

The frightened workers did as they were told. When the king, as he passed, admired the rich harvest, they called, 'This corn belongs to the Marquis of Hereandthere!'

The king was delighted, as was the miller's youngest son. His eyes never left the king's daughter, and he was glad that thanks to his cat, the king thought him a noble lord. In the meantime Puss in Boots ran on, issuing the same order to everyone he met. So the king never stopped marvelling at the marquis's wealth.

Puss in Boots now came to a castle. This was the home of a wicked ogre, and one of the wealthiest creatures on earth. It was he who owned all the land the king was travelling through. The artful cat had himself announced, stating he wished to pay his respects. This amused the ugly giant, and he greeted him as cordially as was possible for an ogre. He smacked his lips, rolled his eyes and ground his teeth, but he asked the cat to stay and rest.

'I have heard, my noble lord ogre,' the cat began, 'that you are a master of magic. They tell me you can change into the largest of beasts, like the lion or the elephant. I can hardly believe it!'

The ogre roared with laughter and turned instantly into a terrible lion, sending the cat spit-

ting and hissing to the roof. But Puss in Boots forgot that cats to not know how to walk in boots on roofs, and he almost crashed to the ground. The ogre found this very funny.

'Ha, ha, ha, that frightened you,' spat the ogre, back in his own shape.

'It certainly did,' the cat admitted. 'But I wager you cannot turn into a little animal, like a rat or a mouse. That must be harder.'

The ogre only laughed, and a moment later there was only a tiny mouse scuttling across the floor. Thereupon, Puss in Boots pounced and gobbled it up in one gulp. And that was the end of the ogre.

At that moment the king was driving past the castle. Puss in Boots ran out of the gates, bowed and cried 'Welcome, Your Royal Highness, to the golden castle of my lord and master, the Marquis of Hereandthere!'

The king could hardly believe his eyes. 'What a fine husband he would be for my daughter,' he thought, looking approvingly at the marquis. But he dared not say so aloud. And when he was led to the dining table, his eyes nearly popped out of his head. So much food and drink, so much silver and gold — all prepared for a feast for the ogre's friends. When they saw the royal coach outside the palace, they did not dare to enter. So the king, his daughter and the marquis feasted on the ogre's food, drank and were merry.

At last the king had the courage to ask the marquis, 'Would you like to marry my daughter and become my honoured son-in-law?' And needless to say, the youth joyfully agreed. They held the wedding the same day and it lasted for a whole year.

As for Puss in Boots, he became a very noble gentleman at court. But when no one was looking, he sneaked off to catch a mouse or two. For it is true that food fit for a king is not always fit for a cat.

The Little Girl on the Moon

When it is full moon, a little girl walks across it. If you look carefully you will see her. Her hair falls to her feet, and she is smiling, always smiling. 'And now,' said the West Wind, 'I will tell you how she got to the moon.'

Once upon a time there was a little girl who had no mother or father, no grandmother or grandfather. She was quite alone in the world. A wealthy merchant took her in, but he was not a good man. He was a miser, and day after day he would order the little girl to work and work till she was quite exhausted. His wife was no better. Poor little girl! She hardly had time to sleep.

One wintry day the merchant's wife sent the little girl to fetch water. The well by the house was frozen solid, so the little girl had to wade through the deep snow all the way to the pond where the ice was not so thick. It was freezing hard. The little girl cut a hole in the ice, filled her pail with water and stumbled home. When she was nearly at the house, her foot slipped and she spilled all the water. What now? She did not dare go in empty-handed, yet she had no strength left to return to the pond. At that very moment the bright wintry sun was going down.

'Sun, dear Sun, shining up high, take me with you to the distant sky, or of sadness I shall die,' the little girl begged.

But the Sun, having heard her plea, rolled behind the hill and suddenly it was night. The silver moon now swung into the sky.

'Moon, silver Moon, take me with you to the night sky, or of sadness I shall die,' the little girl begged. The Moon heard her pleas and stepped down to earth, changing immediately into a handsome silvery youth.

'Hold on to my silvery hair, and I shall take you up into the sky,' he said to the little girl. All at once another youth in a golden robe appeared by his side. He was the Sun.

'Come with me, little girl, for you called me first.' But the little girl replied, 'Oh, shining Sun, beautiful Sun! When I called you, you did not listen. I shall go into the sky with the silver Moon.'

'Since that day you can see her walking when the moon is full. Look hard, and you will see,' said the West Wind.

The Two Old Women and the Boastful Fish

Once upon a time there were two old women who were both as thin as fish fins. Their cottage was built of ice and snow and they kept warm in polar bear coats and hoarfrost gloves. How frail these two old women were. They swayed and trembled like thin little twigs in the breeze, their eyes barely seeing, their ears hardly hearing.

One day a perch swam up from the sea. Stretching out by the side of the snow cottage, it began to sing in a loud voice, intending to frighten the old women.

'I smash the ice, conquer the sea,
eat anyone who dares to oppose me!'

But the old women were too deaf to hear, and were fast asleep anyway. So the perch tried again, singing even more loudly.

'I crush rocks, tear up clouds,
giants I've devoured,
now your turn has come!'

Now the old women were wide awake and trembling with fear.

'Who can be trying to scare us with his song? Do you think it is the polar bear?' whispered one old woman.

'More likely it is an evil spirit,' stammered the other. Cautiously, they peered out of their snow cottage, but they saw no one, for their eyes could barely see and the perch was such a small fish that it could be tossed by the tiniest wave on the sea. But the old women did not know this, and they were terribly afraid.

'Hurry, hurry! We must flee from this evil spirit and set sail across the wide open sea!' cried one. And loading all they needed into their kayak, they pulled it over the snow to the sea.

'Wait!' cried the second. 'We have forgotten the lamp with the whale oil.' And she turned back towards the ice cottage. She almost trod on the small perch which was still singing its frightening song.

'Come back,' she called to her friend. 'That is no evil spirit, but just a little fish.'

So the old women moved back into their little house, and put a pan on the fire, to cook that perch.

When the perch heard what they were planning, it sang in a strong voice,

'Those thin old women I'll let go free;
a nice fat giant my next meal will be!'

And with that it slid back into the sea.

Prince Asraf and the King of the Spirits

In the land of the endless desert there once ruled a wise king, who had an only son, the noble Prince Asraf. He was a handsome, courageous youth, but hot-blooded and reckless. The days he spent in revelry and a round of pleasure and his escapades caused the old king much pain. When his life was nearly over and the wise sovereign was preparing for death, he summoned his son to his bedside.

'My son,' he said, 'there are as many of your unwise deeds as there are grains of sand. Take care that they will not turn your heart into a parched desert. Thoughtlessness is not a good adviser to a king. But I advise you to reign wisely and justly, to make our kingdom wealthier still and to work for the welfare of our people. Above all else, safeguard your honour, always keep your royal word, no matter how hard this sometimes may seem. A given promise must never be broken! Remember this, and may Allah protect you!' With these words the old king died.

Prince Asraf became the ruler of the kingdom. But he did not heed his father's words, and reigned recklessly, till he had spent all the riches of the kingdom. When now at night he went to bed, and heard through the window the weeping and moaning of his hungry subjects, he blamed himself bitterly for not listening to his father. For in spite of his pride and wild ways, his heart was kind, and so he suffered too on account of his thoughtless actions.

One night, in an uneasy sleep, a kind old man with a flowing beard appeared to him. 'Sadness and regret walk at the heel of evil deeds, Prince Asraf,' the aged man said. 'But with true repentance comes forgiveness and happiness. If you wish to atone for your mistakes, you must go through the desert without a drop of water to the distant city of Cairo, to lie in the noon sun at its gates. If you do this, you will be rich again.'

Prince Asraf did not hesitate, but had his mount saddled and rode out alone into the desert. He ignored the fierce sun, which beat down on him like a flame. When his exhausted horse collapsed in the sand, he crawled on alone, half dead with thirst and hunger, through the parched land to the gates of Cairo. Conquering his yearning for water, he sank to the burning

The next morning Prince Asraf rose as if reborn, and hastened to carry out the old man's command. Great was his surprise when he found iron gates under the floorboards of his father's chamber. Beyond, white marble stairs led downwards. A lighted torch in his hand, the prince descended, and came upon an underground palace of clear crystal. Walls glittered

sand to fulfil his mission. He fell into a feverish sleep, and in his dream saw the old man again.

'Your suffering is not yet at an end,' he said. 'If you wish to atone for your sins, you must now turn round and walk home!'

Prince Asraf obeyed. His feet covered in sores, he stumbled over the burning sand, while the impatient vultures tried to tear his flesh from his body. Yet the prince carried on, till one day at last he collapsed into his mother's arms. For many days he hovered between life and death, then one night the old man came to him again in his dream.

'Your test is at an end, and you have passed. When you awake, take an axe and dig up the centre of your father's chamber. There you will find happiness,' he said with a smile.

with gold and silver, and floors and ceilings were studded with diamonds and rubies. Everywhere stood jugs of jasper filled to the brim with gold. In the far corner was an ordinary earthenware jug and in it a rusty key. It fitted the lock in a little door. Prince Asraf opened it and was greeted with a dazzling blaze. He saw eight glittering statues, each on a base and all made of diamonds. These statues represented maidens of untold beauty. The ninth base was empty, but on a fragment of white satin there were written in the deceased king's hand these words: 'At last you have learned wisdom, my son! My wealth is now rightfully yours. But if you wish to own the most beautiful of all the diamond statues, you must hasten to Cairo to find my former slave Mubarak. He will lead you to the distant kingdom of spirits where you will find what you most desire. May Allah go with you!'

Prince Asraf, who was bewitched by the diamond statues, journeyed to Cairo without delay. He found his father's old servant and asked him to lead him to the kingdom of genies. Mubarak, who over the years had become rich, granted Asraf's request out of respect for his former master. Long and hard was their journey! They had to conquer seven steep mountains, cross seven deserts, withstand many dangers, before they came to a great black lake. In its centre a shimmering white isle towered to the skies, with a gleaming golden palace studded with emeralds and rubies.

'We have arrived,' Mubarak said to the weary prince. 'Before us lies the palace of the king of the spirits. When his ferryman takes us on his boat, we must not utter a single word, or we shall turn into snakes.' Mubarak then whistled loudly and a pearly boat appeared, at the helm a hideous monster with a lion's body and an elephant's head. With its octopus-like arms it pulled the two travellers into the boat, and they flew like an arrow to the island. None of them uttered a single word.

The moment they struck the shore, they were welcomed by the roar of the strangest creatures with spiderlike bodies. They had the heads of beasts, and from their mouths thick smoke escaped. The loyal Mubarak spread two rugs on the ground, and as soon as he and Prince Asraf sat upon them, the monsters fled in all directions.

'These are magic carpets,' Mubarak explained. 'They protect good people from all things evil. Be patient, the king of the genies will be here soon. If we are welcomed, he will come in the form of a man. Otherwise we shall be met by the most hideous monster.'

A terrible storm then descended and day turned to night. Lightning flashed in the sky and wild monsters howled in tune with the thunder. Silence followed, daylight broke, and before the bewildered Prince Asraf appeared the old man who visited him in his dreams.

'I welcome you to my kingdom, Prince Asraf,' he said, smiling kindly. 'I know why you are here. Your father often stayed in my palace, and each time he took from me a diamond statue as a keepsake. The loveliest one has been left for you. But I do not know whether you are worthy yet of such a valuable gift. A young mind is

more capricious than the desert wind. Listen to my will! Go and seek the maiden with the purest heart and give her to me for a slave. Then you can have the beautiful statue you so desire. As it is not easy to look into a human heart, take my magic mirror with you. Only the maiden whose face the mirror will reflect, is fit to be my chief slave.' Having thus spoken, the king of the spirits turned into a flowering shrub.

And so Asraf had once again to set out into the world with the faithful Mubarak. As the word spread that he was seeking the maiden with the purest heart, lovely women rushed forth to show their face to the mirror. But it remained dull. The prince was near despair when they came to the house of a rich vizier.

'Let my only daughter gaze into the magic mirror, so that we can see into her heart,' the vizier begged the prince.

Asraf agreed, and a face appeared in the mirror, so lovely that it took his breath away. 'She alone is worthy of the greatest king,' he cried, and asked the vizier to give his daughter to the mighty sovereign. The vizier gladly consented, not realizing that Prince Asraf did not mean himself, but the king of the spirits.

Before long the vizier's daughter was on her way to the distant isle of spirits. The nearer they came, the quieter Prince Asraf was, for he had fallen in love with the beautiful maiden, and he could not bear to think of what life would be like without her.

'I cannot give the vizier's daughter as a slave to the king of the spirits,' he confided to Mubarak, 'for my life is worthless without her.'

Mubarak was aghast. 'How can you, sir, break a promise given to your father's friend?' The prince sadly hung his head and continued the journey in silence.

'You have come through your most difficult test,' the king of the genies said in welcome. 'Now return in peace to your home. There, in the underground palace, you will find what you desire most.'

Prince Asraf bade the vizier's daughter a sad goodbye, and turned for home. His steps led him straight to the underground palace, to lighten his sorrow with the sight of the precious gift. The king of the genies had kept his word. On the ninth base stood a statue of untold beauty. And suddenly it came to life, and knelt at his feet. With immense joy the prince saw that it was the vizier's daughter whom he loved so deeply. Till their dying day they remembered with gratitude the noble king of the spirits who filled their lives with endless happiness.

The Giant with Three Golden Hairs

Long, long ago a little boy was born to a poor couple. His hair was golden and on his brow was a strange little sign in the shape of a silver moon.

'This child must have been sent by Heaven itself!' said the village seer, who was also the little boy's godmother. 'Look at that silver moon! It is a good omen!' Then the wise old woman gazed up into the sky and added, 'When your son reaches his sixteenth year, he will marry the king's only daughter.'

On that same day there was born at the palace a lovely little girl, and the queen and the king were full of joy and pride. But the king heard of the godmother's strange prophecy and he grew extremely angry. His daughter to become the wife of some pauper!

'The boy must die,' he decided, and disguised as a wealthy merchant, he knocked one day on the door of the boy's parents.

'I lost my way in the forest,' he said. 'Good people, please let me stay overnight with you.'

The poor couple made him welcome, not suspecting his evil intentions, and shared with him their simple meal. The disguised king suddenly leaned over the crib and spoke admiringly.

'What a beautiful child you have and what a shame that he should grow up in such poor surroundings. Entrust your little son to my safe keeping, and I shall raise him to be a nobleman.'

The wife protested, not wishing to part with her infant for anything in the world. But at last her husband persuaded her.

'Remember the words of the wise old woman, wife!' he urged. 'The king's daughter will be waiting for our son. Some young fellow from a poor cottage such as ours could not tempt her. Believe me, our son will be better off with this rich gentleman. He will have an excellent upbringing and education, and fine manners. Why should we stand in his way?'

Heavy-hearted, the mother bade her infant goodbye and handed him to their wealthy visitor. The king mounted his horse and turned towards the palace.

He did not ride far. When he came to the banks of a deep river, he let the fierce stream carry away the crib with the infant. 'You can have the boy, river! Let some cold fish princess dance with him at her wedding,' he cried, and continued on his homeward journey.

The king was sure the baby boy would drown in the deep river. But the crib sailed safely and gently with the current, and it seemed as if the waters were cradling and protecting him. It floated on and on, till it came to an old mill.

'Look, wife, what the river is bringing us,' the old miller called in surprise. 'You have so longed for a baby, and now your wish is coming true.' So the miller and his wife saved the life of the infant boy. They cared for him as if he were their own, calling him Hans and raising him with kindness and love. The years passed and the boy grew into a handsome youth.

He was sixteen years but a day, when a sudden storm, more fierce than any anyone could recall, lashed the countryside. There was a hammering on the door and the king himself entered.

'I have been caught by the storm in the forest. Prepare me a bed,' he said curtly to the miller. He and his wife did not know what to do first, so anxious were they to please such a noble visitor. And Hans helped them willingly. The king, noticing the strange sign on the boy's brow, started asking questions, and the miller told him truthfully how the baby had been brought to them by the river. The king then realized who he was. Frowning heavily, he called for writing materials.

'You are to take this letter to the queen tonight,' he ordered Hans. The letter said, 'The bearer of this letter must die at once!'

The youth bravely faced the storm, but very soon he lost his way, and was glad when he came upon a lonely hut in the dark forest. 'Good people,' he begged, 'please let me rest my head here till morning.'

At a window the face of a little girl appeared. She was a robber's daughter, unwashed and uncombed. 'Run for your life!' she cried. 'My father and his robber friends will return soon, and if they find you, they are sure to kill you.'

Hans felt his blood run cold. But then he thought, 'Shall I let the wild beasts of the forest tear me apart, or shall I throw myself on the mercy of the robbers? Perhaps there is a spark of kindness left in their hearts.' So he refused to be turned away from the door.

The robber's little girl eventually let him in. Telling him to stretch out on a bench she then hid Hans under all the cloaks and bed covers. Hans was in a deep sleep when the robbers burst into the room. 'Bring the food, girl!' her father, who was the leader, cried, while a long-

nosed comrade prowled in a suspicious way round the room, sniffing.

'There's the smell of a mill here,' he growled. 'You'd better tell who you are hiding, girl.'

Another robber with batlike ears listened and said, 'What do I hear? Snores which sound like the rattle of a mill wheel! Whom have you here? He'll not wake again, never fear, for I am going to end his life with my sharp knife.'

The robber's daughter started to weep. She begged that the handsome youth's life be spared.

'Very well,' agreed her father. 'But as we are robbers, we must go through his pockets at least.'

The thieves then threw off the cloaks and covers and set to work. They were so quick and deft that the youth did not even wake up.

One robber with eyes like burning coal found the king's letter. 'A note from the king himself,' he exclaimed, and they all started to read.

'What a wily fellow that king of ours is,' the robbers' leader muttered. 'He is sending that unsuspecting lad to his death. But he did not reckon that we would intervene!' Hastily he wrote another letter, which said, 'Dear wife! I wish the bearer of this letter to marry my daughter immediately! That is the will of your king!' Sealing it, he put this letter into Hans's pocket.

When in the morning the youth awoke, the robbers bade him a friendly goodbye and even accompanied him for a little of the way. They were laughing under their whiskers, so pleased were they with the trick they were playing on the king. The young man decided that these robbers were not wholly wicked and thanking them warmly, he turned towards the palace.

When the queen opened and read the king's letter, she was astounded, but she did not dare oppose the king's will. And that very day Hans married her daughter. As for the young man himself, the princess was so lovely that his astonishment turned quickly to joy.

When the king returned to the palace, he roared with fury and despair. He demanded to know where Hans had spent the night. When the young man told him the truth, the king immediately sent his guards into the forest to arrest the robbers and hang them from the nearest trees. But the robbers and even their hut completely disappeared.

The unhappy king pondered and wondered how to rid himself of his unwelcome son-in-law. One day he called Hans to his presence and scowling angrily, said, 'You have forced yourself into my household in a dishonest manner. I should like to cut off your head, but if you bring me three golden hairs from the head of the terrible Giant Knowall, who lives far off in an underground cave, my heart will soften.'

The youth agreed, and the king rubbed his hands in satisfaction, for no man had ever returned alive from the giant's kingdom. But Hans was not afraid. He set out at once on his quest. In the depths of a forest he came to a spot where two paths crossed and there under an oak tree the three robbers sat arguing over their last gold coin. Hans gave them two more coins and said, 'Now tell me the way to the cave of Giant Knowall.'

The robbers recognized the youth who had spent the night with them.

'Follow your nose!' the long-nosed robber advised him readily.

'Be led by your ears,' the bat-eared robber suggested.

'Go where your eyes take you,' said the one with the burning eyes. The youth listened to all three, and very soon came to a strange town.

'Stop!' cried the guard at the gates. 'No one may pass through our town, unless he tells why the water has dried up in our magic well. Until recently it flowed with wine. If a dead man's lips were moistened with it, he was brought back to life. And now you must tell why the spring has ebbed away!'

Hans could not give a reason, but he promised to ask Giant Knowall. The guard then let him pass through, and the youth walked on till he came to the next town.

'Stop!' exclaimed the guard at the gates. 'I cannot open the gates to anyone unless he can say why the royal apple tree no longer yields golden apples. They brought youth to anyone who tasted them. But the tree is now withered and fruitless. Tell me why!'

Hans promised once again to ask Giant Knowall, and the guard let him pass. After a time he reached the bank of a river so wide he could not see the opposite bank. Suddenly an old ferryman appeared of the mist. Hans asked to be rowed across to the other bank.

'Certainly,' the latter agreed, 'but first you will tell me why I must always ferry people from shore to shore. I am old, but never may I step on dry land. When will my suffering come to an end?'

When Hans gave his word that he would ask Giant Knowall, the old man willingly took him to the opposite bank. 'Take care,' he warned, 'I have rowed many men across, but no one has ever returned.'

Hans walked on, till at last he came to the giant's cave. An aged, white-haired woman stood at the entrance. She was the giant's grandmother.

'Flee for your life, before my grandson returns!' she cried.

Hans then told her what fate awaited him if he were to turn back without three of the giant's golden hairs. He told of the king, of the aged ferryman, the golden apple tree and the dried up well and he begged the woman to help him.

'Very well,' she agreed, 'I shall help you as you help others. But my grandson must not find you here.' Next moment she had turned Hans into a little ant and hidden him in the pocket of her apron.

It was not a moment too soon. On a great gust of wind, a fearsome giant rushed into the

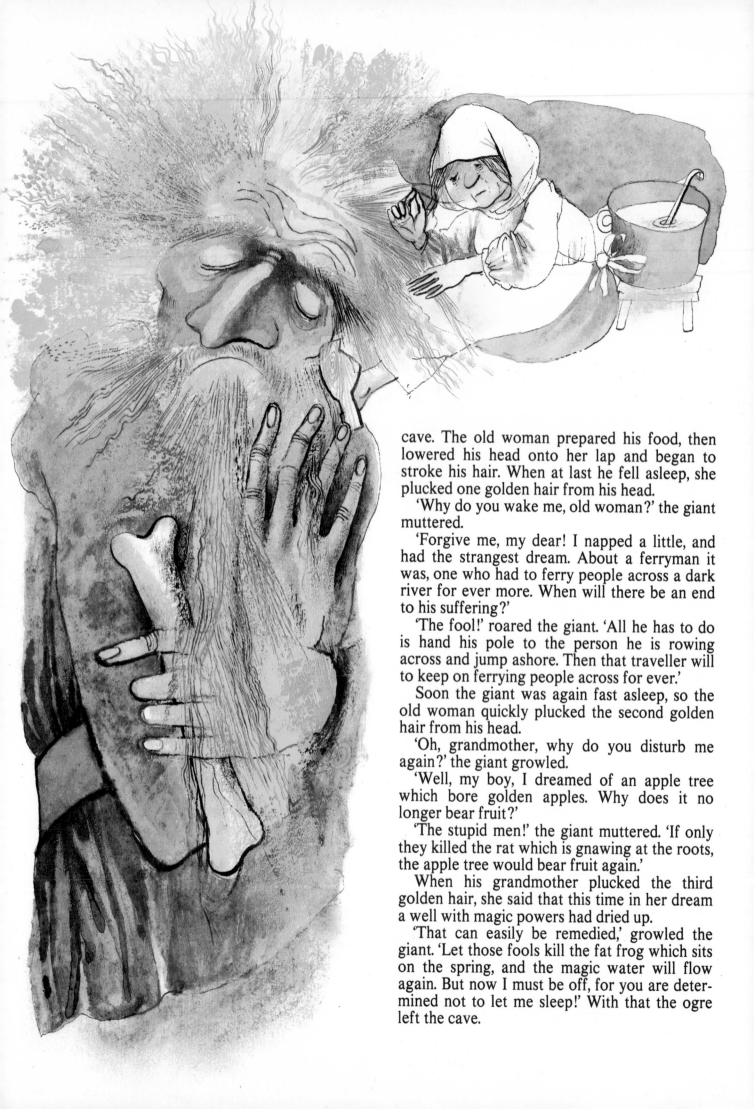

cave. The old woman prepared his food, then lowered his head onto her lap and began to stroke his hair. When at last he fell asleep, she plucked one golden hair from his head.

'Why do you wake me, old woman?' the giant muttered.

'Forgive me, my dear! I napped a little, and had the strangest dream. About a ferryman it was, one who had to ferry people across a dark river for ever more. When will there be an end to his suffering?'

'The fool!' roared the giant. 'All he has to do is hand his pole to the person he is rowing across and jump ashore. Then that traveller will to keep on ferrying people across for ever.'

Soon the giant was again fast asleep, so the old woman quickly plucked the second golden hair from his head.

'Oh, grandmother, why do you disturb me again?' the giant growled.

'Well, my boy, I dreamed of an apple tree which bore golden apples. Why does it no longer bear fruit?'

'The stupid men!' the giant muttered. 'If only they killed the rat which is gnawing at the roots, the apple tree would bear fruit again.'

When his grandmother plucked the third golden hair, she said that this time in her dream a well with magic powers had dried up.

'That can easily be remedied,' growled the giant. 'Let those fools kill the fat frog which sits on the spring, and the magic water will flow again. But now I must be off, for you are determined not to let me sleep!' With that the ogre left the cave.

The old woman swiftly changed the ant back into a handsome youth and took him to the dark river where she bade him goodbye.

The ferryman asked how Hans had fared. 'I will tell you as soon as we reach the other shore,' said the youth. And when Hans jumped from the boat he cried,' 'Next time you have a passenger, let him hold your pole! Then he instead of you will have to ferry men across.'

On his return journey Hans, thanks to Giant Knowall, made the apple tree spring to life again and the magic water in the well flow again. And in both towns he was amply rewarded with gold and jewels.

So Hans returned to the palace not only with three golden hairs from the head of Giant Knowall, but with an abundance of riches. With tears of joy in her eyes his young wife fell into his arms. She had thought that never again would she see her beloved.

But her father, the jealous king was furious that Hans was still alive. 'How did you acquire such riches?' he stormed. 'Did you steal them?'

Hans smiled. 'If you want to acquire the same fortune, you must follow your nose, go where your ears lead you and your eyes take you. Beyond the dark river there are mountains of pure gold and diamonds.' The greedy king did not have to be told twice. Without a word of farewell he set out.

When he reached the wide river, the ferryman gave him his pole, while he himself jumped ashore. And to this day the wicked king is ferrying travellers across that dark river.

The Little Talking Animal and the Shining Blue Fish

Once upon a time there were two brothers who lived at different ends of the same village. The younger one was quiet and dreamy and liked best to talk to and make friends with the little wild animals of the jungle. He did not work very hard, but his heart was kind and good, and he would not harm anyone. But his elder brother even envied the fly her wings, and had not a good word to say for another human being. The younger one they called Slowcoach, the elder one did not have a nice name.

One day a little jungle animal visited Slowcoach — Cibet was his name. He came to steal a few black nuts, knowing well that Slowcoach would not be angry, that at the most he would only smile and murmur a few scolding words. But Slowcoach caught Cibet as he was creeping away and persuaded him to stay and be his friend. He taught the little animal to talk and to sing and many other clever things. Cibet was very happy. After all, no other jungle animal could do the things he could do.

One morning Slowcoach and Cibet went into town. On the way they met wealthy merchants.

'Where are you bound for?' the merchants asked.

'I am taking Cibet into town. He will sing there at the market,' Slowcoach replied.

The merchants laughed at him. 'If that little animal of yours sings for us,' they said, 'we shall give you all our riches. If it doesn't, you shall get a hiding with a bamboo stick.' Slowcoach then told Cibet to sing, and Cibet sang. And the merchants had to part with all their riches.

When Slowcoach returned to the village and related what had happened, his brother heard of it and was very envious. He asked Slowcoach to lend him Cibet, for he too wanted to grow rich. But on his way to town he was too lazy to carry the little animal in his arms. He made him walk and shouted angrily at him for going too slowly. Then he met some merchants. He told them where he was going, and why, just as his brother had done.

When he ordered Cibet to sing, the little animal stayed dumb. The merchants then gave him such a good hiding with their bamboo sticks that he thought his last hour had come. So furious was the brother that he seized a stick and killed Cibet with one stroke.

When Slowcoach heard this, he wept bitterly. He buried Cibet under a palm tree and every evening he prayed at his grave. Whenever he said his prayers, the palm tree trembled and a shower of silver rain fell from its leaves. This went on day after day and Slowcoach grew richer and richer. His brother was full of envy.

One day he decided that he too would go and pray under the palm tree. And as he said his prayers the palm tree trembled. But instead of a silver shower, there poured down upon him a deluge of evil-smelling mud. The brother was so furious that there and then he fetched an axe and cut down the palm tree.

Poor Slowcoach wept again. But so that he would have something to remember his Cibet by, he carved a fine trough for his swine from the trunk of the palm tree. And wonder of wonders! The little pigs grew rounder and fatter so quickly, that before a week had passed he could sell them at the market.

The envious brother borrowed the trough for his swine. But instead of growing fatter his pigs grew thinner and thinner till they were nothing but skin and bone. The angry brother did not hesitate. In his fury he burned the trough and all Slowcoach managed to save from the ashes was a little splinter of wood. He made a hook for his fishing rod from it and went to the lake to fish. Soon he had caught so many fish that he could hardly carry them all to market.

The envious brother borrowed the rod, but as soon as the hook touched the water, the lake burst its banks and he nearly drowned in the flood. The rod disappeared from sight in the deep waters.

And Slowcoach sat on the shore and wept. Suddenly a beautiful maiden rose from the lake and spoke. 'I am the daughter of the dragon king,' she said. 'Your hook is embedded in my father's mouth and he cannot get it out. Will you help him?'

Slowcoach agreed at once. The maiden breathed on him and next moment he was turned into a silver bubble and carried down to the depths of the lake. The dragon king, moaning and groaning with pain, welcomed him. Slowcoach quickly pulled out the hook and as a reward the dragon king gave him a jug containing a little blue fish which shone like a bright flame.

At home again, Slowcoach put the jug on a shelf. And soon he found that the fish had magic powers. Whenever he left his cottage was cleaned and his pans were filled with food. 'How can this be?' he wondered.

One day he only pretended to leave for the fields, and peeping through a crack in the wall of his cottage, he saw to his amazement the little fish change into a lovely maiden. It was the daughter of the dragon king. Slowcoach burst into the cottage just as she set to work, and seizing the jug, broke it in pieces.

The maiden smiled at him. 'Now I must stay with you,' she said. 'But I have no bones in my body. You must make some.' And Slowcoach broke some utensils made of bone and gave them to the maiden to eat.

'Now I am like other people,' she cried happily. 'Now I can be your wife.'

As for the envious brother, he too wanted a lovely and clever bride. So he dived to the bed of the lake and the dragon king turned him into a fish. And a fish he will remain, unless he mends his wicked ways.

The Magic Fruit

There was once a young lad who looked after pigs and whom everyone in the village called Swineherd. One day, he decided to go out into the world. When he had walked for one whole day, his nose was still filled with the smoke from his cottage. 'Never did I realize how far it was into the world,' he muttered and as it was growing dark, he settled down for the night among the roots of an old oak. But something was sticking into his back and much to his surprise he found it was a fine saddle. And what was this shining nearby? A gold ring! And over there a purse, and it was not empty. Two gold coins clinked inside. The happy Swineherd stretched out under the oak and soon was sound asleep.

But he had a rude awakening with the arrival of three robbers. 'One moment, fellows,' croaked one. 'I hid a magic saddle under this oak. Whoever sits in it can fly wherever he wants!'

'I left a ring here,' drawled another. 'Whoever turns it will have any princess as a bride!'

'Who cares about your toys, you fools!' spat the third. 'I hid a purse with two coins somewhere here. As soon as they are spent, two more appear. So I can be rich without having to steal.'

When Swineherd heard this, he climbed like a monkey up the oak tree, clutching the three treasures. But the robbers heard him and their hands flew to their pistols.

'Come down, thief, or we'll shoot you!' they raged.

But Swineherd had the magic saddle and the minute he sat in it, he found himself flying through the air towards the royal city.

The king just then was looking out of the window, a very mournful princess at his side. This princess had never laughed in her life and the king was determined to give her in marriage to the first man who would make her laugh. At the sight of Swineherd riding through the air on a horseless saddle both she and her royal father roared with laughter.

'Meet your bridegroom!' cried the king, tears of mirth rolling down his royal cheeks. But the princess did not want to marry this unknown young man. Swineherd, however, thought the princess was beautiful, so he turned the magic ring and in a trice the royal maiden jumped through the window right into his arms and kissed him warmly on the lips. The king prepared their wedding at once, but it worried him that the lad probably had no noble blood in his veins.

'Do not worry about noble blood,' Swineherd

said proudly. 'My father has such a vast army that no one can count the men!' So the king told him to invite his parents to the wedding. What could Swineherd do? He had to write a letter bearing the king's seal, asking his parents to come to the royal city at the head of the army. His father thought his son had lost his reason, but a royal letter could not be ignored. So he drove together his swine, while his wife rounded up their goats and off they started for the royal city. When the king saw this comical army, he laughed so heartily that his sides nearly split.

But the proud princess was offended and, swelling up like a frog, she croaked, 'Get out of my sight, wretched swineherd!' And there and then the guards chased Swineherd and his parents with their goats and swine out of the city gates. The lad did not even have time to take his magic treasures with him. Father and Mother returned home in shame, but their son went off into the world again.

One day he came upon a very strange garden, where golden pears and apples were a joy to behold. Swineherd hungrily bit into a golden apple. Next moment, his arms and legs were covered in hair and he had hooves instead of feet!

'Eeeooh,' he cried, startled at his own voice. To his horror, Swineherd had turned into a donkey! In despair, he bit into a golden pear, and turned instantly into a goat. 'Maa,' he bleated,

and in sheer desperation he chewed a simple thorn from a bush. As soon as he swallowed it, there stood Swineherd as young and handsome as before.

'This is very strange magic,' he said to himself. He picked some fruit, put it in his shirt, then disguising himself he returned to the palace. He offered the golden fruit to the princess and her proud lady-in-waiting. The princess bit into an apple, the proud lady-in-waiting into a pear.

'Eeeooh,' neighed the princess, 'Maa,' bleated the maid. The noise brought the king.

'My daughter has turned into an ass!' he cried in horror. 'And the other into a nanny goat!' Swineherd then appeared, dressed as a doctor, saying he knew how to rid them both of the spell as long as the king entrusted them to his safe keeping. The anxious father agreed and even helped to harness the donkey and the goat to a cart, and off they trotted.

Swineherd drove them hard, till they could hardly raise their hooves. When he decided they had been punished enough, he let them munch the magic thorn. Instantly they returned to their former selves. But their pride had evaporated. The princess sank to her knees to beg Swineherd's forgiveness and led him back to the palace as her husband.

Sometimes when they had nothing better to do, swineherd and his princess would drive their swine to pasture together.

The Golden Cranes

Somewhere in the Far North, a thousand sleeps beyond the Land of Many Rivers there lived a tribe of huge golden birds called cranes. Wise Manitou, the Indian God himself, gave them their golden plumage long ago. It was then he summoned Latakini, their chief, and said, 'Latakini, you are chief of the most beautiful birds. I have not given golden feathers to any other bird tribe. But in return, you must never leave the territory I have assigned to you. If you disobey, your plumage will lose its golden glitter!'

Latakini promised. But the summer was growing old and soon came the day when the first flocks of Canadian geese and wild ducks began to assemble to migrate to the distant south. Latakini grew restless. His eyes wistfully followed the migrating flocks, and night after night he was excited and disturbed by the sound of the countless wings in the dark sky. One morning, when he saw that his tribe was now alone in its homeland, he could no longer resist the temptation and gave his tribe the command to fly south.

When Manitou saw the golden cranes migrating, his anger knew no bounds. He was aware that the birds were flying to the Land of Many Rivers, and he therefore instructed all the waters in that land to take away the golden plumage from the disobedient Latakini and his tribe. For many days and nights the cranes sailed across the endless sky, till at last they glimpsed below silver threads of rivers and splashes of glittering lakes. They had reached their destination at last.

At the head of the flock, Latakini circled majestically over the largest lake, then slowly descended to its surface. Before they touched the water, a mysterious storm broke. Waves rose, almost drowning the unfortunate birds, tearing the beautiful golden feathers from their bodies, scattering them over the whole lake. Too late Latakini ordered them to retreat. With their wet, featherless wings, the birds rose with difficulty. Now, instead of the golden flock, white birds were flying under the shining sun.

Latakini then remembered Manitou's warning and assembled his flock for the return flight to the Far North. He believed Manitou would forgive. When, after their long journey, the cranes at last flew down and landed on their cold homeland, the ground looked as if it was covered with freshly fallen snow. Their feathers remained white for ever. This was how the Great Spirit punished the disobedient golden cranes.

The Dandelion

There came a morning when he wanted again to cheer himself with the sight of his beloved. To his surprise, the maiden's beautiful golden hair had turned to silver during the night, as if it had been coated in hoarfrost.

'Kabibonocca has bewitched the lovely maiden with his midnight stories, tied her with icy bonds and covered her golden locks in hoarfrost,' Shawondasee sighed bitterly and passionately. Then suddenly it seemed as if a snowstorm had whirled over the prairie. Something silky and white like a snowflake floated through the air, and the lovely maiden melted like a puff of smoke.

To this day Shawondasee does not know his love was only a yellow dandelion. As it was about to shed its blossom, the South Wind scattered its silver hair with his passionate sighs. But they say Shawondasee is too lazy even to think. He only lies on the prairie and sighs gently to himself. So say the Indians.

'The South Wind is called Shawondasee by the Indians in their distant land, and in their language Kabibonocca is the name of the North Wind,' said West Wind, starting another story. 'They say those two do not like each other. They are forever bickering and forcing one another out of the prairie to other hunting grounds. What a shame, say the Indians, that Shawondasee cannot chase the freezing Kabibonocca to the Far North for ever, to his kingdom of the eternal snow and ice. How wonderful it would be for the warm summer to last all the year! But they say Shawondasee is too lazy for that. As soon as the last snow flakes melt on the fur coat of his icy brother, Shawondasee makes himself comfortable in the grass and does nothing but roll from side to side, puffing contentedly. But as autumn nears, the South Wind becomes gloomier and gloomier. He lies and sighs. The Indians say that he is missing his great love. Who was his great love? That I am about to tell you,' smiled West Wind.

One day Shawondasee was rolling lazily over the prairie as usual, yawning and dreaming by turns. Suddenly he saw in the distance towards the north a beautiful golden-haired maiden in a flower-strewn meadow. She was as slender as the stem of a flower and glowed so brightly that she almost blinded Shawondasee. He was completely bewitched. You would think that Shawondasee would have flown after her. But no! He just lay back in the grass and sighed and yearned and feasted his eyes on the distant, dazzling miracle.

East of the Sun, West of the Moon

(The Tales of the North Wind)

'Oh, you little telltale,' said the old woman jokingly to West Wind, 'you should not gossip about your brothers!' West Wind smiled impishly. 'You know very well, Mother, it was only a fairy story. Anyway, it was not mine, but the Indians'! Now I must be off, for I can feel the rain in my eyes freezing to snowflakes. My brother North Wind must be returning.' With that the West Wind flew off.

'My kind, good lady,' sobbed the young woman, who was searching for the way to lead to her prince, 'I no longer believe that I shall ever learn how to reach the secret castle east of the sun and west of the moon.'

And the old lady comforted her again and wrapped her in a white fur cloak. 'Do not fear, my dear,' she said, 'for my eldest son is the wisest one. He will surely lead you to your prince.'

Suddenly a magnificent glow lit up the sky, and a transparent old man flew down to the ground on snowflake wings. His face was wrinkled like an old iceberg and instead of a beard, a fringe of tinkling icicles hung from his chin. He breathed on his hands, and the first snow filled the skies. The old man was smiling kindly.

'Be welcome, my son the North Wind,' said his mother, embracing him. 'Tell us the secret way to the palace in the transparent sea! To the east of the sun and west of the moon the wicked stepmother keeps the handsome prince prisoner. This unhappy girl is searching for him.'

North Wind stroked the young woman's hair very gently, so as not to harm her with his icy touch. Then he said, 'I know the way to the transparent sea. It passes through stories from the whole world. You are almost at the end of your pilgrimage, but you still have to hear my tales.'

The young woman's eyes filled with tears. 'I am afraid your stories will be icy and sad like your freezing kingdom,' she said.

North Wind consoled her. 'Have no fear, my child! Like my brothers, I too hear tales from all the world in my icy kingdom — from regions of everlasting sun, as well as from lands of ice and snow. They are told by fishes and birds, by waves on the sea and clouds in the sky. Pray listen! The last tale we shall tell together.' North Wind began.

159

The Sleeping Beauty

Once upon a time there was a king and a queen who were very unhappy because they had no children. At last one day fortune smiled upon them, and the queen gave birth to a lovely daughter. A joyful christening was held at the palace and to it all the fairies of the kingdom were invited. They would be the princess's fairy godmothers, and they would bestow upon the baby girl gifts and blessings which would bring happiness for the rest of her life. There were seven fairies in all.

The sovereign himself led the fairies to the lavishly laden tables where each place was set with beautiful plates and a golden casket, containing gold spoons, forks and knives, set with rubies and diamonds. Unfortunately the king had forgotten to invite the oldest fairy, who for the past fifty years had not left her lonely tower. Perhaps he thought her dead or bewitched.

But suddenly in the midst of the celebrations she appeared and demanded her place at the feast. Everyone gasped in astonishment at her arrival. The king quickly ordered a place to be set in the seat of honour, but he could not present her with a golden casket, for he had ordered only seven to be made. The aged fairy, greatly insulted, thereupon mumbled under her breath a terrible curse.

One of the younger fairies heard her muttering, and knew that the old woman was planning something evil for the little princess. She slipped away quietly and hid behind the curtain near the cradle, where she could hear the promises and blessings of the other fairy godmothers. She hoped that if she spoke last, she could avert any evil curse pronounced by the angry old fairy.

The fairies crowded round the cradle to bestow their gifts upon the baby princess. The first promised that she would be the most beautiful princess in the world, the second, that she would be the sweetest and most charming, the third that she would be full of grace, the fourth that she would dance like an angel, the fifth gave her the voice of a lark, the sixth said she would make music divinely. Then the old fairy leaned over the cradle and croaked, 'To you this gift I endow! When you have blossomed like a flower and are sixteen to the day, for the king's insult you shall pay! You will prick your finger on a spindle and die!'

Hearing this, everyone present started to

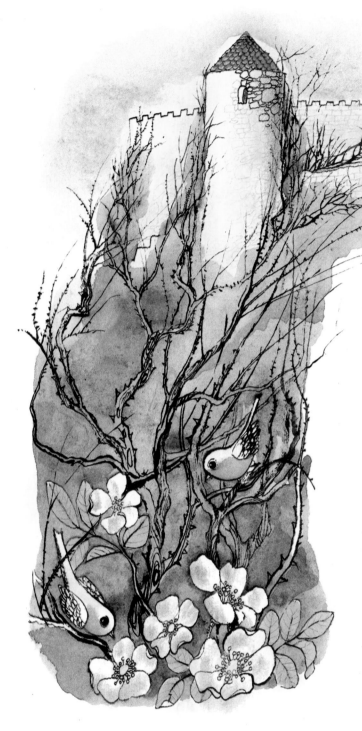

kingdom. Anyone caught spinning would be put to death. But, alas, he was powerless against the evil curse. One day, when the princess was sixteen years old, the king and queen drove into the countryside in their golden carriage. The princess amused herself by wandering all over the palace. As if led by an invisible hand, she at last found herself in the oldest, derelict tower, where an old, white-haired woman sat spinning. The king's law against spindles had never reached her ears, for she had not for many years left her little room.

'Is not this pretty! What are you doing, old woman?' asked the princess, marvelling at the delicate thread.

'I am spinning, my child, spinning of course! Can't you see?' laughed the old woman.

The curious princess begged to be allowed to try this strange work, but as soon as she took the spindle in her hand, she pricked her finger and at once fell into a deep sleep.

When the king returned and heard of his daughter's misfortune, he recalled immediately the curse and the promise of the fairies. His heart full of grief, he ordered the princess to be taken to the finest chamber and laid on a bed embroidered with gold and silver. In her deep sleep she looked like a beautiful angel.

The king then announced that no one must disturb her long sleep, and after kissing his dear daughter farewell, he and the queen prepared to leave the palace where the princess would lie for a hundred years.

It was then that the good fairy who had saved the life of the princess appeared. At that time she was living many thousands of miles away, but a little dwarf in seven-league boots had hastened to tell her what had happened. And in a chariot drawn by fiery dragons she sped

weep and lament, but then the young fairy stepped out from her hiding place and in a clear voice, said, 'I have not the power to break entirely the curse of the oldest fairy, but hear me, my King, hear me, my Queen! When your daughter pricks her finger on a spindle, she will not die, but will fall into a deep sleep which will last for a hundred years. Then a noble prince will come to wake her from her long sleep.' As soon as she had spoken these words, all the fairies disappeared.

The unhappy king immediately ordered all spinning wheels to be destroyed throughout the

through the sky to the palace. The king welcomed her warmly and the fairy praised him for the arrangements he had so far made. Then she thought how lonely the princess would be when she awakened in the old palace in one hundred years time. For a time the good fairy pondered, then suddenly she knew what she must do.

She touched with her magic wand everyone who was in the palace — servants, noblemen, pages, guards, cooks, soldiers, the horses in the stables, the doves and the pigeons, and the princess's little dog, who snuggled at the feet of his mistress. At once they too had fallen into a deep sleep. Even the fire in the hearth and the smoke above the chimneys fell asleep. The king and the queen were left awake to rule over the kingdom.

As soon as the king and queen left the palace, there sprang up around it a dense wood, interlaced with briars, thorns and bracken. It was so tall that only the very tips of the palace towers could be seen. This too was the work of the good fairy, who had now made sure that no living creature would penetrate the wood and disturb the princess.

Time passed. The king and the queen had died long ago. All the people of their generation had also died and the younger ones soon forgot

what had happened in the past. Nobody remembered about the palace in the Sleeping Wood. Some said it was a haunted place, full of ghosts, others that it was the home of the witches. Some believed that a terrible man-eating ogre lived there, who caught and ate little children. Only he would be big enough to get through the enchanted wood.

But when a hundred years had passed, the mysterious wood blossomed with thousands of flowers. Each fragrant bloom held a golden-haired dancing little fairy, who drank from transparent upturned hands the honey-sweet scent. It was this heavenly fragrance which tempted a young prince to the edge of the Sleeping Wood.

'What is that mysterious palace?' he wondered, and advanced towards the thicket. Lo and behold! As soon as he entered the wood, the trees and brambles parted in front of him, and the tiny fairies and birds swept the leaves from under his feet. The prince strode bravely towards the palace and the wood closed again behind him like a magic gate.

An eerie silence as in a tomb reigned in the palace. Wherever he looked the prince saw the still bodies of men and women and animals, looking as if they had all died at the same moment. But when he came close, he saw they were still breathing and in the grip of an enchanted sleep.

'Wake up, you lazybones!' laughed the prince, shaking the guard till his armour rattled.

'It is too soon,' the guard muttered in his sleep and snored noisily.

Thus the prince passed through the whole palace, without being able to wake a single person. Then he entered a golden chamber, where lay the loveliest maiden he had ever seen. In her sleep she looked as beautiful as an angel. And the prince knelt by her bedside and gently kissed her forehead.

Next moment the princess opened her eyes and smiled.

'Is it you, my prince?' she murmured. 'I have waited a long time for you.'

The prince was so overcome with joy and wonder that he could not speak. But the princess, smiling, took his hand in hers and next moment the prince was asking her to be his bride.

The whole palace had come to life with the princess and there was much laughter and rejoicing! Everyone finished whatever they had

been doing a hundred years ago. The servants went about their tasks, the pages paged, the soldiers and the guards sprang to attention, the cooks cooked a magnificent repast, the horses in the stables stamped their hooves and neighed happily, the doves cooed and the princess's little dog barked for joy. And when the palace guard threw open the gates, the dense wood, which for a hundred years had surrounded the palace, had magically vanished as if it had never been.

And the prince married the beautiful princess and the celebrations went on for many days and

nights. No one slept during these rejoicings, for everyone thought they had had enough sleep to last them for the rest of their lives.

One day there arrived at that happy palace a golden coach drawn by fiery dragons. Out of it stepped the good fairy who had saved the life of the beautiful princess. With her she had brought a golden cradle as a present for the prince and princess. And not long after, there lay in that cradle a baby daughter who grew up to be as lovely, as charming and as graceful as her mother, the Sleeping Beauty.

The Wooden Horse and the Painted Jug

Once long ago there was a youth called Shersod who went to work as an apprentice to a carpenter. The old carpenter soon looked upon the hardworking lad as his own son, and it pained him greatly when the boy one day unexpectedly came to bid him goodbye.

'Do not be angry, Master,' Shersod explained, 'but I must go into the world. I have seen in a dream a flock of doves, all of them ash grey, but one, which was white. The doves turned into slender maidens, each beautiful, but one the most beautiful of them all. I shall know no peace till I find her.'

'I shall not prevent you,' replied the wise carpenter, 'but before you leave, I shall teach you what no one else can do.'

Together they set to work and in a few days they had made a wooden horse. He was a joy to behold, with a polished body, eyes of glass, hoofs of ebony. They gave him a golden mane and added a few coloured horsehairs to his tail.

All they had to do now was to give him a saddle.

'Take him as a keepsake,' said the old man, 'for he is a magic horse. When you turn the left ear, he will rise into the clouds. If you turn the right ear, he will return to earth.'

Shersod bade his master farewell and jumped into the saddle. He flew over mountains and lakes, over deserts and barren lands, till he saw far below golden domes and slender minarets. Directing his horse towards the ground, he found himself in a deserted city. An aged woman, a black veil hiding her face, sat before the palace gates, spinning.

'Welcome, my son,' she said. 'The one who comes to my city across the deserts and the mountains, is allowed to become the ruler here. But he must wed the white dove. Tonight, when she flies with her companions to the lake and turns into a beautiful maiden, you must take away her dove robe. Then she will remain with you for ever.'

The happy Shersod hid by the lake. As the sun was sinking, a flock of doves circled over the lake. Except for one white dove, they were all ash grey. The moment they touched the ground, they turned into slender maidens, all beautiful, but one was more beautiful than all the others. Shersod recognized her immediately as the maiden of his dreams. But suddenly a twig cracked under his foot, and in a trice the maidens spread their dove wings and flew away.

'Do not be downhearted,' the old woman comforted the heart-broken Shersod, 'the doves have to land somewhere again. Fly after them, and when you find your maiden, place this ring on her finger. Then she will never fly away again.'

Shersod thanked the old woman and flew on his horse into the clouds. Once more he soared above mountains and barren lands, rivers and lakes, till he saw below a silver palace by a silver lake. Beautiful damsels were sleeping on the shore, their heads resting on their dove robes. In silence Shersod descended to the ground and placed the ring the old woman had given him on the finger of the most beautiful maiden. She woke and said with a smile.

'I know you, Shersod, for I have visited you in your dream. Now I shall be forever yours, but hurry and carry me away from this city, for if you are caught, my father, the cruel shah, will have you executed!'

Holding the maiden in his arms, Shersod turned towards the city.

'Welcome, Shersod,' the aged woman with the black veil spoke. 'You are now the master of my palace. Reign justly and wisely,' she added. With that she disappeared as mysteriously as she had come.

Thus Shersod became the sovereign. He and his wife lived happily and soon a little son was born to them. Shersod then decided to take his dearest ones to visit his aged parents in his old home. On the wooden horse they flew above a vast desert for so long, that with the approach of night, his wife begged to be allowed to rest with her son on the ground. Shersod put them both down in the middle of the barren land, and flew off on his horse to search for fire.

Soon he saw smoke rising beyond a distant mountain, and before long was on his way back, holding a burning branch, which some shepherds had given him. The faster Shersod flew towards his beloved, the greater were the flames which shot from his fiery torch. All at once the golden mane caught fire, then the burnished back, and to Shersod's horror, the wooden

165

boy whispered sadly. 'It is so long since he left us.'

His mother then selected her most beautiful jug and with loving care drew Shersod's face upon it. 'This is your father,' she said. 'Go and wait till he comes.'

From that day the boy sat at the city gate horse fell crashing to the ground and became a handful of ashes. Shersod was alone in the desert, far, far away from his loved ones.

His wife waited and waited in vain, then began to walk aimlessly with her little son in her arms, so that they might not die of starvation in the desert. It was a miracle they escaped alive.

After much suffering they stumbled through the gates of a strange city, where the woman asked for help. And because she did not know where else to go, she decided to stay there. And so that her little son and she would have enough to eat, she learned to paint little jugs, which she and her son, when he grew older, sold by the city gate.

One day her son asked, 'Where is my father? I will go and search for him.'

But his mother begged the boy not to leave her. 'If your father is alive, he must surely be looking for us. One day he must surely wander into our city,' she said to her sad son. 'Look at the faces of all newcomers, so you do not miss him.'

'I do not know my father's face, Mother,' the from morning till night, looking hopefully at the faces of all passers-by. At last one day an exhausted wanderer staggered towards him along the dusty path. His face was wrinkled and worn, his shoulders were bent and his eyes were sadder than a rainfilled sky. The boy looked up from his jug, gazed into the weatherbeaten face of the traveller and exclaimed happily, 'Father! At last you have found us!'

Thus Shersod, who in despair had roamed the world, was at last reunited with his beloved family. One day, however, Shersod asked his son to help him build a wooden horse. 'I have tried it many times during my search for you, but my horses never would fly. Perhaps we will be luckier.'

Before long the horse was completed. His eyes were of glass, his hoofs of ebony, and he had a lovely golden mane. Shersod sat his wife and son in front of him, turned the left ear, and the horse rose into the sky. They flew all the way to their deserted palace. Shersod then went on his horse to fetch his aged parents, and they all lived happily together.

The Real Princess

bedstead. Then she placed twenty mattresses on top of the pea, and twenty featherbeds on top of these.

That was the bed where the princess was to sleep that night. Wearily she climbed to the topmost mattress and lay down.

The next morning they asked how she had slept.

'Very badly!' the princess complained. 'I hardly closed an eye all night! Goodness knows what was in that bed, but I lay on something hard and now I am black and blue all over!'

This proved beyond all doubt that the visitor must truly be a real princess, when she could feel a single pea through twenty mattresses and twenty featherbeds.

The prince married her straightaway of course, and the little pea was placed among the royal treasures. People came from miles around to gaze in wonder at this smallest but most greatly prized possession of their family.

Once there was a prince who wanted only a real princess for his wife. For many years, he searched the world to find such a bride, but he was never satisfied. Each time something was not quite right. Princesses there were in abundance, but according to this very particular prince, they were never good enough and he always had objections.

He returned home at last, a sad man indeed, for he had so very much wanted to find a real princess.

One evening a fierce thunderstorm broke over the palace. Jagged lightning pierced the sky, the thunder crashed and echoed like a thousand drums and the rain cascaded from the heavens like a million rivulets rolled into one. There was such a deluge outside that it was not fit even for a dog to be outside. Suddenly someone knocked at the palace door, and the old king went to open it.

A princess stood there miserable and bedraggled. Water trickled from her hair to her toes. Her clothing was heavy with rain and splashed with mud. In fact she looked like a little scarecrow. Nevertheless she said she was a real princess.

'We'll see about that!' the old queen muttered under her breath, but aloud she said nothing. She went into the bedroom, took all the featherbeds off the bed, and laid a single pea on the

Long, Wide and Hawkeye

Once upon a time there lived an aged king who had an only son. One day, when he felt his strength ebbing away, he sent for his son and said, 'Before I die, I should dearly love to see the face of your wife. Take this key, climb to the top of the tower and from the portraits you will see there, select a bride.'

The prince obeyed. He had never before been in the tower and was therefore curious to see what he could find. The golden key opened iron doors which led into a great hall. There were twelve high windows in the tower and in every one the picture of a maiden with a crown on her head, and each one was lovelier than the last. The prince noticed that a curtain was drawn over one window. Drawing it aside, he saw a beautiful, sad young girl in a white robe, with a crown of pearls on her head. She was the most beautiful of all.

'She is the only one for me,' the prince exclaimed. As he spoke, the maiden smiled, bowed her head, and all the portraits disappeared.

The old king frowned when his son told him of his choice. 'You have chosen unwisely, my boy,' he said. 'That maiden is imprisoned by a wicked wizard in the iron castle. Many have tried to rescue her, but none have returned alive. But if you insist, go out and try your luck!'

The prince bade his father a fond goodbye and set forth to seek his bride. As he rode along, he heard a voice calling him from the bushes, 'Take me into your service! You will not regret it!'

'Who are you and what can you do?' the prince asked.

'They call me Long,' was the answer, 'and I live up to my name.' With that a strange lean fellow stretched himself till he reached the very tip of the tallest fir tree, and handed the prince a bird's nest.

'I would be more grateful if you could tell me the quickest way out of this wood,' the prince remarked with a smile. Long stretched himself again till he was taller than the highest tree. 'Follow me!' he cried, each stride stretching the

width of a field. The prince on his mount could hardly keep up with him. Soon they were out of the wood.

'Here comes my friend Wide! You should hire him too, sir. I shall bring him to you!' In three strides Long reached his friend, put him on his shoulders and was back again. The prince was looking at a fat little fellow, as round as a barrel.

'Who are you and what can you do?' asked the prince.

'My name is Wide and I can grow wider and wider,' the stranger replied and, to demonstrate, he began to swell to such an enormous size that he resembled a bulging mountain. Long and the prince barely managed to get out of the way in time. Wide then shrank to his normal size. The prince agreed to take him into his service, and on they travelled till they came to a heap of rocks. There they met a man whose eyes were covered with a handkerchief.

'Sir,' said Long, 'this is another friend of mine. It will pay you to employ him too.'

'Why do you keep your eyes bandaged? Surely you cannot see the way?' the prince asked.

But the newcomer replied, 'I have to keep my eyes covered, because I see too well! They call me Hawkeye.' To demonstrate what he could do, he took off the handkerchief and stared at the rock opposite. The rock straight away be-

gan to crumble till it was but a heap of sand and among the sand fragments of gold glittered in the sun.

'You're an invaluable fellow!' exclaimed the prince. 'But I should prefer you to look and see how far it is to the iron castle, and what my bride is doing!'

Hawkeye gazed into the distance and said, 'In a high tower, behind bars, guarded by the wicked wizard is your princess. On your own it would take you over a year to reach her. With us you will be there before nightfall.'

Hawkeye spoke the truth. With the aid of the three friends, all obstacles were conquered. Long stepped over mountains, Wide drank up lakes, and Hawkeye burned paths through rocks. As the sun went down, they were crossing the drawbridge into the iron castle. Behind them the drawbridge closed with a noise like thunder. All around were noblemen and servants, but not one of them moved. They had all been turned to stone by the evil magic of the wizard, in the middle of whatever they had been doing. One had just tripped, and had not quite reached the floor. Another was yawning, and the head cook was about to box the ears of the kitchen boy. Even trees and flowers were of stone. The prince and his friends entered a dining room, where dinner was laid, almost as if they were expected. Nobody came, and as they were very hungry, they sat down and began to eat.

Suddenly the door flew open and the wizard stood there. He wore a long black robe and his beard flowed down to the floor. Instead of a belt he wore three iron bands round his waist.

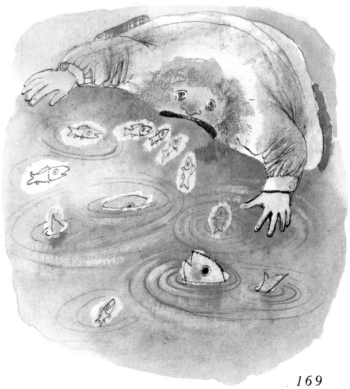

By the hand he held the lovely sad maiden with the crown of pearls on her head, the maiden whom the prince had last seen in the portrait.

The wizard eyed them with an evil glance. 'I know why you have come!' he cried. 'You can take your princess, if for three nights you can guard her so well that I shall not be able to steal her back. If you fail, you will all be turned to stone.'

The wizard disappeared, after leading the princess to a chair. The prince spoke to her, trying to make her reply and smile, but she remained still and silent as if made of marble.

The prince was determined not to close an eye during the following night. Just to make doubly sure, his friend Long wound himself like a rope round the room, then Wide puffed himself up till he covered the whole door, and Hawkeye stood on guard in the centre of the room. But in a moment they all began to doze, and when just before dawn they awoke, the princess was gone.

'Do not worry, sir,' Hawkeye cheered the prince, 'I can see her. A hundred miles from here is a deep forest, and in the middle of it there is an oak tree with an acorn on top of it. Our princess is that acorn.'

With Hawkeye on his shoulders, Long strode out, each step ten miles. It was not long before they were back with the acorn and the moment the prince dropped it on the floor, the acorn turned into the princess. The sun was just rising as the wizard burst into the room. He was furious to see the princess and one of the iron bars round his waist snapped and thundered to the floor. He seized the princess and led her away.

The following night everything happened as before. Try as they might, the prince and his companions could not keep awake. It seemed that some force made them fall asleep, and when they awoke just before dawn, they found the maiden had gone.

But Hawkeye rubbed his eyes and cried, 'Yes, I see her! Two hundred miles from here lies a mountain and in it, upon a rock, is a jewel. She is that jewel. Do not worry, we will soon have her back again.'

Long stretched himself out into the clouds, and with Hawkeye on his shoulders, strode out, each step twenty miles. When they reached the mountain, it turned with the rock to dust under Hawkeye's stare.

Soon they were back with the beautiful jewel. The prince dropped it on the floor just in time, for the wizard burst into the room as the jewel turned into the princess. The furious wizard terribly frowned, and the second iron bar round his waist snapped and thundered to the floor. Muttering under his breath, the wizard again led the princess away.

That night, when he set the maiden in the chair once more, he chuckled. 'We shall see who will win this time!'

The prince and his friends were determined to walk about all night, but they fell asleep as they walked. Once again the maiden disappeared. Hawkeye saw her, just before daybreak. 'Three hundred miles from here is a black sea, and right at the bottom lies a little shell holding a gold ring. She is that ring. Let me take Wide with me today, I shall need his help.'

Long, with both his friends on his back, strode out, each step thirty miles. By the black sea, though Long stretched his arm as far as it would go, he could not reach the bottom. So Wide took a deep breath, and began to drink up the ocean, and soon the sea was so shallow that Long could pick up the shell and take out the gold ring. But as Wide was so heavy with all that water in his stomach, Long dropped him. So much water spilled out from his mouth that they almost drowned in it.

The sun was already rising, and the wizard was striding into the empty room, laughing victoriously, when Long threw the gold ring from afar through the window, shattering the glass. The ring fell to the floor, turned into princess, and the wizard, cursing loudly, turned into a crow, as the last iron band burst open. As the crow flew away through the shattered window, the whole castle came to life. The one who had tripped fell right on to his nose, the kitchen boy got his box on the ear from the cook and everyone finished what they had been doing.

When the prince returned home with his bride, his old father cried with joy, and soon a merry wedding was held. The prince begged Long, Wide and Hawkeye to stay with him, but they refused. They did not fancy an idle life, and soon were off again. They are still wandering about the world, helping people when they can.

The Two Little Cottages

There once was a little cottage made of salt. It gleamed and glittered like a sparkling mirror. A salty grandfather and a sugary grandmother lived inside. Sometimes they loved each other, sometimes they hated each other; they quarrelled, they made up, just like lots of people do.

One day the couple had an awful argument. Grandfather picked up a big salty stick and chased grandmother out of the cottage.

'Go and build yourself a cottage of clay, you sugary old woman,' he raved. The sugary grandmother went away, weeping, but not too much, in case her sugary cheeks should melt. She built a clay cottage. It was comfortable but she was lonely. She thought of the salty grandfather, and sighed and sighed. One day she gathered courage and knocked on the door of his salt cottage.

'Grandfather, dear, give me a little salt for my soup,' she begged. Grandfather grasped the big salty stick instead and chased her from his doorstep.

'Go where you have come from, you pestering old Grandmother!' he cried. 'If you have no salt, you can sweeten your soup with sugar.' The sugary grandmother went home, weeping, but only a little bit, in case her sugary cheeks would be washed away. But as she became sadder and sadder as time passed, she asked the sky to cry instead of her.

As soon as she asked, it started to rain. It poured and poured, the rain just flowed from the skies. And grandfather's beautiful shimmering salt cottage was washed away. The salty grandfather ran for all he was worth to the grandmother in her clay cottage.

'Let me in, Grandmother,' he begged, peering through the window, 'or I will melt in the rain.'

'I do not care!' snapped the grandmother. 'When I asked you for salt, you took the stick to me. Go away, and give me peace. I want nothing to do with you.'

But grandfather pleaded so nicely, begging for kindness, apologizing for everything, that sugary grandmother's heart melted, and she let him into her clay cottage. Then they gave one another a big sweet and salty kiss. But as grandfather was soaking wet, they stuck to each other, and if they had not eventually dried, they would still be stuck today. After that day salty grandfather had a sugary mouth and sugary grandmother had a salty mouth. No longer did they argue, and quarrel over silly little things, but like true sweethearts they loved each other for the rest of their lives.

Cook, Pot, Cook.' !

In a village at the edge of a forest, there lived a poor widow, who had an only daughter. They lived on what the forest gave them. In winter they gathered firewood, in summer they collected berries.

One bright summer's day the daughter picked up the basket and a piece of black bread, and went to gather wild raspberries in the forest. All at once she met an old woman. In her hand she held a little pot, and she begged, 'Oh, my dear child, I have not eaten since yesterday. Would you be so kind as to give me a small piece of your bread?'

'You are welcome to the whole slice,' the girl replied. 'I only hope it won't be hard for you.'

'The Lord will reward you,' replied the old woman. 'As you have been so kind, please take my little pot. If at home you put it on the table and say, "Cook, pot, cook!" you will have as much sweet gruel as you want. All you have to do then is to say, "Enough, pot, enough," and the pot will stop cooking. But don't forget what you must say!' the old lady reminded her, then disappeared.

When she went home, the daughter related everything to her mother. She then placed the little pot on the table and said, 'Cook, pot, cook!'

Lovely sweet gruel rose up in the pot, and soon was right up to the rim. The daughter then said, 'Enough, pot, enough!' And at once the pot stopped cooking, and mother and daughter sat down to eat their fill of the sweet gruel. How delicious it tasted!

The next day the daughter went to the forest to pick wild strawberries. After a time her mother grew impatient and hungry so she said to the little pot, 'Cook, pot, cook!' She ran to the kitchen for a plate and a spoon, and was quite taken aback on her return, for the gruel was spilling onto the table and onto the floor. In her fright the woman forgot the words she should say. She tried to stop the flow with a lid, but it was no use. By then the gruel was pouring through the door and windows like a flood. It flowed on into the village square. The mother only just managed to jump out of its way. Goodness knows how it would all have ended, had not the daughter returned just then and cried, 'Enough, pot, enough!'

By then there was such a mountain of gruel in the village square that the farmers could not drive through. In the end they had to sup their way to the other side, and they did not eat again for seven days and seven nights.

173

The Magic Candelabra

A meagre hut once stood at the outskirts of a great city. It was the home of a poor widow and her son Abdullah. One day an aged, sick man, a travelling sage, passed by, dragging himself along the dusty road, his eyes sunken with fatigue and fever. The widow felt pity for the sick old man, and though she herself could not keep hunger from her door, she offered the dervish shelter till he was well again. Thankfully, the old man accepted, and when, after some time, his strength returned, he bade her a grateful goodbye.

'Good woman, I have seen your poverty, I have heard your whispered prayers. I shall repay your kindness. If you trust me, place your son Abdullah in my safe keeping! On my journey through the world I shall teach him wisdom and the meaning of truth. If he heeds my words, he will return to you as a noble, learned man.'

The woman gladly agreed, said farewell to her son and told him to do all that the wise man said. Abdullah roamed the world with the old dervish. Days and months passed, and all the time the sage cared for the boy as if he were his own son. He taught him kindness, truth, and modesty. One day they came to towering rocks.

'We have reached the end of our journey together, Abdullah,' the sage announced. 'I cannot give you anything else, for you have learned all the wisdom within my head and my heart. Now you will have to use what I have taught you. Before we part, prove your gratefulness, as I once did to your mother! These rocks hide an underground cave, which is full of fabulous riches. I shall show you the way down, but it is too narrow for me to pass. All I ask in return

for my love and care of you is that you fetch from the cave an old candelabra with twelve candle-holders. But do not touch anything else you may see. Remember that wisdom, modesty and love are the greatest human treasures.'

Abdullah swore his undying devotion and gratitude to the old man. Then the dervish lit a small flame and tossed into it a handful of strange herbs which he carried in his worn bag. He chanted some magic formulae, the words of which even Abdullah could not understand. Suddenly thick smoke rose from the flame, turning first yellow, then green, then purple, like a wizard's cloak. When the smoke dispersed, there was an opening in the cave, so narrow, that Abdullah could barely squeeze through it. The old man handed a flaming torch to him, and the boy bravely descended to the heart of the earth.

Following a twisting path, he came to an iron door. Without hesitating, he turned the heavy handle, and was met by such a blinding glare that he was forced to close his eyes. When he opened them again, he could hardly believe what he saw. The whole cave was filled with magnificent, coloured frescoes, far more beautiful than the boy had seen anywhere on his journey with the old sage. Then the light of his torch showed him heaps of gold and diamonds, surrounded by cedar chests, overflowing with strings of glittering pearls. He walked through a gleaming land of rubies and magnificent emeralds, where everything shimmered like the stars in the midnight sky.

The sight of so much rich splendour aroused a yearning for wealth in Abdullah's mind. Forgetting the sage's teaching, he was soon up to his elbows in these fairytale riches. Quickly, greedily, he stuffed his shirt with gold and jewels, till he could scarcely stand up with the weight of all the treasures.

Only then did Abdullah remember the old man's request. Looking round the cave, he saw in a corner an old iron candelabra, so battered and so rusty, that the boy sneered scornfully. But he did not dare disappoint his benefactor and he stretched his arm to take it. The moment his hand touched the cool metal, there was a crack of thunder, as if the earth itself was being torn apart, and the passage through the rock closed abruptly. Abdullah was imprisoned in the heart of the earth. At long last he recalled the sage's words of warning, and in terror he cried for his mercy and his help, but it was in vain. The torch was flickering and Abdullah felt as if death was near. Then suddenly he noticed

a gleam of light above his head. With his remaining strength he climbed to the roof of the cave and discovered a tiny opening, through which he escaped into sunlight.

The moment Abdullah realized he was safe, all his good resolutions flew from his head, and he hastened home with his new wealth. He did not even glance back to see if the poor sage was still waiting, so afraid was he that he would have to share his spoils.

Imagine his surprise, when the roofs of his

was left was the hideous candelabra, as cold as the old man's accusing eyes. Too late, Abdullah regretted his greed. He knew this to be the sage's revenge for his ingratitude. After that day the boy often sat near the old candelabra, pondering on the uselessness of wealth.

One day he took the notion to light the twelve candles in the candle-holder. No sooner were they lit than he and his mother cried out in terror. In the flames there appeared the shapes of twelve ancient dervishes and they began an eerie dance, turning and spinning on the tips of the flames like silvery eels. When the dance ended, each of them tossed a small shiny coin at Abdullah's feet. The candles then went out and the apparitions disappeared.

'So this is the secret of the candelabra,' Abdullah thought. 'No wonder the old sage wanted to have it so badly.' Thanks to the magic candle-holder, Abdullah and his mother no longer feared poverty.

Yet as time passed, Abdullah once again became obsessed by greed. He remembered with longing the incredible riches in the underground cave, and so he decided one day to go and seek out the old sage in his distant home.

'If I give him the candelabra he so desired, he may let me enter the rock and load myself with treasures. This time the old man will be grateful, so my wealth should not melt away,' he reasoned, as he set off.

After a long journey he came to a fine city. Upon enquiring the way to the home of the old sage, he was shown a fine palace, which glistened against the sky like the rising sun. Abdullah was speechless.

native village suddenly appeared before him! It was as if some magic hand had carried him half-way across the world. No words can describe his mother's joy, when after so many lonely years she was reunited with her beloved son. Abdullah proudly showed off his wealth and told her of the adventures he had had on his travels. But he kept silent about the way he had deceived the aged dervish.

'This treasure must be the old man's reward for your loyalty and courage,' his mother cried joyfully. But her joy was shortlived. For as soon as Abdullah poured all the spoils onto the table, the gold and the jewels melted away before their horrified eyes like drops of rain. All that

'Can this be the home of the impoverished old man, my teacher?' he muttered to himself. Just then the well-remembered old man came out of the palace, dressed in a magnificent robe. The youth fell face down on the ground, not daring to raise his eyes. The sage looked at him sternly and beckoned Abdullah to follow him into the palace. Then Abdullah related humbly how much he had had to suffer in order to return the iron candelabra to its owner.

The dervish frowned. 'Do not pretend that respect and gratitude has led you to me,' he said. 'I know you were driven here by greed. Had you known what wealth the iron candelabra holds, you would not have come to me.' Having spoken, the old man lit the twelve candles in the holders, and when the dancing dervishes appeared, he raised a thick stick and beat their backs with all his might. In the middle of their dance, the dervishes suddenly disintegrated into twelve piles of gold and jewels.

'This is the true secret of the candelabra,' smiled the old man. 'I do not want more riches, but I should like to amuse my guests with its magic. You do not deserve my gratitude, yet I shall reward you.'

And the sage handed Abdullah twelve gold keys, telling him to take out of his treasury a chestful of gold and jewels, as much as he could carry. 'But you are to leave the iron candelabrá in the twelfth room,' he added.

When the greedy Abdullah entered the rooms, he could not believe his eyes. His grasping hands stuffed the chest with gold and precious stones, magnificent robes and glittering pearls. The last room was empty. Abdullah was about to leave the old man's candelabra there, when he heard the voice of temptation. 'Should I give up the most valuable object just for an old man's amusement?' he pondered. And the ungrateful youth hid the iron candelabra at the bottom of the chest, bade the sage a hasty farewell and hurried home.

Once in the house, he placed the candelabra on the table and lit the candles. The moment the dancing dervishes appeared, he beat them with a heavy stick. But what was this? Instead of turning into piles of gold and jewels, they took truncheons from their beards and pummelled Abdullah till he was black and blue all over and begging for mercy. Suddenly they vanished like puffs of smoke, and all the treasures and the magic candelabra vanished too. And, thanks to Abdullah, no one ever saw them again.

Lini the Lost Prince

Once upon a time there was a handsome prince called Lini, who like most princes, lived in a palace. A lovely maiden named Signy lived next door to the palace, in a poor, tumbledown little cottage. Poor little Signy owned nothing. She did not even have a hole in her stocking for she had not a stocking, nor a flea in her bed, for she had no bed — in short, she had nothing.

Prince Lini and little Signy argued continually over the garden wall. Once it was over who was the shortest, then who was the tallest, next who had more freckles, which berries were sweetest. And so it went on. They argued so much that they fell in love.

One morning Prince Lini went hunting and disappeared.

The king immediately announced that Prince Lini must return to the palace at once, otherwise he would disinherit him. But day followed day and there was still no sign of the prince. At last the king announced that he would give half his kingdom to anyone who would bring the prince home.

Signy heard this over the garden wall and she said, 'I shall bring him home, because now I have nobody to argue with!' And she went off.

Signy walked and walked till she came to a huge icy cave, and the walls were hung with gold and silver icicles. There was a gold bed and on the headboard white swans were drawn, and underneath was a magic inscription. Prince Lini lay fast asleep in the gold bed. Next moment there was the sound of heavy footsteps, and two ogresses burst into the cave. Signy barely had time to hide behind a large gold icicle.

The ogresses stepped up to the bed and cried, 'Sing, swans, sing! Let your voices ring and bring back the prince from his deep sleep!'

The swans sang and the prince awoke. 'Which one of us will you marry?' the two ogresses screeched. But the prince only pulled a face at both of them. 'Sing, swans, sing, and put the prince back into a deep sleep!' The swans sang and the prince again lay as if dead.

As soon as the ogresses left the cave, Signy stepped up to the bed and ordered the swans to rouse her dear prince. The moment they began to sing, the prince opened his eyes and embraced Signy. Then he related how the hideous ogresses had kidnapped him in the forest, telling him that he must marry one of them.

Signy thought for a moment or two, then said, 'When the ogresses return, say you will do as they ask, on condition that they tell you what is written above your bed, and where they go when they leave this cave.' Prince Lini agreed, and Signy ordered the swans to put him back to sleep again and she went back to hide.

Before long the ogresses returned. Again they cried, 'Sing, swans, sing! Let your voices ring and bring back the prince from his deep sleep!'

The moment the prince opened his eyes, he told them he had changed his mind, that if they explained the writing on the headboard and confessed where they went when they left the cave, he would marry one of them.

The ogresses were delighted and straightaway told him the secret of the inscription. 'Take me where I wish to go, little swan bed,' they read. Then they confided that each day they went into the forest to play with the golden egg of life. 'If someone broke that egg, we would die,' they whispered. Then they sent the prince to sleep again and left the cave.

Signy quickly brought him back to life, sat on his bed and cried, 'Take us into the forest, little swan bed!' And in the twinkling of an eye they were there. They climbed to the top of a high tree, and Prince Lini cut a strong lance from a thick branch.

Quite soon the ogresses appeared and at the foot of the tree where Lini and Signy were perched, started playing ball with the golden egg. Lini took aim, down flew the lance, and next moment the egg was shattered. The ogresses slumped down and were no more.

Lini and Signy ran back to the cave, filled their pockets with gold and silver icicles, then asked the little bed to take them home.

There was great rejoicing when they returned to the palace, alive and well. The king, true to his promise gave Signy half the kingdom.

What a wedding there was! Prince Lini and Signy enjoyed every minute — for throughout the celebrations they argued — who was the shortest, who was the longest, who had more freckles, which berries were sweetest and so it went on and on and on and on ...

The Gingerbread House

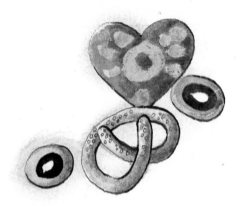

Once, long ago, a little cottage stood on the edge of a dense forest. It was the home of a poor woodcutter, his wife and two children, Hansel and Gretel. They loved one another dearly, but this did not help them in their poverty. They grew poorer day by day and sometimes as there was not even a crust of bread to eat, the children would cry themselves to sleep at night.

Once, when their mother thought the children were asleep, she said,

'Dear husband, I cannot watch them suffer any longer. Tomorrow we shall take the children into the depths of the forest and abandon them

there. Perhaps they will find the way to better things. If not, it would be kinder that they should fall into eternal sleep in the forest, than die slowly of hunger before our very eyes.'

At first the woodcutter would not hear of this, but eventually, with a heavy heart, he agreed. The unhappy parents had not realized they had been overheard. Gretel was sobbing under the bed covers, clutching Hansel tightly round the neck.

'What will become of us, brother?' she cried, and Hansel consoled her. 'Do not cry, Gretel, I shall think of something.'

When the parents fell asleep, Hansel crept on tiptoe out of the cottage and filled his pockets with pebbles from the brook. Then he crept back into bed and stroked his sister's head until sleep closed her eyes.

At daybreak, their mother cut each child a slice of bread, as thin as a cobweb, and told them both to get ready to go into the forest to gather wood. The parents and children walked further and further into the forest. The trees grew higher and higher, the forest darkened and in the topmost branches the wind whistled and whined. Gretel was near to tears, but Hansel whistled merrily to hide his fears, and kept glancing behind him. Whenever he glanced

round, he dropped a pebble on the ground.

'Why are you lagging behind?' his mother scolded him. Hansel's excuse was always the same: he wanted to know if their cottage chimney was still in sight.

'When will our cottage be out of sight?' the mother said. 'Stop dawdling and hurry!' They came to the darkest section of the forest, from which no paths led.

himself bitterly for deserting them in the forest. But his wife only frowned. When the children had been put to bed, she insisted.

'Tomorrow we will take them further still into the forest, so that they will not be able to find the way back. There is only one piece of dry bread left in the bin. Do you want your children to die of hunger in our arms? It will be kinder for the dark forest to take them. It will be easier

Their mother now said, 'Wait for us here! I am going to help your father cut firewood in the clearing. You can pick berries till we return!' The woodcutter lit the children a little fire, and then left with his wife. The children obediently picked berries.

'Maybe our parents will think better of it,' they hoped, particularly as from the nearby clearing came the echoes of a tree being felled. But when their jugs were full and darkness was falling and their parents still had not returned, the children followed the sound. All they found in the clearing was a wooden mallet tied to a tree. The strong wind was knocking the mallet against it, making sounds as if the tree was being cut down. There was no sign of their parents. Gretel started to weep.

'Please don't cry,' Hansel pleaded. 'I shall take you home, never fear.' Suddenly the moon came out, and the pebbles he had strewn along the way gleamed like jewels in the darkness. Hansel took Gretel by the hand and followed the shining pebble trail to their cottage. Their father joyfully embraced them, for he was reproaching

for us two to manage somehow.'

The woodcutter could not soften her heart, and at last agreed to her plan. But under the covers, the children had again heard their conversation, and as soon as their parents fell asleep, Hansel went to fetch more pebbles. But alas! This time the doors were locked.

'Don't be afraid,' Hansel comforted his tearful sister. 'When we go into the forest, we shall leave a trail of breadcrumbs!' And this is what they did, and their parents noticed nothing. Again they were abandoned in the depths of the forest, but when the children looked for the trail of crumbs, there was not a crumb to be seen. The birds of the forest had eaten every one. Poor Hansel and Gretel were completely lost and alone in the darkness of the black, eerie forest. The wind moaned in the branches, the owls screeched, and trembling with fear, Hansel and Gretel lay down in the moss, clutching each other tightly.

When the sun rose in the morning, the world seemed a happier place and the children felt happier too. A lovely white bird appeared on

'I'll tell you what we shall do, Gretel,' Hansel said. 'I'll climb onto the roof and break off a little marzipan. You can take a little piece of window frame. Nobody will notice.'

In a trice he was on the roof, picking off a piece of gingerbread here, a piece of marzipan there. Suddenly a hideous old hag peered out of the window.

'Who is helping himself to my gingerbread and my marzipan?', she croaked.

'The breeze, Grandmother, the breeze,' Gretel replied in a faint voice, hiding quickly behind a big toadstool. The old hag disappeared and the children went on eating. But suddenly there she was, on the doorstep, glaring at them with her shortsighted eyes, threatening them with a stick.

'What a thing to do, to eat an old woman's house before her very eyes,' she stormed, scowling at Hansel and Gretel. Then suddenly she smiled, and said, 'Come on in, and don't be afraid. You can have as many sweet things as you can eat. You poor little creatures, you must be starving!'

The children were quite taken in by her kindness, and they followed her into the house. But once inside, the old hag grasped Hansel and pushed him into a wooden cage!

'Thank you, my servant bird,' she called through the window to the white bird, 'thank you for bringing me such a delicacy. I cannot remember when I had anything so tasty to eat!'

Hansel and Gretel were at the mercy of a wicked old witch, who lived on little children, and the white bird was her servant. As soon as the old hag had locked Hansel in the cage she turned on poor Gretel.

'You are to keep my house clean and tidy and feed your little brother. When he is fattened up, I shall roast him in my oven!'

a branch above. He sang so joyfully, and fluttered from bush to bush, as if inviting the children to follow him. So the children walked behind him, and all at once came upon a little house. But this was no ordinary house. It was made entirely of cakes and buns and gingerbread hearts, with a marzipan roof, nut-pastry window frames, crystal sugar window panes and nuts, raisins and sweets were scattered everywhere. Candyfloss smoke poured from the chimney and fresh cream filled the well. At the sight, the hungry children became hungrier and hungrier.

And so poor, unhappy Gretel was forced to serve the old witch, and feed Hansel with the tastiest goodies. But she herself was not allowed to taste a single raisin.

'Please don't eat so much,' she begged her brother, 'or that wicked witch will roast you.' But Hansel loved sweet things, and he could not resist eating everything up, especially the gingerbread. He grew fatter and fatter, till he was almost too big for the cage.

Every morning the old hag came to the cage and said, 'Give me your little finger, so I can see whether you are plump enough!' And each morning Hansel pushed out an old gnawed bone. The shortsighted witch bit into it and frowned, 'Well I never! He eats as if he has a bottomless stomach, and yet he is still no better than skin and bones!'

After a time, the old hag muttered that she had waited long enough. 'Fat or thin,' she said to Gretel, 'tomorrow I shall have him roasted for my dinner!'

The next morning Gretel had to light the oven. When it was red hot, the witch brought a huge spade, set Hansel on it, and ordered Gretel to open the oven door. But Hansel rolled off the spade.

'Can't you sit on it properly?' snapped the witch crossly.

'No, I can't. I have never sat on a spade before and I've never been roasted before,' Hansel said. 'Please show me how it is done.'

Without thinking, the old hag sat on the spade and that was just what the children were waiting for. They gripped the spade and pushed the witch into the oven. In a few minutes all that was left of the hag was a cloud of black smoke. The gingerbread house fell to the ground and turned into a heap of gold and jewels.

Hansel was a little sad to lose the lovely gingerbread, but Gretel with cries of joy quickly filled her apron with as much treasure as it would hold, and the children then set off to find their way home.

The path led them to the shore of a wide lake. How were they to get across? But Hansel found a sweet nut in his pocket. He offered it to a swan, and in return the swan carried them to the other side.

At last they saw their cottage and the children raced the last few steps. What a welcome they had. Their parents could not forgive themselves for leaving the children in the forest. They had not slept since that day. Their mother begged forgiveness and promised never to forsake them again.

But thanks to Gretel's apronful of treasure, they were never poor or hungry again and only now and then Hansel would sigh, as he thought longingly of the witch's lovely gingerbread.

Sikulume and the Seven Brothers

Once upon a time there lived in Africa a chief, who had eight sons. The youngest whose name was Sikulume was still a boy when one day all seven of his older brothers died in battle, struck down by the magic arrows of their enemy. From that time, Sikulume was dumb, as if his tongue had turned to wood. The chief called on all witchdoctors, asking them to return words to his son's mouth, but they tried in vain to cure him.

Time passed, when one day a wise old man came to the chief and said, 'Seven strange birds have flown to our village. They are different from other birds, for they sing with human voices. You lost seven brave sons in battle when magic arrows took their lives away. Therefore have these birds caught; let their human song cheer you in your grief.'

The following day the chief sent seven youths to catch with nets the strange birds. Sikulume, his son, was among them. The youths stalked the birds for six long days and nights, trudging along through thorny, dense thicket, till at last, on the seventh day, they managed to trap them. At that very moment Sikulume cried, 'Thank you with all my heart for coming, brother birds!' Speech had miraculously returned to his mouth.

It was evening by then, and as the youths were far away from home, they lay down in the bushes to sleep. Only Sikulume stayed awake to guard against the lions. When midnight approached, the thundering voice of a fearsome, man-eating ogre boomed from the bushes.

'Just look at all this lovely, tender meat! I must fetch my brothers, and we can have a feast!'

Sikulume was the only one to hear, and the minute the giant left, he woke his companions and helter skelter, they took to their heels. Sikulume suddenly remembered the bird he had trapped in the bushes. He hastened back to save him. The ogres were already there, arguing with the brother who had fetched them for nothing.

'You have tricked us! There is no one here,' they fumed. 'For that we will eat you!'

Sikulume sneaked past them like a mouse snatched up his net and ran for his life. But the giants saw him and ran after him, making the earth tremble. 'We will catch you,' they roared.

Sikulume ran on as fast his legs would carry him, till he came to an old hut. An aged woman sat outside it holding a pan of butter in her lap.

'Please hide me, grandmother,' the boy pleaded. 'Man-eating giants are after me.'

The old woman shook her head and said, 'Save you? What nonsense, my boy! Those ogres would swallow us both, and my cottage too. But take this pan of butter. When the ogres have almost caught up with you, spread butter over a boulder behind you. Then run on, and do not look back!'

As soon as Sikulume held the pan of butter, the giants were upon him. 'We have you now!' they roared, making the boy's hair stand on end.

But the brave Sikulume quickly smeared a huge boulder with the butter and flew like the wind. The giants started fighting over the buttered boulder. The biggest ogre won and swallowed the boulder in one gulp. With such a weight in his stomach it was now not easy for a giant like him to run. So he stayed behind and went to sleep.

Sikulume used the butter over and over again, but soon it was all gone and there was still one remaining ogre hot on his heels, one arm outstretched to capture him. The clever Sikulume then untied a bright scarf from round his waist, and let it float off in the wind. The ogre followed the scarf and Sikulume raced on and on till he caught up with his companions. Quickly he told them what had happened, and hurried them on.

The ogre was following them again, when they met a dwarf. 'Have no fear,' he nodded to them, 'I do not like those giants. I shall hide you in this rock.' The dwarf knocked once and the rock opened and swallowed up the boys. Seeing this, the ogre flew into a fearsome rage, biting and gnawing at the rock, till he had broken all his teeth. Furious with anger and shame, the ogre retreated.

The youths thanked the dwarf for saving their lives, and hastened on to their village. On the outskirts they threw the birds to the ground and, lo and behold, they turned into Sikulume's seven dear brothers! All the youths embraced joyfully, and went off to their huts. But the village was deserted, except for one terrified woman.

'I had gone to the well, when Inabulele the water monster rose out of the river and swallowed every single soul in the village,' she sobbed.

Armed with a spear, Sikulume ran to the river bank and cried, 'Come and get me too, hideous Inabulele!'

The river swirled and rose and Inabulele's head appeared with mouth agape. In one gulp Sikulume was gone.

The monster's stomach was crowded with villagers, their cows and horses. They were astonished to see Sikulume and he told them the story of his adventures. Then they wanted to know if the rains had come.

'We shall soon see,' Sikulume replied, and taking his spear he slit the monster's stomach and led out all the people and their beasts to the river bank.

'The rains have come indeed,' they all cried gladly and happily to be alive and went off to their huts. Their chief was happiest of all, for now he was reunited with all eight of his beloved sons.

The Farmer
and the Bear

An old bear once lived in a hollow tree in a forest. This bear was so enormous, that when he wanted to scratch behind his ears, he had to stand on tiptoe to reach. One morning this great bear woke up very hungry and began to sniff about for something good to eat. As he prowled about, he saw a poor young farmer gathering beet at the edge of the forest. A very fine crop of beet it was too!

'Look there,' muttered the bear to himself, his tongue shooting out so greedily it touched his ears. 'That crop must be really good, since that farmer is working so hard. I certainly must taste those beets!' Baring his fangs, the bear pounced from the bushes, growling and snarling, 'Give me your crop, or I'll eat you up!'

The young fellow gaped as if struck by lightning. He had never seen such a monstrous creature, had never seen such a thick coat of fur, such cruel fangs, such menacing claws! Could this be the Devil himself?

But that young farmer was no coward. Recovering from his shock, he wiped his nose on his sleeve and said, 'Help yourself, Bear. I don't care! But if I were you, I'd leave some for the farmer, so that he doesn't die of hunger. Otherwise who would work the field to give you the next crop? You would be wiser to share with me. If you take everything that grows above the ground, I'll make do with the roots.'

This plan appealed to the bear. The wily farmer then gathered the beet, leaving only the leaves for the bear. What a surprise the bear had. As his great teeth crunched the leaves he thought he was biting into a lemon. He ranted and raved about the way he had been tricked, and the young farmer was careful to keep well out of his way.

Some time later the young farmer was reaping corn near the forest, when suddenly the bear appeared again! There he stood, licking his lips, baring his fangs, roaring with rage.

'This time I'll take everything, you rascal!' he growled menacingly. 'This time you won't swindle me!'

'Take what you like, Bear. Eat it all. I don't

care!' the farmer said with a shrug of the shoulders. 'But what good will it do you, if I die of hunger this winter? Are you going to plough the field in the spring? Take my advice, and share with me. But this time you can choose which half you want. Then you can't accuse me of swindling you again.'

'Very well,' agreed the bear, already gloating over his victory. 'You take what grows above the ground, I'll keep what grows under it.'

'Whatever you say,' the farmer said, smiling under his whiskers. And he cut the corn, stacked it in his barn, and all that was left for the bear was the stubble. It stung his tongue like the sting of a wasp. The bear crashed through the forest, ranting and raving on his way to cool his stinging, greedy tongue and snout in the well. 'Just wait, you sly farmer, I'll get the better of you yet,' he threatened.

Before long the farmer went into the forest for firewood. With him he took his billygoat, so that it could graze in the bushes. But before the farmer could swing his axe, the bear stood before him, determined to eat up the farmer there and then.

'My last hour has come,' muttered the horrified fellow, 'for even if the bear agreed to take only half of me, what good would half of my body be to me! I couldn't even light a pipe!'

As he was thus lamenting, the billygoat stuck its head out of the bushes and bleated.

'What is that?' the bear wondered aloud. 'I have never before seen such a strange creature.'

'Pay no attention to him,' the sly young man replied. 'That is only my friend, the fearsome killer and hunter of bears. He has just asked me what sort of a tree you are, so big and strange and hairy, and why don't I cut you down, load you on my cart and tie you up, so that you won't fall off on the way home.'

'Hurry, hurry, do as he says, before he finds out I am a bear,' the great cowardly beast pleaded, shaking with fear.

'Since it is your own idea and you seem to be serious, I agree,' said the artful farmer.

He pushed the bear over, loaded him on the cart and tied him down securely.

The whole village cheered when they saw the farmer and his cart. 'What a catch!' they cried and everyone gave the greedy bear such a hiding that he remembered it for the rest of his life.

Since that day he has never dared to show his snout outside the forest. What if that fearsome horned killer of bears was waiting for him!

As for the farmer? Often he tells his grandchildren the story of the billygoat who nearly frightened the great cowardly bear to death.

Ali Baba
and the
Forty Thieves

There were once two brothers, Cassim and Ali Baba, who lived in the land of Persia. Cassim, the eldest, was a miser who amassed great wealth, whereas the kind and honest Ali Baba was the poorest of the poor. Good fortune seemed always to pass him by, no matter how hard he worked. In the end all Ali Baba possessed was a good wife, the roof over his head, a skinny donkey and the black slave, Morgiana. They barely managed to scrape a living.

One day Ali Baba summoned up his courage and went to see his brother Cassim. 'Please help me, good Cassim,' he begged, 'give me at least a handful of flour and a few sesame seeds, so that we do not die of hunger.'

But Cassim dismissed him curtly. 'Leave me alone, Ali Baba. I have nothing to spare! If you want to eat, then sell your slave, Morgiana. She should fetch a good price.'

'How can I do that?' cried the horrified Ali Baba. 'My wife and I love her as our own daughter. Do not suggest such a vile deed!'

Ali Baba returned home sad and dejected. He told Morgiana what had happened at his brother's house.

'I am glad you did not listen to Cassim,' she said. 'I shall repay you well, you will see!'

Acting on his servant's advice, Ali Baba set out next day for the mountains to gather wood to sell. He worked all through the morning, but when the noonday sun became too hot, he went with his donkey to rest in the shade of a clump of bushes.

He was disturbed by the distant stamping of hooves, and shortly a band of wild looking riders appeared. They were armed to the teeth and cruel, hard eyes gleamed in their stony faces. Ali Baba guessed at once they were rob-

188

bers, and crouched where he was, out of sight.

The robbers dismounted and their leader turning to a nearby rock cried, 'Open, Sesame!'

To Ali Baba's astonishment the rock opened with a loud rumble and one by one the thieves entered, carrying with them their bulging saddle bags. Then the rock closed behind them. Ali Baba counted forty thieves in all. Full of curiosity, he decided to remain where he was to see what would happen next. He did not have to wait long. The rock shook, and the robbers scrambled into the daylight, their saddle bags now empty. Then they mounted their horses and disappeared in a cloud of dust.

Ali Baba watched them out of sight, then walked over to the rock and cried, 'Open, Sesame!' The rock opened and Ali Baba went inside. He felt as if he had been struck by lightning, for he found himself in a cave filled to overflowing with gold, gems, rare china, magnificent robes and materials. They were so dazzling that the glare almost blinded him and he stood transfixed at the sight of such riches. But fear that the robbers might return brought him to his senses. Gathering as many bags of gold as he could carry, he turned to leave. He found the entrance closed, the rock immovable. Remembering the magic words, he called, 'Open, Sesame!' and next moment he was out.

Ali Baba's wife could hardly believe her eyes when he emptied the bags of gold before her. She agreed that her husband should lose no time in burying the treasure in the garden. The world was full of evil, envious people who might rob them. But she begged that she might first count and weigh the gold. Yet, try as she might, with such a huge pile of coins, it was an impossible task. So she ran to Cassim's house, to borrow his grain measure.

'I shall lend you the measure gladly!' said her sister-in-law, 'but where will you find enough corn to weigh?' Ali Baba's wife was so confused and excited that Cassim's wife became suspicious. She therefore smeared the base of the measure with sticky wax, and asked no further questions.

It took almost the whole night to weigh the gold. When next morning the measure was returned to Cassim's house, his wife found one gold coin stuck to its base. She ran at once to tell Cassim.

The envious brother rushed to Ali Baba and stormed, 'Tell me where you got so much gold that you have to weigh it in a grain measure! If you do not tell me, I shall denounce you to the judge as a thief.'

Now the secret was out, and Ali Baba told Cassim everything. The miserly brother immediately saddled his mules and went up into the hills to the secret rock.

'Open, Sesame!' he commanded, and the moment the rock opened, he rushed in. Greedily he stuffed his sacks with gold, pearls and jewels, and when there were no sacks left to put them

189

in, he swallowed gold coins, till his stomach nearly burst. At last he turned to the entrance, but to his horror, he could not remember the magic words.

'Open, Barley!' he called. 'Open, Corn!' he tried. 'Open, Oats!' he cried. 'Open, Wheat!' he stormed. But the rock remained firmly closed. The terrified man went on till he had named every type of grain — except sesame. He sank to the ground and began to weep.

Suddenly the rock split open and the thieves rushed inside. The moment they saw Cassim, they knew he was there to rob them. The leader's sword flashed and plunged deep into Cassim's heart.

'Leave his corpse by the entrance of the cave, as a warning to anyone who might wish to uncover our secret,' the leader said to his band of men before they rode off.

Cassim's wife waited and waited for her husband to return. When she could not bear her anxiety any longer, she ran crying to Ali Baba. He set out immediately for the hills. When the rock opened at his command, he gasped with horror. Cassim lay there lifeless at his feet. Ali Baba hurriedly loaded his brother's corpse onto one of his mules and hastened home.

'You have not acted wisely,' the wise Morgi-ana reproached him. 'When the thieves discover you have taken the body, your life will be in danger. You must bury Cassim quietly and quickly and spread the word that he died after drinking infected water.'

Ali Baba heeded her advice and after the burial he moved with his family to his late brother's house and took over the running of the business.

When the robbers discovered that someone else had found their secret hideout, they searched the whole region for clues, but in vain. Then the slyest, cleverest thief, disguised as a merchant, rode into the city where he heard of Cassim's sudden death and of Ali Baba's newly found prosperity. He was sure then that Ali Baba was the man he sought. So that there would be no mistake, as all the houses in that street were identical, the robber marked the door with a white cross and hastened to join the others in the hills.

But the clever Morgiana noticed the white cross on the door, and though she was not sure what it meant, she chalked a cross on every house in the street.

When that night the thieves crept into the city to punish Ali Baba for his audacity, they vainly looked for the right house. The disappointed

and angry leader sentenced his unfortunate scout to death there and then.

The second member of the robber band fared no better. He marked Ali Baba's house with a drop of his own blood, but the observant Morgiana was not slow to notice it, and she sprayed all the doors in the street with the blood of a fish. And so once again the thieves failed and another scout lost his head.

The furious leader himself now thought of a plan. He had forty leather oil containers fastened to twenty mules. Two were filled with oil, but the others held his men. Disguised as a rich merchant, the robber chief then led his mule caravan into the city, where unsuspecting neighbours showed him Ali Baba's house.

'I have heard of your wealth, noble Ali Baba!' said the leader, when Ali Baba opened the door. 'I am a merchant from foreign parts and would be pleased to sell you the oil I am carrying. If you would kindly give me shelter for the night, we can attend to business in the morning.'

Ali Baba welcomed the visitor, led him into his house, and ordered the servants to attend to the mules and leave the containers in the yard. The trusting Ali Baba was most hospitable and they ate and drank and talked far into the night. At last the oil lamp was burning low, and there was not a drop of oil to be had in the whole house. Morgiana remembered the oil containers in the yard, and went to fetch some.

As she touched the first one, she heard a voice, 'Is it time, chief?'

The quick-witted girl answered in a deep voice, 'Not yet.' Going round all the containers she counted thirty-eight robbers in all. What was she to do? But when Morgiana discovered the two oil-filled containers at the end of the line, she had an idea. Lighting a fire under a huge cauldron, she filled it with the oil, and when it was boiling hot, she poured some into each container. And so the robbers died.

Morgiana then calmly returned to the house, filled the lamp and suggested she should dance in honour of their guest. She had heard rumours, that the leader of the robbers wore a magic dagger, which made him invincible. In perfect rhythm she swayed nearer and nearer to the unsuspecting man. Suddenly she pounced on the dagger and thrust it through his evil heart.

When Ali Baba realized the terrible danger she had saved him from, he granted Morgiana her freedom, and gave her as a bride to his son Muhamad. From then on they all lived together in peace and happiness. Never again did Ali Baba return to the robbers' cave. Perhaps the riches lie there still.

The Clever Nikorima

Far away on a distant island there lived a nation of tattooed people. They wore their tattooes on all parts of their bodies uncovered by clothes. They were beautiful people, like women adorned with jewels.

Nikorima was a young man who lived long ago in one of the villages. He was the finest warrior of his tribe, the wisest of all the men. But some mocked him because only one half of Nikorima's face was tattooed. People said, 'Here comes Nikorima, here comes half a face, half a man. Half a man is no warrior.' Thus they sneered and said he was not a whole man. They never saw the bare side of his face. And when the warriors went to war, Nikorima had to stay behind with the women and children. The warriors did not want Nikorima, who was half a man.

One day, when they had all left to fight, enemies surrounded the defenceless village. The deserted, terrified women hastened to close the gates. 'What shall we do,' they wept, 'we only have Nikorima, half a man, but no warrior.'

But Nikorima was not afraid.

He covered himself in fine mesh matting, gripped his spear and shield and tore through the gates towards the enemy. He danced a wild war dance, his arms and legs flashing, his sharp spear flying up behind the shield. But the artful Nikorima showed the enemy only one side, only one cheek, the tattooed one. The attackers' feet turned to stone with terror when they saw his hungry spear and his wild face, and decided to retreat.

Nikorima returned to the village, smiling. 'I want other clothes and other arms,' he cried. 'I shall feed terror to the enemies.' The women dressed him in matting with brightly coloured designs, wove feathers into his hair and placed a fearsome club in his hand. Out flew Nikorima through the second gate. Facing the enemy he performed a terrifying, frenzied war dance, brandishing his huge club above his head. To the attackers he showed only his bare cheek. They gasped with fright. 'Look at that man with his frightful white face! He is as fearsome as an evil spirit,' they cried in horror.

Smearing the tattooed half of his face with red clay, he said to the women, 'I want other clothes and other arms, for I want to feed our enemy with fear.'

The women dressed him in a cloak, adorned his hair with dove feathers and put two spears with a leather shield in his hands. Nikorima rushed through the third gate towards the enemy. He stooped dead before them. Then with one step and a leap he began the frightening dance of vengeance. He showed only one cheek to the enemy, the tattooed one, smeared with red clay. The attackers again retreated.

'What a fearsome warrior is the one with the bloody face,' they cried.

Nikorima only laughed, and later he burst through the fourth gate clad in a cloak hemmed with string. Boar's fangs decorated his head, bow and arrows were in his hands. Behind him, women and children applauded, encouraging the clever Nikorima in his fearsome war dance.

Hearing the cries of many voices the enemies' bones turned to water. It sounded as if countless

with a rope. Whenever he tugged at the rope, the forms moved as if they were alive.

Darkness fell, the enemies approached. Their chief gazed at the forms of the guards, illuminated by the fires. 'I wonder how many warriors there are in the village?' he thought, and sent a scout to find out. But Nikorima pounced on the scout, tied him up and changed into his clothes. Protected by darkness, he ran to the enemies.

'Run for your life,' he cried. 'The village is full of warriors, anxious to plunge their lances through our hearts.'.

And the enemy took to their heels. But Nikorima stopped the chief. 'Come,' he said, 'let us creep into the village and capture the guards!' The war-loving chief willingly followed Nikorima — to captivity!

When the village warriors returned from battle, they were astonished at the number of enemies one man, the clever Nikorima, had forced to retreat — and had even captured their chief. Never did they sneer at him again.

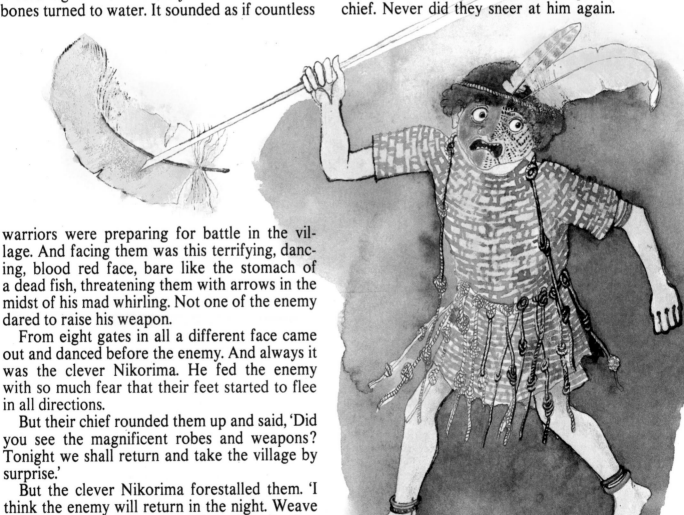

warriors were preparing for battle in the village. And facing them was this terrifying, dancing, blood red face, bare like the stomach of a dead fish, threatening them with arrows in the midst of his mad whirling. Not one of the enemy dared to raise his weapon.

From eight gates in all a different face came out and danced before the enemy. And always it was the clever Nikorima. He fed the enemy with so much fear that their feet started to flee in all directions.

But their chief rounded them up and said, 'Did you see the magnificent robes and weapons? Tonight we shall return and take the village by surprise.'

But the clever Nikorima forestalled them. 'I think the enemy will return in the night. Weave from reeds the forms of men, dress them in matting and at dusk light a fire by the side of each one,' he said to the women and children. When this was done, Nikorima tied them all together

Roly Poly

Once there was an old man and woman, who had two sons and a daughter, who was as pretty as a field of flowers. Everyone adored her.

One day the brothers set off to plough a distant field. They had to pass through a dark forest and step through the undergrowth of tangled roots. The lads took enough bread to last three days.

'Your work should take nine days,' said the old father. 'When the bread is gone, your sister will bring fresh loaves.' 'How shall I find you, dear brothers?' worried the girl. 'I have never ventured so far.' And they promised to leave a trail of birch chippings, so she would not lose her way among the tangled undergrowth.

The Sevenheaded Dragon lived in the black forest. He saw and heard everything, and he gathered the chippings the brothers threw on the path, and put them on a different track.

On the third day the daughter set out to follow her brothers with fresh bread. She walked from birch splinter to birch splinter, never hesitating, while the forest grew deeper and darker, and all was silent. Suddenly, without warning, a golden palace towered before her, its copper gates open wide. Inside stood the Sevenheaded Dragon, spitting fire from every head.

'Welcome, dear maiden, welcome, white dove! I have been expecting you. The feast is ready. Come, you will live with me for ever.'

The girl burst into tears, pleading with clasped hands, falling to her knees, begging for mercy. It was all in vain. The dragon breathed his fiery breath and immediately the forest behind the girl was alight; not even a mouse could have escaped. The poor maiden had to stay in the golden palace, the copper gates firmly closed.

In the meantime the brothers had eaten their bread, and as their sister had not appeared and they had nothing to eat, they left the ploughing and went home.

'Have you forgotten us, mother?' they said. 'Why didn't you send the fresh bread as you promised?'

The mother grew frightened. 'What are you saying, my children? Surely your sister brought you bread.'

The brothers then cried sadly, 'Alas, alas! Our dear sister did not reach the field. She must have lost her way in the forest.'

The oldest brother then put some bread, salt and onions into a bundle and left to search for her. He walked on and on, following a silver brook over dark boulders, over tangled roots, into the burnt-out forest. Suddenly the golden palace glistened before him, with its diamond roof shining like the sun. The youth opened the copper gates, and courageously stepped into the silver-paved courtyard. And there, in a crystal garden, his sister was sitting on a gold seat, combing her long, thick locks and crying bitterly.

'Go back, dear brother, you cannot help me! The Sevenheaded Dragon guards me day and night. If he catches you, he will devour you,' she sobbed when she saw him. But the brave youth would not listen.

'Let the creature kill me, as long as I can be with you! Go to your ugly master and tell him to welcome his relative, as is proper!'

The monster roared with laughter, causing a storm to break out in the sky. 'My doors are open to anyone who is dear to your heart. Bring food to the table, dear wife. We shall have a feast! Prepare metal beans and a copper loaf of bread. And you, dear brother-in-law, come in and eat whatever you wish!'

But the eldest brother did not touch any of the food prepared for him.

'You have offended me by rejecting my hospitality,' frowned the dragon. 'Come, let me show you my wealth instead; then you will see your sister has not fared badly by marrying me.'

The dragon escorted his brother-in-law throughout the palace, where every room glittered with pearls and gems. The stables had twelve gold horses, the cow-shed twelve silver cows, which gave fiery milk.

'Tell me, brother-in-law, who is the richer of us two?' said the dragon. 'You must agree your sister is better off with me.'

'I haven't even a pinch of your wealth, but my sister would be happier at home with us,' the youth proudly replied. The dragon flared.

'You shall pay dearly for your audacity. See this oak log? It is twenty-four feet wide and seventy-two feet long. If you can chop it up

without an axe and burn it without a fire, I shall let you and your sister go free. If not, you will pay with your head.'

'You may as well kill me now,' said the brother sadly, 'for I cannot do as you ask.' The dragon roared with laughter, till lightning flashed in the sky, and with one blow of his hideous paw he killed the unfortunate youth, and hung him on the copper gates.

The younger brother fared no better. He followed the same path, refused the same food, was unable to break up the oak log without an axe or to burn it without a fire. He too was killed and hung on the copper gates.

When the brothers failed to return, their aged parents cried, 'For what have we survived into old age? We are now completely alone. Only poverty sits with us in our wretched cottage.'

One day the despairing old woman went to the well for water, dragging her feet, swallowing her tears. Suddenly a little pea rolled towards her. She picked it up and put it in her apron, and at home she put the apron on the stove.

All at once a faint little voice cried, 'Mother,

Father, help me down please! I am so hungry, I could eat a horse!'

The old couple could not believe what they saw. A tiny boy, as small as a little pea was rolling on the stove. And because he had rolled to them along the path, they named him Roly Poly. How fast he grew! Not by the day, but by the hour! Soon the cottage seemed full of him. Where he could not reach by jumping, he reached by rolling. So beautifully rounded was he.

When he had grown so round that he could hardly squeeze through the door, he said, 'I shall go, Mother, to look for my sister and my brothers, about whom you have told me so much. But first ask Father to get the blacksmith to make from your hair-pin a hammer!'

Hearing this, the father did not complain, but thought, 'That boy of mine is a strapping lad with a heart of gold, but he has as many brains in his head as there are in a pea. How can anyone fashion anything out of a simple hair-pin?' So instead he bought with the last of his money enough iron to make a hammer and took it to the blacksmith. When the hammer was made, he took it home to his son. Roly Poly weighed it, tossed it into the sky and returned to his supper in the cottage. He ate for three whole hours, then returned to the yard, put his ear to the ground and cried, 'I can hear a swishing and thundering in the sky. That means my hammer is returning to earth!'

Roly Poly put out his right knee, the hammer flew down, and broke in two. 'Didn't I ask you to have the hammer made from Mother's hairpin?' Roly Poly said crossly to his father.

So his father took the hair-pin to the blacksmith and the blacksmith toiled and toiled, his face getting redder and redder, till a hammer was made. It was a joy to behold.

Roly Poly slung it over his shoulder and off he went, following the silver brook, crossing the black boulders, the tangled roots, the burnt-out forest, till he came to the dragon's palace. There he hammered on the copper gates till they flew open.

'I am Roly Poly, your youngest brother and I have come to fetch you home,' he cried to the weeping maiden in the garden. 'And you, Dragon, prepare a feast in honour of your relative!'

The dragon roared like thunder, and had iron beans and copper bread brought to the table. 'Take what you want, brother-in-law, Roly Poly,' he smirked. Roly Poly licked his lips and in one sitting downed five copper loaves and three barrels of iron beans.

Then he remarked, 'Your hospitality was poor, brother-in-law Dragon. Into a meagre house my sister has married. I shall take her back to our cottage.'

The infuriated dragon led his guest round his palace, showing him all his riches, but Roly Poly only sneered, 'I wouldn't even have a goat spend a night in such a meagre hut. You are a true beggar.'

The dragon had had enough. He took Roly Poly to the oak log and said, 'If you break it without an axe and burn it without a fire, I shall allow your sister to go home. Otherwise you will die!'

But Roly Poly with his little finger broke the log into pieces, blew onto them, and they caught fire and burned to ashes.

'Your turn now, Dragon,' he then cried. Grasping the monster in his arms, he wedged him in the silver paving of the courtyard up to his waist, and then with his hammer he cut off his hideous head. Then he stamped on the floor, and water from the spring of life gushed forth. This he sprinkled on the dead bodies of his brothers and at once they came to life.

Gathering all the gold, silver and jewels they could carry, all four hastened home.

What joy there now was in their cottage! Everyone hugged and kissed, and danced around the stove, till in all the excitement they knocked it down and had to build a new one.

How the Citizens of Gotham Paid their Taxes

It is no idle saying that the citizens of Gotham have as many brains under their caps as saucepans have under their lids. They say that when brains were brewed and handed out, some of them queued up twice, others thrice, so as not to be outdone.

But instead of swallowing the brew, the citizens smeared their mice holes with it. Ever since, the Gotham mice have been wiser than the Lord Mayor himself. I must say, the Gotham citizens are loyal, obedient subjects to their Royal Majesty, they keep their word and pay their taxes. Except on one occasion, when they all forgot about paying taxes. Perhaps the town hall clock went backwards, perhaps the mayor overslept, but whatever the reason, suddenly the mayor struck his head with his hand and exclaimed, 'Gracious me! Tomorrow our king will expect our messenger with a pouch of honestly earned Gotham gold coins! What shall we do? It is a long way to the royal city. Nobody can reach it in one day.'

The Gotham folks were scared. 'Whatever will His Royal Highness think of us? Perhaps he'll assemble his army to attack the disloyal Gotham!' they whispered to each other. But they put their heads together, trying hard not to lose them, and they debated and debated who in that town was the fastest runner. But they could not think of anyone.

A traveller was passing by, carrying a fine hare in a sack. 'I have an idea, good people', he said. 'Why not send the hare to London with the money? He is the fastest animal I know. If you give me a good price, he is yours!'

The people were delighted. They paid the man the price he asked, tied the pouch with the gold and greetings to the king round the hare's neck and put him down on the road to London.

'Run, messenger, run, to our noble king! And tell him, please, that we respect and love him.'

The hare raced off, but not along the road to London! Straight for the forest he turned. The Gotham citizens stood flabbergasted.

'Not that way, you fool! To London!' they cried.

The mayor suddenly smacked his brow and laughed. 'That hare is not stupid', he said. 'He knows he could meet a dog on the road. That is why he took off through the forest.' And the people of Gotham, pleased with the hare's wisdom, turned for home, quite content.

How did it end? A poacher caught the hare. He roasted him, spent the money, and sent a friendly greeting to the king. So the Gotham citizens still owed their royal taxes.

How Porridge Was Cooked in Gotham

One day the mayor of Gotham was inspecting the town. While he walked, he wondered how he could make Gotham even more famous for its wisdom. A passing vagrant was dawdling on the bridge, his eyes fixed absentmindedly on the river.

'Why do you stare like that? We do not need

you to mesmerize our river!' the mayor snapped.

'I am watching it because I am bored,' the vagrant replied with a smile. 'Just look how the water here froths and whirls and boils! I vow one could cook porridge in it.'

'That is a good idea!' said the mayor with a chuckle, rapping his brow with his knuckles, till it had a bump on it the size of an egg. 'We won't have to use stoves, we'll save on wood, and there'll be plenty of porridge for all!'

The announcement was made all over the town. Soon every citizen knew it was the mayor's will and command that the next day porridge would be cooked in the river at the council's expense. 'What a wise mayor we are blessed with,' the people remarked.

Impatient crowds flocked to the river in the morning, every man with a sack of oatmeal over his shoulder, so as to cook plenty of porridge for now and to keep in reserve. The mayor marched about the bridge, as proud as a peacok, graciously supervising the townspeople, as one by one, they emptied their sacks of oats into the whirlpool.

'No pushing, please. Everyone will have his turn,' the mayor called, already excited at the thought that perhaps the news of his incredible wisdom would soon reach the ears of the king.

The whirlpool, of course, dragged all the oatmeal to the bottom, and swirled and frothed on merrily, as if nothing out of the ordinary had happened. And the Gotham citizens all stood gaping at this miracle.

'Do you think the porridge is cooked yet?' they asked one another. One fool offered to dive in to see. He did just that, and before you could blink, the whirlpool had seized his foot and dragged him to the river bed.

'I'll wager that he's helping himself to our porridge,' grumbled the others. Then the poor man's head bobbed for a moment above the surface, gasping for breath.

'Is it cooked?' they cried impatiently. But the poor fellow could not utter a word, but spat and choked and gasped before the whirlpool dragged him under again.

'Did you see that? His mouth is full of porridge. He'll eat the lot!' the Gotham people cried, and one after the other they too jumped into the river. The whirlpool dragged them to the bottom, the river carried them out to sea and the sea took them to every corner of the world. That is why today fools are scattered over the earth all because the citizens of Gotham once cooked porridge in their river.

Maidens
in a Mirror

When you go from fairy tale to fairy tale, you will arrive at an enchanted land where exquisite flowers sing under a blue, silky sky. An aged woman once lived in this land. She had two sons, strong, handsome youths with eyes like deep pools and hearts kind and gentle. The mother was proud of her sons, but it pained her that they did not want to hear of getting married. When one day she stood on the door-step, thinking silently that perhaps she would not live to see her grandchildren, a shining cloud flew down from the sky. An aged, trans-lucent man sat on the cloud, smiling kindly.

'I know why you are sad, old woman,' he said. 'But have no fear! Give your sons these two mirrors and ask them to look into them at full moon. They will see two beautiful maidens, so gentle and sweet that they will fall in love with them at first glance. If your sons decide to seek them, they must turn the mirrors towards the moon and its light will show them which path to follow.'

Having spoken, the old man rose on his shin-ing cloud into the sky and the mother hastened to her sons, to tell them her story. The youths laughed, not believing her words, but curiosity got the better of them. At full moon, both brothers secretly glanced into their mirrors. The elder youth saw such an exquisite maiden, that the sight took his breath away. Clad in a glim-mering, translucent robe, ruby-coloured roses shone in her hair.

'Oh, mother,' cried the elder son, 'I must have that beautiful apparition for my wife!' The youngest brother too had seen a girl of such loveliness, that his head spun. Dressed in a sea-green robe, her hair was circled by a garland of emerald-hued blossom. 'Oh, mother,' he exclaimed, 'I must have the Sea-green maiden for my bride! I cannot live without her!'

The woman told her sons how to find the way to their chosen brides.

'I shall go first to look for the Ruby maiden,' the elder brother cried. 'If I fail to return by the end of the year, let my brother seek his bride.'

When it was again full moon the youth turned his magic mirror towards its glow, and suddenly a silvery path appeared. The young man walked on and on, till he came to high mountains. By a deep forest he met the translucent old man, who was smiling kindly. From what his mother had told him, the elder brother realized this must be the good spirit who had spoken to her.

'I am waiting for you,' the aged man whispered. 'Your journey is not yet at an end. A wicked witch has turned your bride into a peony rose. She blooms in her garden and sheds tears of dew. You will change her back to her human form if you shine the light of your mirror towards her. But the journey is beset with perils. Take my magic whip and this ball of magic yarn. Without their help you will not succeed.'

The old man explained how to use his gifts, then melted like the morning mist. The youth set forth into the mountains.

Exactly at noon the skies suddenly grew dark and through the blackness he saw a tiger's bloodshot eyes gleaming from the bushes and heard its blood-curdling roar. But the valiant youth showed no fear. He cracked the magic whip and cried, 'Oh, mighty tiger, master of the mountains, let me use your hunting trails, for I wish to set free the rose maiden, my bride to be!'

The sky cleared as suddenly as it had darkened and the fierce tiger tamely rubbed itself against the youth's legs, as if they had always been friends. The young man continued on his way, climbing sheer rocks till he reached a bottomless abyss. It was the gully of the spirits. In its depths a wild river swirled full of treacherous whirlpools.

This time the youth untied the ball of yarn and dropped one end into the abyss. As it touched the whirling waters a mermaid swam to the surface, gripped the end of the yarn and swam to the other side. As she touched firm rock, a narrow bridge spanned the river. But as

the young man stepped onto it, he heard from below such hideous shrieks and wails that his blood turned cold. He could not resist looking down at the waters and found himself staring into the bulging bloodshot eyes of the spirits which dwelt there.

Too late he realized that he had forgotten to ask the spirits for their help, and his knees trembled with fear. At the same moment the little bridge became again a length of fine yarn, and the unfortunate youth fell head first into the spirits' abyss. The river swirled as if in victory and the red eyes of the spirits disappeared under the surface.

Days passed, and mother and brother waited for the youth's return in vain. When a year had gone by, the younger brother could not bear to wait any longer, though his mother implored him not to leave her.

'I must find my bride, and also my elder brother,' he reasoned, 'for without them the world for me is an unhappy place.' And at full moon, he turned his magic mirror to its light, and followed the silver trail which led him to the translucent old man in the mountains.

'Your brother did not heed my advice,' he said. 'He forgot to ask the spirits for their help. If you have greater wisdom and courage, go and seek out the wicked witch. A green peony flowers in her garden, shedding tears of dew. If you turn the light of your mirror upon it, it will turn back into your lovely bride. Take my magic whip and my magic ball of yarn with you! And remember my advice!'

When everything had been explained to him, the young man went to the mountains. He tamed the man-eating tiger without effort, and

without mishap reached the spirits' abyss. Like his brother, he too dropped one end of the yarn into the swirling current, but he remembered to ask at the same time for the spirits' help.

'Mighty spirits, good and evil, let me pass, help me to set free the Sea-green princess, my bride to be!'

Once again the mermaid rose to the surface, carried the yarn to the opposite side, and once more a footbridge spanned the abyss. The younger brother crossed it without hesitation, without glancing into the swirling depths. Once on firm ground, he saw before him a hideous hut built of bones. Round it was a beautiful garden filled with many flowers. In the centre two peonies shone in full bloom, one a rosy colour, the other sea-green. The youth turned the mirror towards the green peony and the moment the light touched it, the flower changed into the enchanting maiden with a garland of emerald

202

blossoms round her head. Sinking to her knees, and with tears in her eyes, she thanked the youth for saving her.

Suddenly, overhead a storm broke, bringing with it the hideous witch on a black cloud. But the youth was not afraid. Following the old man's advice, he cracked the magic whip and flashed the magic mirror in the face of the ugly hag. She screeched with pain and fear.

'You, daring one, have won! You are stronger and mightier than I!' rasped the witch, 'but no magic tricks will help you to escape from my garden. It will hold you prisoner, until I allow you to be released. But if you should succeed in taking a herd of my horses to pasture, I shall let you and your Sea-green bride go free.'

'Do not take them into the mountains,' the maiden begged, 'for they are not horses, but bloodthirsty tigers, poisonous snakes and scorpions.' But the youth was not afraid. He had promised the witch to look after the herd, and when it was attacked by wild, ravenous beasts, he cracked the magic whip and asked the mighty lion for his help. The beasts instantly disappeared.

'So you have fulfilled the task I set you,' screeched the witch. 'I shall release you from the magic garden, but the rose peony will not turn into its human form! Only your brother can achieve this. Take me with you; I will try and persuade the evil spirits to let us have his body from the bottom of their river.'

The witch intended to push the youth and his bride into the abyss, but the Sea-green maiden was clever too. 'You are too old to climb mountains,' she said. 'And if you turn into a black cloud, we shall not be able to keep up with you.

Change into something very small, then we can carry you.'

The unsuspecting witch shrank till she was no bigger than a spider and the youth put her into an old bottle, which they took with them to the river of the spirits.

'Spirits good and evil, I bring you this witch to give in exchange for my brother,' he called, tossing the bottle into the swirling current. Immediately the mermaid swam to the bank, carrying the elder brother.

'Where have I slept so long?' he wondered, as soon as he opened his eyes. But the Sea-green maiden quickly led him to the enchanted garden. With the light from the second mirror, the rose peony turned at once into the beautiful rosy princess with rubies in her hair. Joyfully they all embraced, and returned home to the old mother in that enchanted land where exquisite flowers sing under a blue, silky sky.

The Wise King and the Honest Thief

Everyone knows that there are countless crooks, thieves and swindlers in the world. And now and then such a villain steals into a fairy tale and something is sure to disappear: the chimney sweep loses a chimney, the night watchman his lantern, the king a copper or two, or maybe his crown! But there is one kingdom in the world where no one ever steals; not even a grain of salt goes missing. And this is how it came about —

Once upon a time a very wise king ruled over a northern kingdom. To his subjects he was kind and understanding, so it pained him all the more to find out that frequently objects disappeared from his treasury. Once it was a pearl necklace, the next time a gingerbread stick, a pair of royal underpants, warm and thick, a golden ring, a silver spoon and even a brand new broom, not to mention precious jewels and other royal valuables.

'Oh dear, oh dear,' cried the king, 'all my life I have taught my subjects to lead an honest life, and this is how I am rewarded. But just you wait, thief, I'll get the better of you yet!'

He had thought of a plan, and he put it into operation at once. He got the royal tailor to make him the shoddiest, raggediest suit ever seen, the royal cobbler to put together a few shreds of worn old leather to serve as shoes, the barber to fix on his chin the bristliest stubble of a beard.

Then he stuck a paper nose on his own nose, a paper beret on his head, picked up an old walking stick, and there he stood — the most beggarly looking vagabond in the world.

That evening the disguised king hid in the treasury and waited.

The clock on the churchtower struck ten, but there was not a sound to be heard. It struck eleven, and still all was silent. But at the stroke of twelve there was a noise in the great chimney, and a thief slid down into the room. He crept to a chest on tiptoe, lighting his way with his robber's lamp, his bunch of robber's keys jangling in his hand. And in the twinkling of an eye the lid flew open.

The silent thief carefully took out one large jewel and hid it under his tongue, he took another and hid it in his left ear. But into the right ear he put a finger and twirled it round and shook it as if he had gone deaf. It was at that moment that the vagabond king came out of hiding.

'Hey, brother thief, leave something for me!' he whispered hoarsely.

The scared robber jumped, then shone his

lamp on the beggarly figure. The king's appearance at once put him at ease.

'Are you of our trade?' he enquired.

'To be sure,' answered the king. 'I steal like the magpie. But I've never learned how to pick locks on chests. I'll make it worth your while, if you teach me.'

'You strike me as a clumsy oaf,' the thief said sternly, 'but what have I to lose! If you have a bunch of skeleton keys, try opening that chest over there! It is sure to be full of gold and jewels.'

The disguised king showed his bunch of keys and pretended to be trying hard to open the lock — but without success.

'I knew you were a hopeless good-for-nothing,' laughed the thief. 'Move over and I'll show you how it is done!' But at that very moment the king put the right key into the lock and the lid opened.

'So you're not such a fool after all,' the thief praised him. The king paid him no attention, but began to stuff all the valuables into a sack.

'One moment, friend,' the thief cried. 'Surely you don't intend to take the lot?'

'Of course not, I'll halve everything with you,' the king replied soothingly.

At this the indignant thief jumped at the king, boxing him on the ears, the chin and the nose till he lost the false beard and the false nose.

'Take that, and that, and that, you greedy thief!' he cried hoarsely.

'Shame on you for wanting to bring misery on our good old king! Don't you know that an honest thief only robs for his livelihood? Isn't it enough that our ministers, generals and so-called noblemen rob him whenever his back is turned? I've beaten you so that you won't forget what I say!' The light of his lamp suddenly fell on the king's face, and the robber sank to his knees in fear.

'Have mercy, Your Royal Highness,' he cried. 'Had I known it was you, I wouldn't have struck you so hard!'

The king smiled and said, 'Thank you for letting me know who the real thieves are. You are indeed the most honest fellow. From now on you shall be Highest Guard of all my treasures. Just make sure that nobody steals even a grain of salt!'

Nobody did. The honest thief knew his trade inside out, and he saw through every crook in sight.

No one got a chance to steal, try as he might. And that is why it is now the most honest kingdom in all the world.

East of the Sun, West of the Moon

North Wind had finished the last tale and the glow in the sky was starting to fade. Freshly fallen snow glistened all round. The countryside was silent and completely white. The mother of the four winds rose. In her eyes there was a sad little smile. 'I am glad you came here, my dear,' she said to the young woman. 'But it is now time to say farewell. Your last story has just started. But you still have a long journey before you. Take these small gifts, for you will have need of them.'

The old woman gave her a gold spindle, a distaff and gold yarn which she had spun from sunbeams. Then she stroked the young woman's silky hair as gently as the sigh of South Wind and turned into a snowflake.

The North Wind then picked up the wandering, deserted bride, set her between his snowy wings and soared towards the clouds. Wherever they flew, rivers froze, the earth fell asleep under deep snow and there was wailing and moaning in chimneys. They passed over lowlands and high mountains, forests and endless seas. Colossal waves rose under North Wind's powerful breath and fishermen's frail barges danced on them like tiny shells. They flew on and on, till North Wind's strength began to ebb. He sank lower and lower towards the sea, till the frightened young woman could feel the icy tongues of the waves licking her feet. All at once a glass island with a crystal palace appeared before them.

'We are here,' breathed the exhausted North Wind. 'This is where the wicked stepmother imprisons your prince and the fishermen who lost their way at sea. Go to the palace window, and place the gold gifts my mother gave you under it.' Having spoken, the North Wind sank among the rocks and immediately fell into a deep sleep.

The young woman sped to the palace window and laid her gifts below it. Before long a hideous princess with a long nose looked out of the window.

'How much will you take in exchange for the lovely distaff?' she cried.

'It is not for sale,' the young woman replied, 'but if you permit me to spend one night in the room of the handsome prince, you can have it as a gift.' The princess frowned.

'He is my bridegroom,' she snapped. 'If he fails to marry me within three days, my mother will turn him into a polar bear for ever. But if you insist, I shall grant your request.'

The ugly princess kept her word, but that evening she doped the prince's wine. He fell so soundly asleep, that he could not hear the sweet words of his beloved, could not feel her soft hands stroking his hair. The young woman was near despair.

The next day she offered the gold spindle to the ugly princess, but again that night the prince slept. In vain she called him, in vain she shed tears - she could not wake him.

But the next morning the imprisoned fishermen asked the prince who had called him so plaintively all through the night for a second time. The prince thought deeply and when that evening the ugly princess offered him the wine, he only pretended to drink it. Then sinking back, he feigned sleep. Soon afterwards the hideous princess again brought the young woman into the chamber, in return for the gold yarn.

The prince gazed at his bride through half-closed lids, and the moment the doors closed behind the ugly princess, he leapt out of bed and, smiling happily, embraced his true wife.

'My stepmother means me to marry my stepsister tomorrow, but first she must fulfil my wishes, otherwise she must set me free,' he said.

'Have no fear, for I shall ask the wicked women to wash my shirt which you soiled with wax in my palace. If it is not lily-white, you must take the shirt and plunge it three times in the sea.'

The following day the prince said to his stepmother and her daughter, 'At my wedding, I want to wear my very old shirt which is soiled with wax. I will marry only the maiden who can make it lily-white.'

Impatiently, the ugly princess soaked the shirt in rose water, but the more she scrubbed, the dirtier the shirt became. When the furious stepmother tried, the shirt turned as black as night. Suddenly the true wife tore the shirt from her hands and ran to the sea. She plunged it in the waves once and the dirt was gone. She plunged it under the second time and the wax disappeared. The third time the shirt shone like freshly fallen snow.

'You cursed ocean!' the enraged women stormed at the sea, spitting like wildcats into the waves. The fiendish noise woke North Wind from his slumber. Crossly he blew into the water, causing gigantic waves to roll over the shore, swallowing for ever the wicked stepmother and her ugly daughter. Now the brave young woman had truly liberated her beloved prince.

Far, far away, to the east of the sun and west of the moon a glass island floats in transparent seas. A crystal palace stands upon it, where a handsome prince lives with his beautiful wife, and they tell each other this, their favourite, fairy tale over and over again to their hearts' content.

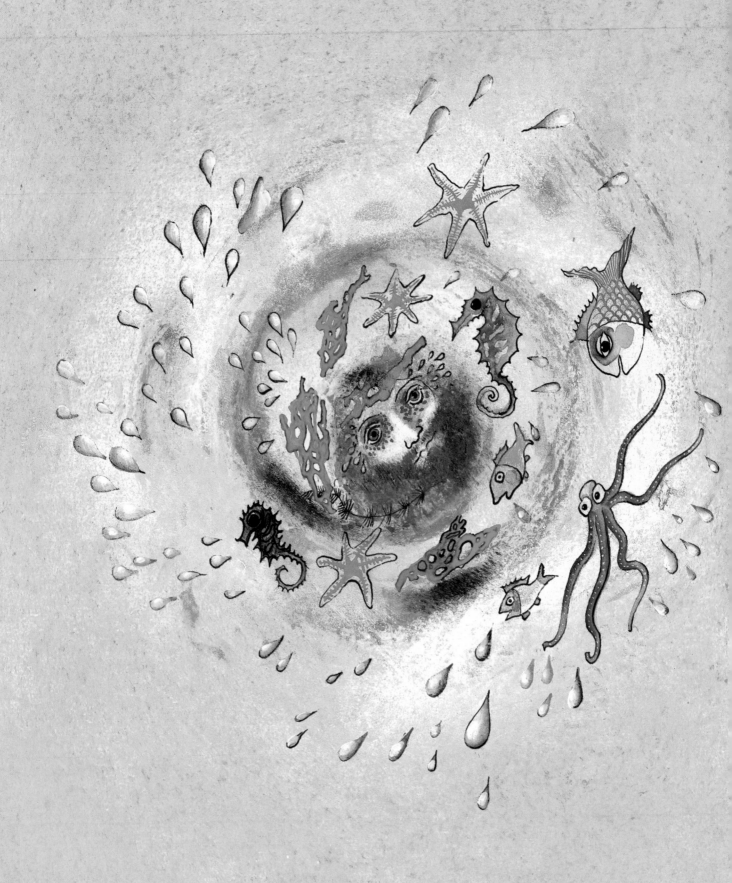